INTO THE GRAY SCALE

A DARK FANTASY NOVEL

OGE MOBUOGWU

Reboshke Publishing

Dedicated to all that is and all that could have been.

1

The itch was sudden and felt more like a burning sensation, or was it pain he mistook for an itch? He wasn't exactly sure. He dug into the spot on his forehead and scratched intensely with his fingertips, at the same time being careful not to hurt himself any further. It stopped hurting, then hurt some more, or was it an intense itch? He still wasn't sure.

In the dark he felt his fingers were dry. There should have been blood but he felt nothing. The adrenaline rush and the pain were too real, as real as his own body, yet he felt no blood.

"Oh, I get it, it's a dream," he thought, coming to a comfortable realization, still not sure if that was truly the case. It had to be a dream. He'd had dreams like this before, with the plots so vivid that even after he awoke, he still trembled. On some of those days he was grateful they were just dreams, and they happened so often he had come up with an exit routine to get out, and it was simple.

"Okay, AJ, it's just a dream, wake up now," and he always did.

It didn't work.

Perhaps this wasn't a dream, or maybe it was, but just needed a new exit.

As he racked his head for this new method, he felt his way around in the dark and then touched a wall, a smooth, cold, hard wall, unending on both sides to the extent his stretched-out arms could feel, and to the top. It felt deliberately impermeable.

Suddenly, a voice let out a loud piercing scream. Hearing his mother's voice broke his heart, leaving him even more confused. He screamed in turn, hoping to be heard. He suddenly drifted away from the sound as he tried to cling onto reality desperately in his head, screaming his mom's and Jessica's names. Not hearing him, they remained inconsolable even as their sorrowful voices drifted even farther away from him.

"I trust you two won't give me any problems."

Reginald's calm but stern voice sent chills down his spine, prompting him to pause for a bit and duck. He thought about that monster alone with his family and screamed out for them again. He became surrounded by a palpable silence. In it was a discomfort so overwhelming he needed to scream again just to keep out the sense of hopeless oblivion.

He did.

Silence. His mouth moved but he heard nothing. He felt around the cold wall aggressively, desperate for any way around it, even a crack to peep through, groping far to the left and returning to grope to the right. Touching nothing, he kept groping and moving, then started running, still keeping his hands on the wall. He stumbled, fell, and stood up as hastily as he could.

Upon standing, the area suddenly had brightened. The wall had stopped and behind it was nothing but empty space; arid, gusty, and carrying sand with it. He walked behind the wall hoping to see where the voices came from. Nothing. He turned to his right, making a full circle turn, taking in the confusion. By the time he made a full turn, the wall was gone, leaving only a vast, empty, arid space as far as his eyes could see. He'd never had a dream like that, and his head still hurt or itched, he still wasn't sure.

Despite the confusion, he felt a sudden calmness, as if an active removal from the previous calamity he had been surrounded by. He tried to hold on to it for his mom's and Jessica's sakes but didn't know how. He needed to stay alarmed to find another exit route since the one he knew no longer worked.

The wind came from behind and pushed him as if demanding he walk on. He held back, still trying to see the vanished wall and hear their voices again, but from within him came a further peaceful and unlabored acceptance of the situation that was not his own doing. He didn't want to accept it but didn't know how not to. He paused, looked around, letting out a hopeless sigh and prayed.

"God, where am I?"

In the newfound tranquility, he took time to observe. The sun was setting; perhaps the very last sighting before it would disappear, yet it hung there like an act of rebellion, or maybe obedience, however grudgingly. Somehow, he knew the sun was supposed to set but didn't and wouldn't or couldn't. That would-have-been last sight of the setting sun seemed perpetual. How he came to this conclusion was unclear to him.

In the corner of his eye, he saw something move. He turned to see an old woman walk by, casually, like she knew where she was going. He tried to call out but cautioned himself to not be rude. Something about her strides seemed solemn and purposeful. She turned to take a casual glance at him and continued on her way.

Someone else walked by in the distance, then more people followed. Everyone was headed the same direction and in the direction they all headed was a multitude of people already far ahead.

"How didn't I see this before?"

Now they were all around him, numbering at least a hundred, many more ahead, many more on either side, and even many more coming from behind.

Some of them had tattered clothes, some looked healthy and normal, others pale. Some were rather bizarre; a noose mark around the neck, a woman with a swollen face as if she was being strangled, he also saw a male body with its head floating just about an inch above it. Everyone was of different ethnicities and wore attires from different cultures. He thought about the Olympics opening ceremony, but there was nothing pleasant about this scenario. Curious, though, it wasn't unpleasant either. It just *was*.

Now they were starting to push past him, looking straight ahead as if totally oblivious to him. He decided to walk with the crowd, it seemed like the right thing to do. Clearly, someone knew where they were going.

***

From the attendant ahead, the line forked into two. Both went into two small, single-story structures standing opposite each other that ordinarily would hold only a tiny fraction of the number of people entering them. Beyond the buildings were two pedestrian bridges crossing over a small, heavily fogged body of water. He could see the exits from behind the buildings to the bridges. His thoughts came back to the queue.

It wasn't supposed to be his concern, but he couldn't take his eyes off the attendant ahead by whose instruction the line forked. As he followed the line closer to his turn, he found himself preoccupied with whether this was a man or woman. He couldn't even make out his or her ethnicity. In ordinary circumstances, he would have thought it was a robot with high intelligence and advanced design features. He decided he would probably try using one of those AI software to recreate it when he woke up.

"Andrew Jackson."

"How do you know my name?" he asked.

He'd been staring and also not realized it was his turn.

"If you'll please follow the line to your right."

He turned to inquire further but stopped at the sight of an old man behind who looked at him with a plain face that still somehow carried a degree of restiveness. He held his peace and walked on to the line to his right. Ahead of him were, amongst others, the woman with a swollen choke-like face, a little boy with a gash behind his head, and ahead of him was the body with the floating head. He winced and rubbed the painful itch on his head again.

***

The setting looked familiar, quite like what you'll find at a Department of Motor Vehicles or any other public utility office. This however was significantly larger. To either side he looked, he was sure he couldn't see an end, as bright light poured in from the exits down much of the hall.

"Where's this light coming from?" he wondered, looking around and remembering the weather seemed rather dreary when he stood in line outside.

Some of the people behind the desks looked human yet others looked just like the attendant on the queue outside with indistinct gender and ethnicity. The people they all attended to looked abnormal, as if they'd all suffered tragic deaths. He winced and scratched his forehead again. Inside his head, he felt a combination of a hollow and burning sensation at once and desperately wanted to be free of it. He hoped a fever, or some terrible flu wasn't waiting for him when he woke up.

At one of the work desks, a severely burnt man walked away from a cubicle beside the body with the floating head. The attendant behind the desk looked straight at him. He looked away.

"Andrew Jackson." His voice was medium-low in volume, yet crystal clear. It didn't sound like the general nature of a loudspeaker but more like a direct audible whisper. Again, Andrew wondered why everyone knew his name. Reluctantly, he stood and walked over.

"Study this. It contains the rules of *Animmo*, breaching them will get you in trouble and could make for a problematic passing."

"A what?"

The attendant paused in acknowledgement of the question but chose to finish.

"The rules are generally in your best interest and of everyone else here. If you have any questions, there are liaison stations around your *domain*."

"My what?"

He paused while they stared at each other, the attendant expecting any other questions from him. AJ remained silent.

"This is your domain situation; it's been pre-coded with your *being*. So only your hands can unlock your door."

He handed AJ a metal like material with the string "2023-08-13, 19:47:01:25." He couldn't wrap his head around the numbers.

"What's this?"

"Your *situation*."

AJ's concern grew.

"Sir, I'm really confused. Please tell me what's going on."

The attendant's voice was husky, and he still couldn't tell if "he" was male or female.

"It'll all be clear right now. Your situation is what you would have called an address, look closely, it's the exact time of your death."

"My death? Like I'm dead in my dream?"

"No, Mr. Jackson, you're not dreaming. Your reaction is normal, that's why you're being processed in Sudden Death."

"Sudden Death." AJ let out a short disbelieving laughter. "I'm sorry, what?"

"Yes, Mr. Jackson, that's the painful itch you've been nursing on your head."

AJ stared back at him, pondering as realization hit him. Suddenly, he grabbed his head again and toppled as the pain came back more forcefully, accompanied by a very bright flash.

***

Saint Matthew College never came across as built for anything other than strictly study. It could be argued that whatever sporting or extra-curricular activities approved by the institution that went on in the school only happened in the more recent years due to the student body's need for progress. This idea didn't need to be true but felt true to him. The school carried an unwelcoming quiet that seemed unnatural and forced, as if to deliberately shut out the public and the corrupt world within which it found itself. Maybe it was designed that way from the beginning since it was supposed to be a religious institution after all. Was it a religious institution? I mean, Saint Matthew. He knew of course all that was a façade. The students were his biggest customers. As a matter of fact, his co-hustler, Kester, used his grandma's old basement along South Street to organize his iconic Bake Atmosphere, which is basically a marijuana plus orgy mix. Such parties were a favorite amongst even the pretty, daddy's girls next door from the hostels at Carobene but they all knew to leave the dirt outside of the school's premises while they returned to their pristine educated lives. Even the black and Latin students had some air around themselves. How dare they?

Some have said there were no rich folks in Jisike. Surely some could claim to be middle class, yet Saint Matthew just seemed completely detached, not just from Jisike but especially from its immediate environment. From Gidney to Savage, Elmwood to Demola, and Isiaka to Liberty streets, Saint Matthew was in the midst of standard American poverty. Perhaps it made sense that the school would find a way to detach itself from the environment. It had a reputation to protect, after all. He understood this but still, it annoyed him.

AJ realized he'd stood there at that street corner for no other reason than just letting his angry thoughts take shape against the innocent students who had no hand in his personal struggles. He was returning from a delivery. There was something about that day that left him a weird feeling he couldn't shake. He'd had a fight with his mom earlier that morning about finishing college. Going back to school at twenty-six to rub shoulders with teenagers wasn't something he felt enthused about. When you looked at the world through his eyes, you were certain to see some things differently, at least that's what he believed but all the muddled thoughts in his head just couldn't be the source of his inner turbulence. Maybe it was Kester's disappearance.

Making his way slowly along Liberty, approaching Elmwood, past the houses lined to the right and occupied mainly by students, he noticed one of the windows on the ground floor was open and the girls inside were dancing in a very carefree manner, all without rhythm. Life was good, wasn't it?

His phone beeped, a text message from Jessica.

"We've got a problem. Reginald is here and mom is losing it."

"Shit!!"

Home was less than two blocks away. Running as fast as his legs could carry him, all he thought about was his fight with his mom that morning, his missed opportunities and how he ended up a twenty-six-year-old drug dealer in a world where his own cousins and neighbors had taken advantage of a better life while he slacked. Perhaps his internal turbulence was right. Thinking of his folks alone with Reginald made his life flash before his eyes.

The pair of Escalades, with out of state number plates, parked in front of his building were rather conspicuous. His neighbors didn't need to be nosy to peep because such occurrences just didn't happen in that side of town. As he walked to his door, past the cars and men in suits standing guard, he wondered how much courage they would display if he actually had the balls to call the cops.

He rested his head on the door to allow his raging heart calm down while he rehearsed his speech to Reginald. He finally pressed the bell, Jessica peeped from the window upstairs and disappeared back into the house.

***

Reginald wasn't a man who easily fit in a box. In his suit and tie, some took him for an investment banker, sometimes, a private school principal.

AJ's mother was sobbing deeply and angrily, seated on their only sofa in the corner while Reginald sat on a dining chair beside a wall calendar with a plastic square showing the date, Sunday, August 13, 2023. Two others of Reginald's men, Victor and Maurice, stood closer to the door. In his right hand, calmly resting above his leg, Reginald held a 45mm, with his face completely blank of any emotions.

AJ remained at the door, still wide open, his head empty as he tried to decide between telling his mom and sister to run, tackle Reginald and all his men or just go on his knees and beg. Reginald calmly raised two fingers and urged him forward. His weak legs carried him into the house while one of the other men shut the door behind him. He went straight on his knees right in front of Reginald, searching his face and hoping for a sign of appreciation for his displayed contriteness. Reginald remained blank.

"Reginald, I'm not the source of the leak. You know me. I didn't sell you out, I swear."

Reginald's expression remained unreadable. His voice was calm.

"Every organization is built on structure. Words of scripture, 'If the foundation be destroyed, what can the righteous do?'"

Sarah was offended by his reference to the Bible, not because the Bible offended her but because a man as vile as Reginald should not dare quote from it. "How dare he not burst into flames?" she thought.

"Reginald, I was approached by the police, but I told them nothing. I know the drill." AJ tried desperately to reassure him.

"You had your place. Maintain your retail position. Target the Saint Matthew students and the junkies around. Was the instruction not clear?"

AJ stole a glance at his mom who was clearly heartbroken by what she'd heard. She always knew some of his choices were unscrupulous but a full-time drug dealer? That wasn't the son she thought she'd raised. AJ decided he'd deal with his mom's disapproval later. He needed to get out of this situation. The problem was Reginald, as complex as he was, was a very simple man. His being in his house was a problem. Evidently, his matter had been discussed and a decision had been made. Reginald was that straightforward.

"Reginald, I had talked it over with Kester, he too believed it was legit."

"I asked you a question."

"Crystal. Totally crystal," he fought back tears.

"Stay in your lane. Man the retail. You were paid for your role not because of your sales skills, because you know what, junkies will do drugs. You were simply a point man for ease of logistics."

"I understand, it will never happen again, you have my word."

"Well, your words translate to nothing and yes, it will never happen again."

AJ's heart sank and his shoulders slumped as it dawned on him what Reginald meant.

"The so-called 'high-capacity' taker you thought you were striking a deal with was the FBI. Single handed, you almost got the Feds, the DEA and all my enemies on my trail."

He leaned out to AJ and spoke in a tone and body language that could have been taken for affection given a different circumstance.

"This has never happened to me before, and I've been doing this a long time. Much longer than you've been alive."

Reginald reached into his suit pocket and brought out a silencer.

Seeing it, Sarah immediately went on her knees beside AJ.

"Look, mister, please, he said he sorry. Whatever my boy done, sure you can let it go. He's young and foolish, but what boy his age ain't? If he owe you money, I promise you I will sell all I got, even take extra shifts to pay it up but we don't gotta let this get so ugly."

AJ looked at Reginald's face and knew his mother's words made no impact.

As he fixed the silencer on the gun, he spoke calmly to Sarah, "You're worth nothing. The value you place on yourself is insignificant. I do not expect you to understand what is going on here. Besides, you do not need to know the rules. It is not in your place to know, and the price is not yours to pay. And now I must clean up."

AJ threw all caution to the wind and leaned in as if begging a best friend's pardon. His eyes became wet with tears.

"Reginald, sir. It was a stupid mistake. It was a wrong turn but not one for greed. I only wanted to move up, yeah, trying to get some attention. I wanted to serve you better, that's all. All the aggression was for you, and I know I screwed up and I swear on my life I will make it up, on my father's grave I'll make up for every loss. I'm real, real sorry.

AJ paused, gauging if his words made any impact. Reginald's face remained unreadable.

"Reginald, are we good?"

Silence. He got scared.

"Reginald?"

"*Pfft!*" Reginald fired the gun.

For a splitting moment she wondered what that sound was, it was supposed to be familiar but there were facts you just didn't accept. The few seconds between then and when AJ's body hit the floor seemed like an eternity. In those moments, she pondered her personal choices from kindergarten; if she should have been a lot more obedient, more attentive at Sunday school; to the high school she attended, if she should have taken other subjects or even skipped gym class, especially the day she met Stephan Jackson, and then got pregnant with Andrew; if she should have aborted him, if she should have married Stephan at all rather than pursuing her college degree; how her life went downhill, and she struggled all the way to raise her children after Stephan overdosed on heroin; and if she should have moved in with her mother; and if it was pride that kept her from doing it because she didn't want to be numbered among the women who did; and if she should have been firmer with her children or perhaps if she should have spanked them or loved them more. As her son's brains spattered around, and his body lay on the floor, her only thought was "Where did I go wrong?"

When she and Jessica screamed, Reginald stood up gently, undid his gun from the silencer and put them away. The two men by the door, Victor and Maurice, had their guns pointed at the two, awaiting instructions from Reginald. He observed his men and turned to the two. Only Sarah showed fear. The defiance on Jessica was something he had seen before. Though she said nothing, her unspoken words were clear, "One day I will find you and I will kill you." He caught himself letting out a hint of smile, as if accepting the challenge.

"I trust you two won't give me any problems."

The guns remained pointed at them.

While Sarah succumbed in fear, Jessica remained defiant, eyes fixed on Reginald. He walked closer to her and squatted.

"I see the thoughts in your head, and I will allow you that sense of vengeance. Perhaps it will give you some drive and propel you out of this wilderness you call a life. Killing you both now is of no benefit to me but do remember I have eyes everywhere and I am very powerful. It will be in your best interest to swallow your sorrow and seek your revenge by other means."

Without another word, he stood, reached out his hand to Maurice who handed him a face mask and they walked out the door.

Then Jessica began to cry but Sarah had become numb all over as she stared at the lifeless body of her son, the very reason her life's path was altered, why she decided against college and even cut her dreams short trying to be a good mother. In that moment, she tried to chastise herself for her thoughts but decided she'd had enough. She should have dumped him with her mother and moved on to college, perhaps the stupid boy would've still been alive. The primary reason for the major decisions in her life was dead, didn't it mean she made the wrong choices all along? Her heart got filled with anger toward AJ for being so stupid, at Jessica for taking his side all the time, at Stephan for getting her pregnant and then having the audacity to die and finally at herself for all her wrong choices. She finally crumbled to the floor, again, and cried with Jessica. With every deep groan Sarah let out, she cursed Reginald and wished him every imaginable pain.

2

Arizona State Correctional Holding Annex (ASCHA) is a collection of dusty, brick-colored, old, sparsely placed buildings inside a very large multi-purpose complex, surrounded by barbed wire fencing, located in the outskirts of suburban Yuma.

The day was mildly windy as dust wafted across, blowing on the few old model cars parked some distance apart from each other within the fenced perimeter.

***

Whenever he was asked to talk about himself, Stanley Weppler liked to jokingly respond saying, "I'm a man of lost dreams." It usually made for some laugh, mostly just polite, but all of it was true for him.

As a child, he wanted to be a pilot when he grew up, then an actor, then a singer. By his teenage years, he'd settled on investment banking and then aerospace engineering by his senior year; and for a while, daydreamed of Embry Riddle Aeronautical University, specifically at Daytona because he also wanted to be far from home and he'd always dreamed of studying in Florida. There was also Aerospace Engineering at University of Southern California. He had received a brochure from USC then and at the back of the page was a funny piece titled "Ten Reasons to Date an Engineer." A couple of the answers were, "Know what those other buttons on your calculator are for," "We know how friction gets results," but his favorite was "Bernoulli's principle, area of high pressure creates lift." He laughed so hard when he first read that and dreamed of when he'd share that joke with his fellow classmates at USC.

The path was supposed to be clear; his commitment passing the mark, his parents supporting his dreams and clear plans. Till that day, he still thought about how everything fell apart. His SAT scores just fell short, his scholarship applications were unfortunately denied, and his parents' finances never quite pulled through. He finally settled for Psychology at Blinn College and again hoped his life would pick up after that. He ended up working for the state prisons and never quite learned to find occupational happiness again. The dissatisfaction that plagued his life hung over his head like a dirty halo and he was done trying to shake it off.

He stood staring out his window when a knock came on his door.

"Yes."

Tana Torres walked in.

Stanley thought about the prisoners, how their lives may have been before then, and how they felt, locked up in a place like AS-CHA. He never let the thought take him too far, it was a principle for him to never involve himself in a prisoner's personal life no matter how tragic it was.

Something about Tana really annoyed him. Many of the prisoners there showed either extreme defiance or much contriteness, hoping to be let off early on good behavior or even if it was just to keep one's head down, but not Tana. There was a nonchalance about her he didn't understand, especially for someone in her predicament.

She looked much older than twenty-five, which was further compounded by her default vacant and distant expressions, her generally unkempt hair, dry face, parched lips, and the sense of hopelessness that followed her every step. She looked like a forgotten gangster girl. She was there for her final psych session.

After she sat down, he went straight to it.

"Are you married?"

Tana wondered why a prison official who had access to all her records would ask such question. It wasn't like he was new and didn't know what to do.

"No."

He checked off an item on his paper.

"Parents?"

"No."

"Fiancé or boyfriend?"

"No."

He deliberately refused to feel sorry for her as he continued to check off the examination sheet.

"Girlfriend?"

Her facial expression said, "Don't be stupid." He allowed himself the chide.

"Okay, anyone at all who can claim your remains after your execution?"

Her eyes reddened and teared up, but her face held resolute.

While he observed her, he once again reminded himself not to take pity on her. Everyone was responsible for their own destiny and her personal failures were not his concern. He was already plagued with his own and again, his thoughts drifted for a bit. He tried to continue from where he stopped. He was already gone past his SAT scores and his parents' financial crises. He looked past her and to around his office; the government worker-ness of it all, to the pants he'd worn a million times and his wedding ring, hanging on like a blood-sucking leech that refused to let go. He allowed himself no pity toward Tana.

His eyes went back to her and saw her brows were knitted with confusion. He'd been distracted more than a moment.

"I'm sorry, you said?"

"No."

"Are we supposed to throw your remains in the trash? We don't have burial space here."

She took a bit to take it in before responding.

"Can you please suggest something?"

He sighed and took to his checklist.

"Okay. It says here that 'in the event that the subject cannot provide any information as to a receiving party in the segment above,' the following options are available: the first here is full organs donation, then there is science for teaching hospitals and research institutes, or any other government approved private institution. There's also the option of cremation, which of course can still occur after the organs donations and research."

"What will happen at the research place or hospital?"

Stanley made certain to lace his response with an extra dose of indifference.

"You'd be used as cadaver. Medical students will cut you open for practice."

It wasn't lost on her. She searched his face, wondering why.

"I'll take it."

"Okay. And what about the organs donation? You should maybe consider that since it'll help more deserving people."

More deserving people. She frowned at him, staring straight in his eyes for so long even Stanley got uncomfortable. She finally broke the gaze while letting out a very long and characteristic hiss.

"I'll do the cremation. Just the cremation."

"You're not donating the organs?"

She shook her head.

"What about research?"

"I said no!" She stared him straight in the eyes, returning the defiance, visibly upset.

He shrugged, ticked the last checkbox, and scribbled a note on the forms and handed over to her.

"Please sign here."

She weakly scribbled her name and paused as if to check if it was nice enough and gave it back to him. As he reached out to take it, she took it back and put a giant "X" paint on the organs donation check box for "No." Then she handed it back to him.

He observed it for a bit, shook his head, made a final note and banged the institution's stamp on it loudly and proceeded to dump it in a folder with other documents.

"That would be all. You're scheduled for Thursday the twenty eighth of next month."

As she walked out, he allowed himself drift away again, reaching for his pack of cigarettes in the drawer.

***

His space had become a numbing static, like the sound that came out of old television sets when the networks closed out for the day. It was like a sad score one heard whenever his mess of a life played out. The muffled sounds coming from the TV in the living room, the loud clicking of the old grandpa clock that hung in the kitchen for no justifiable reason, as if taunting him on how much of a waste of time his existence was, and of course the humming of the microwave, the only source of comfort in his life presently. He was again lost in thought while staring at the takeout pack from the food place.

Beep. His meal was ready.

At the dining, he knew Michelle made every effort to ignore him. Her aloofness, in her nightgown, legs folded up on the sofa, playing with her hair while staring at the TV had become a constant image for him. He knew exactly what he would find her doing every night, no matter what time he came home. He knew the posture and particular positions she took. He wondered if he would ever ask why she watched Jerry Springer every night, however perfectly the chaos from the show mirrored their life. He wondered how surprised he would be coming home one day to find her doing something else or better still, dead. It gave him comfort, thinking about finding her dead, maybe from a heart attack or a razor to the wrist or some freak accident. Who cared? He usually thought about her when he watched "A Thousand Ways to Die."

He chewed on his dinner as he continued to fantasize about her dying. Mentally, he rehearsed his frantic call to 911 or his crocodile tears before her parents. Her mother was just like her, but then again, her father, that old bastard. Clearly, refusing to die ran in the family.

He finished cleaning the countertop and used area then took the food take out pack to the trash. Very conspicuously placed in the open bin was an unwrapped used tampon. It was red and gorged with blood, sitting in the middle and on top on the trash. Clearly, she dropped them just when he was about to get in. He should have gotten used to it already but still, he allowed himself to get shocked every time. It was going to be throughout the current period. From his mental count she had a day or two to go.

He was still visibly upset when he got outside with the trash, a lot with Michelle for being such a psychopath but also with himself and the situation he'd allowed himself to get into.

As he stood beside the trash bin, he looked around as his anger faded to general dissatisfaction. Through a window of a house about half a block away, he watched an old couple dancing, held in each other's embrace. Other than that, all was quiet, no other excitement. It reminded him how much he hated his life, then he walked back in.

As he smoked later that night in a private make-shift man cave behind the house, he let his thoughts travel far still. He thought about Tana and chastised himself for being so callous earlier that day. He thought about his eight-year-old marriage and how quickly it had deteriorated, about Michelle and her lack of forgiveness, and the tampon tantrum she threw every month. He still wished her dead, though. He needed to escape. Sometimes he did envy those in prison for being so far away from it all. He wondered why it never occurred to him to take his own life, if he would ever get to that point or if he'd have the guts if he ever did but, in that moment, he hoped he would have the guts to shoot Michelle instead.

***

It had stopped being because he was horny, the frequency didn't even allow him to get horny anymore. It was more a routine, an establishment of comfortable familiarity and most importantly, an exit point for stress. It wasn't necessarily pleasure either. Okay, of course it was a bit of pleasure, but it was an important handpicked routine to end the day. The last time he didn't masturbate before bed, he did not sleep throughout the night and had a messy day afterward. As he stroked, he focused his mind on his wife, her nonchalance ever so defiant, on ASCHA and its deadness, his chaotic life that managed to stay uneventful at the same time, his disapproving father, Angela Blaine and her smirk-laced stupid face that seemed to say, "I'd have fucked you but you're way below the pay grade," and instead resorted to mocking him with her every gaze; on the ASCHA co-workers and their scheming, the inmates that bored him with their constant meaningless chatter, his dead neighborhood and the prison he found his life in. Eyes tightly closed; he ran these thoughts in his mind like a slide show as his stroking became more vigorous. In his mind, the images and people stopped swirling and finally gathered into a pile, like rubbish, his own failures at the top on that pile. He spread his legs as if in a real simulation, stroking and breathing harder and ejaculated on top all the pile, letting out a deep muffled groan. As he steadied his breathing under the running shower, he allowed himself wonder if he wasn't a psychopath himself, just like his wife. Maybe they were meant for each other after all. Was he the only one who got off on such images? But his was a ritual, a coping mechanism, and a way to say "fuck you" to it all. It was better than taking an assault rifle to Angela's office. That thought only crossed his mind once.

In the bedroom, Michelle lay backing his side of the bed, awake but pretending to sleep, deliberately leaving him little space as if she wanted to be asked to move. Standing by and staring at her, he in turn wondered if it wasn't her deliberate attempt to initiate communication. Was she tired of her tampon tantrums? They actually hadn't had a single conversation in two years. Not one. The house routine was so set they didn't even need to discuss food or bills. They simply found their place and moved on. He took a pillow and walked out. After he left, she opened her eyes and raised her head to glance at the shut door.

T hrough the ripples from the activity on the water and the heavy fog, he tried to focus on his image. His pale looking reflection in the water, moving with the ripples was recognizable yet different. He was certain it was him yet marveled at how different he looked. His dark chocolate skin looked tainted with a gray coating and his eyes were sunken, then he settled on the small round shadow like a hole on his forehead. He thought about Reginald with the gun, that bastard did shoot him after all. The itchy pain came back again, but a bit more gently and he carefully rubbed his finger over it.

As they approached their destination, the street closest to the water, he noticed the place looked oddly familiar. He looked around in the sky for the sun, it hung there still, the very same way he had first seen it. The light rays were gray and melancholic. Everything around regardless of color had a gray tint to it.

The buildings didn't exactly look like anything he'd seen in Phoenix, certainly not in Jisike but surely such building existed somewhere in America. They looked normal, sort of.

"We actually do have all of eternity but still, the dead wait for no one."

AJ raised his head to see the rower waiting for him. Everyone else had gotten off the boat and headed off to a cluster. Behind him, further from the shore, on the water were an innumerable number of boats being rowed their way.

"As was explained to you by the transfer agents at the Exchange, the tablets you've been given carry your situations. It's the exact year, month, day, hour, minute, second and sub-second of your death. So, we're all currently in the twenty-third street of the thirteenth Segment. We will be walking to building number forty-seven, there you will find the domain number that corresponds to the one you're holding.

If you have questions or concerns, there are full rule guides in each of your domains. Read them. Your passing here depends on understanding those rules, there will be no exception, ignorance is no excuse. If anything is unclear, there are officers around. Ask questions. That being said, enjoy your passing and welcome to Animmo."

As they all dispersed, each checking their tablet, AJ lingered.

"Is there a question you would like me to answer, Andrew Jackson?"

"You can call me AJ."

"Of course, AJ."

"I have a question; I hope it doesn't cross the line."

"Everything is laid bare in Animmo, there are no secrets here. We're all of death and rest eternally in it. Ask."

"What is your name?"

"I have no name, but you can address me by my situation, "1875-03-30, 23:15:01:47." AJ knew he'd remember that. Not sure how, but he knew he would.

He looked just like some of the gender-neutral attendants at the Exchange.

"You don't look like anyone I've ever seen or met. I can't even tell if you're male or female. Were you once human?"

His gaze back at AJ was deep and searching, yet without offence.

"I almost was. Those of us that look different were children that were not born. In my case, I was a miscarriage."

"So, all children that were not born become like you?"

"Not all. There are abortions. Those come out as enforcers. Others are more sinister, like the *Ofuukus*."

"Ofuukus?"

"Yes. They, you do not ever want to cross paths with. Go on in and rest your soul, you experienced a sudden death."

"One more question."

"Yes?"

"You keep referring to consequences of breaking the rules. We're already dead, what could be worse?"

He studied him for a bit, "trust me, you have no idea."

He turned and walked back toward the Exchange.

***

Maleek watched the body bag get lifted into the back of the ambulance, the neighbors peeping through their curtains to watch.

The calm in the atmosphere was unusual, especially after a murder so next door. He'd handled homicides in other neighborhoods, regular and rich neighborhoods, and when the neighbors gathered, they usually looked alarmed, afraid, hugging and consoling each other. This was different. A few neighbors were outside, most watched through their curtains, there was sadness of course but there was something different about this grief, a sinister familiarity. He guessed some of them had lost loved ones, near and distant, friends or knew someone who knew someone who lost someone in a similarly violent manner.

He figured this would be one of the many cases that will go cold, but justice would still be served because the *hommie* that did it would most likely end up the victim of another drug related violence or maybe be arrested for an unrelated case.

He let go of his thoughts and walked up to Sarah and Jessica who were still sobbing.

"Hello, I'm Detective Maleek Shapiro. I am truly very sorry for your loss. I need to ask you a few questions."

Sarah had nothing else to tell him and neither did Jessica. They both said, almost with complete similarity, their accounts of that day. He noted their description of heavyset, five foot eleven, two hundred- and fifty-pound black man.

He offered his condolence once more and left, knowing the case would be cold and forgotten in no time.

*****

Seated on the bed, Stanley was dressed in his pants and an inner white t-shirt. His shirt lay on the bed, with his dusty shoes on the floor in front of him. He picked up one of the pairs, took the sock from inside and smelt it, trying to mentally assess how dirty it was. He looked the shoe over and wiped the shoe clean with the same sock, then wore the same sock and then the shoe. He did same for the other pair. While putting on his shoes, he paused to turn on the tv. It was muted, showing a morning news broadcast with the Arizona State Governor, Reginald Tyson, late 50s, African American, addressing the press. At the bottom, the caption, "Breaking News: Gov. Tyson vetoes state minimum wage increase bill," scrolled by. He turned off the TV just as quickly and left the room.

***

As he drove into the ASCHA complex, bobbing his head to the music on the radio, he spotted Lejandro ahead, just beside an open parking spot. He pulled up and parked in the space.

"Hey there, papi," he called as he got out.

"The young man is chilling, amigo, sweet and comfortable just the way my mamma made me," his deep Mexican accent very present. "How you doing?"

"Can't complain," Stanley answered.

"Amen, my brother. By the way, your girl has called for a meeting."

"Angela?" Perhaps he shouldn't have thought about her all night long. It was over a year ago, he admitted to himself that he had a weird sexual interest in Angela, and he hated her as well. She made him feel like a high school freshman who couldn't talk to his crush who was a senior. Also, she made it a point of duty to humiliate him in front of all the staff members. It was like an agenda item she carried out diligently. He admitted the crush to himself the day he got aroused while she was on with one of her usual rants. Since that day, every time she started yelling at or insulting him, he sustained an erection till she was finished. Once, in her office, after another round of insults, he didn't bother to hide it or let it die down. He stood up straight and turned around to leave, knowing she had seen it. He may have been a loser but yes, he was quite meaty. Was showing off his meat print another coping mechanism? Perhaps a middle finger to her sky? Whenever he thought about this, he saw himself seated with the ladies from *The View* and Whoopi Goldberg judging him.

At the general meeting, Stanley and Lejandro sat across each other from both ends. Others present were Michael Hays, middle aged, potbellied; Susan Bethany, mid-forties; Jessica Kirk-Patrick, Mindy Woo, Alicia Stone, Jake Jackson, Eugene Soro, Linda D'Agostin, and Franny Williams, all ranging from twenty-eight to sixty. At the head of the meeting was Angela Blaine, fifty-five. She carried a cunning aura about herself that was present and made some people uncomfortable and guarded around her.

"The summary of it all is that considering past control exceptions noted in our processes, the governor has chosen to pay us closer attention. We have an execution scheduled for next twenty-eighth and we can't fuck that up. So housekeeping people, housekeeping." Angela sounded like a husky bird when she spoke, but she was clearly in charge, however the indifference from her staff suggested she was not very liked.

She continued, "Bethany, Woo, you two are to increase your surveillance, perhaps change your loop patterns. Hays maybe switch the narcotics personnel entirely, so the girls are taken by surprise for now." While talking, she caught Franny rolling her eyes. She paused to contemplate it or possibly address her but decided against it.

She continued, "We've got roughly forty-five days. We haven't had an execution at this facility in almost nine years, still, a high profile one since forever. Soro, did you receive Weppler's report yet?"

"Yes. Estimate for the repairs of the press and visitor viewing area is complete. Should be on your desk for approval before end of day. Also, the room should be set in time for the due date. Phoenix had to delay sending the package because of faulty Pavulon cannisters. Minor setback and not uncommon either. Other than that, everything's as planned." Soro looked satisfied with himself, and Angela concurred with no follow-up questions. She turned her attention to Stanley.

"Weppler?"

"Yes?" Stanley answered after a short pause, just in case a question was following his name.

"How is she?"

"How is who?" Stanley knew it was about Tana, but didn't give into such line of questioning from Angela. He had sworn to always make her clarify her questions before he answered.

"Who else? Tana. Weppler, are you with us?"

"Oh, she's great. I mean, she's scheduled to die in a few weeks from now, maybe losing her shit already but other than that, I'm sure she's having a blast."

Angela tried to maintain decorum, "Anything you'd like to report on her mental state? Anything we can do to help her?"

"Yes, I believe."

His pause irritated her. "And?"

"Perhaps calling off her execution. Or dope her up so she forgets."

Others around the room struggled not to chuckle. Angela gave him a deathly stare and walked away. Perhaps, she wasn't in the mood for him.

***

When he first arrived Animmo, his domain was in the street right next to the stream where the boats had rowed them across. Now, more streets had emerged behind theirs and the stream was no longer in sight. As he stood looking out his window on this gray tinted world of buildings around him, he wondered how long he'd been here, what Jessica and his mom were doing. Here, time was nothing but a concept in a bygone world. Everything stood still and stagnant and it felt like he had only arrived a second ago but, even still, like he'd been here a long time, an eternity, actually. Time, together with its precisions and measures and uses, was for the living. In Animmo, in the absence of all the things that made for life and living, you know, like work, love, trouble, hate, fun; all that was left was stillness, nothingness. Being the primary content with which Animmo was made, nothing therefore mattered.

His domain was a single space of unending grayness, unending to all corners, except one, which had the door. Emptiness, no furnishing. Vanity and comfort were for the living; no kitchen or bathroom; hunger, nutrition, excretion were for the living. Rubbing his hands over himself, his hands felt numb, or maybe the numbness was on his body, again, he wasn't sure. He put his hands down his pants to touch his dick and felt numbness, enough to make him doubt feeling anything, like his arms had been tied to cut off blood supply for too long. This was death, and at its very core was nothing, an eternity of nothing and for eternity to work, time would have to cease to exist as it no longer mattered. And was time not a mere construct, alive solely in the minds of those who were conscious for it? How then could the dead keep time?

Eternity.

He was holding onto but yet to open *Oku Animmo*, the instructional guide for the dead. He finally did.

"For what is death but the proof of life?

Is it not but a finish line, a conclusion to a venture?

Can that which cannot die say it has lived?

Can that which never lived experience death?

Does one have meaning without the other?

The lightening etches its pattern in the darkness, even after its gone.

For what is death but the proof of life?

It is but a finish line, a conclusion to a venture."

He flipped the page.

"Nothing matters. Nothing matters any more. Everything matters.

Nothing, the continuum of emptiness between one thing and the next.

Nothing, the invisible factor around which place and situation is understood.

Does nothing not contribute to the balance of everything?

Does nothing not precede and succeed everything?

Is nothing not then a part of everything?

If nothing then matters, just like everything, then nothing matters any more.

Nothing matters. Nothing matters any more. Everything matters."

Next page.

"It is wise to let the dead bury the dead.

To be without death is to be without form.

For form is no more without death, an end of what gives it form.

For to take away death is to be formless.

So shall be the fate of those who would seek to manipulate death
and the dead.
For their path shall be with death for death to keep its form.
Be warned, for death is for the living but the dead do die, still.
It is wise for the dead to bury the dead."

"The dead do die, still?" Maybe he'd understand it one day? Or perhaps, he never would, since time becomes irrelevant with death and is therefore non-existent. So, if one day will never come, would he *never* understand this?

A knock came on the door, and he opened.

It was Kester, aka "Ice Man", a name he got by providing the best *skooches* anywhere. The ones with the best and longest high left you with a trembling cold for about a minute. The chills from Kester's were the strongest and got him dubbed "Ice Man".

Kester now was truly a ghost of himself. His swag and general brightness were no more. Even his gold teeth, which he apparently died with looked like ordinary metal in the grayness of Animmo. Nothing mattered any more.

"Kester!"

"Seventh."

"You're here? What happened to you?"

"Governor Reginald Tyson, baby. Who else?" He spoke with a tired sad humor.

"I had no idea. I'm sorry." He truly meant his sympathy. Kester looked like he died, trapped in a blizzard and froze to death. The

"Ice Man" alias was very fitting at this point. What could have happened to him, he wondered?

"I, on the other hand, have been expecting you." Kester delivered this almost with some enthusiasm.

"What? Why?"

"Who else, Seventh, but the governor?"

"What the fuck?"

"Yup. And he says this time around, you better not fail him."

"Or he'll what, kill me again? Or tell his dad to torment my soul?"

"His dad?"

"Satan."

"Aha," he replied, deliberately ignoring the intended humor. "Your mom. And Jessica. He'll kill them both."

"What? How do you know this?"

"He's got plans for you, Seventh. Plans, he set in motion even before you got that shadow kiss on your forehead."

AJ stared at him in confusion, rubbing the shadow on his forehead.

***

He couldn't have been more than twenty-three. His ice blue eyes stared far into nothing and even though his mouth was open, his frozen face looked perfectly at peace. As Maleek squatted beside the lifeless body covered in sheet, he couldn't help but wonder what this deceased boy had seen or experienced.

"Detective?"

"Yes." He stood up and walked toward Officer Craig. She walked ahead of him to the dining table.

At the table was Raquel, about twenty-one. She looked calm but had sad, puffy eyes from crying.

"Hi, I'm Detective Shapiro. What's your name?"

"Raquel," she answered and spelt it out.

"Thank you, Raquel." He took notes. "How do you know the victim?"

"Tyler was my boyfriend, a couple of years now."

"I see. Can you tell me what happened here?"

"He overdosed."

"I'm sorry, did you say overdosed?

"Yes"

"Uhm, that person looks frozen."

"Yes, he does. We heard it happened to some guy too, but we thought it was a joke. Apparently, that's what an OD looks like."

"What drug is this?" He continued to scribble.

"It's called skooches," Officer Craig answered. "Not sure of a proper chemical name yet. It's a new drug, hit the streets recently. Was a typical chill party drug and really didn't ruffle any feathers, well, initially."

"So, what happened?" Maleek was waiting for the death turn part. Officer Craig turned to Raquel.

"Word started to spread a few months ago that some guy had mixed his drink with his finger after he cut himself. Its reaction with his blood gave him a trip that was like totally awesome. Unlike any he ever had before. So, we been doing that too."

Maleek was obviously puzzled, "Describe this high to me."

Maleek noticed through her puffy eyes that she was transported to that good place. He also noticed a hint of pleasured smile on the corner of her lips. She spoke calmly.

"It's not just a high. It's a trip, to a different and more beautiful place. Your mind is alive, and you see crystal clear images that you never seen before and in ways you never seen them before. It feels like a long time. It feels like another existence. In that place you feel like you've discovered the secret to life. The happiness is pure ecstasy, and you feel good on every single inch of your skin." She gently rubbed both hands on her upper arms, as if chilly.

"So, how does one overdose on it?"

"Word spread again that mixing the stuff with blood from different people made for better trips. But this only happens if you have the very pure stuff. Also, the more people whose blood are in it, the more intense and longer the experience. When it's really good, you experience the chill,"

Maleek's brows knit up, making the connection.

"The chill?"

"Yes, the chill," Raquel responded calmly.

"So how much of this chill killed Tyler?"

"The experience is usually totally out of body. But word spread around, yet again, that if you do it while you're already, like having sex or whatever, and then have the trip, if you orgasm while on that shit? The scales will fall off your eyes. The orgasm comes with enlightenment."

Maleek could see she was struggling for words to describe it. Anything that made a kid of today's hyper conscious and woke generation this speechless must truly be remarkable.

"It's like you witness and experience the Big Bang all over again." Slowly and with regret she added, "Tyler used to say each time he came, as in nutted, it felt like a spiritual messenger came and took the cum out of him. It was forceful too. Sometimes he felt the pain in that area for days."

"Holy shit!" Maleek couldn't help his exclamation.

"So, what made this happen to Tyler?"

She carefreely eased out of her trance to continue.

"He couldn't get enough. I mean, neither could I. He knew some guy that knew some guy that could get him the very pure stuff. He also made a group of five brothers donate their bloods, word had spread again that if the blood donors are related, it's even much better. So last night, he said he wanted to see God's face."

"The drug makes you see God's face?" Maleek wondered if his asking that question was out of investigative due diligence or from sheer gossip-laced curiosity. Was he getting interested? He wondered what God's face looked like. Would God be attractive?

"Only with a climax," Raquel responded. "The most we had done together, and I think him too, was blood of 3 random guys. But I guess yesterday's being five brothers and the stuff was in its purest form, I don't know. I had taken just a sip of mine because

I was supposed to write a test later today and didn't wanna be too fucked up. But he downed the whole thing."

Raquel looked up and around, eyes lost in thought. Maleek knew she was thinking about the sex they had. Both he and Officer Craig looked on carefully, to let her story fully play out. She was about a full minute.

Maleek finally interjected.

"Raquel. Raquel!"

Carefreely again, she continued. "Anyway."

"I was right," thought Maleek.

"That was the coldest I ever felt in my life, and I grew up in Minnesota. It was strong cold, it really scared me. But as the chills die out, you usually fall asleep. It was when I woke up this morning, I found him like this,"

All three were silent. Maleek wasn't sure how to proceed.

"Do you think you've learnt your lessons?" Officer Craig asked, filled with pity for her.

Her eyes teared up again, helplessly. "No," she said calmly.

"Why not?"

"Cos I'll do it again. I know I will. I believe even sooner than I'm willing to admit."

Maleek and Officer Craig fell silent again.

As Maleek walked away, he paused and turned back to her.

"Raquel, you had said initially that," he investigated his notes, "the stuff, skooches, makes you feel like you've discovered the secret to the universe. What is this secret?"

"That nothing matters. Nothing matters above all," she stated as a matter of fact.

He was rather disappointed with that answer and concluded that skooches or whatever must have really fucked her mind but then, the audacity of her response made him show some respect and not lose his blank face.

"I see. Also, this guy who knew some guy that he got the stuff from, did you get the name of either of them?"

"The guy that knew the main guy was AJ."

"And where can I find this AJ guy?" Maleek was taking notes.

"He lives upstate. Jisike."

Maleek was hit with the realization. "Andrew Jackson?"

"Seventh. Yeah, that's him."

I think we have a case here.

As he walked out of the house, he noticed the body carried into the ambulance. He beckoned to them and ran quickly over there.

In the van, he unzipped the body bag to observe his face again. He unzipped further down and noticed the freeze look had not waned. Even frozen meat should have tawed by now. How deeply frozen was this guy? As he unzipped past the genital area, he noticed the genitals looked extended at the base of the pelvic region. He called for a flashlight.

"What the hell is this?" It looked like his pelvis bone had been broken forward. He looked up at the EMT guys who looked equally confused.

"Any idea what could have caused this"?

"No idea."

"Thanks."

As he walked to his car, he checked his time. It was 11:28 am. He had to get to Jisike.

***

When Stanley arrived at the cell, it was already upside down, with wardens Mindy Woo and Jessica D'Agostin struggling to pin both women to opposite walls of the cell to keep them away from each other.

"I will fucking murder you, you filthy bitch! You dead, you hear me?"

The cell literally stank of shit.

"Bring it on, porch monkey. I ain't scared o'ya."

"Porch monkey?" Stanley was personally offended by this and screamed loud into Gethrude's face. "Shut the fuck up, Gertrude, or I'll have your aged ass in the tank!"

Gertrude was suddenly hurt, totally unaware of her own wrong doings, resting her hand on her chest like she was the only one allowed to be a victim.

"Now, what the fuck is going on here?"

Victoria spoke up first.

"She refuses to use the toilet. She never does. Instead, she'll literally piss and poop in a container and then throw it in the toilet. Why can't she just use the toilet? Why can't she just use the fucking toilet? She does this every day and it's driving me crazy."

"Gertrude, this true?" Stanley demanded.

"Yes?" she answered, defiantly, without even an attempt at denial.

Stanley was already hoping if it was true, that it was because she was just confused or due to some other mental issue but a deliberate action like this?

"Why would you do that, Gertrude? Why don't you use the toilet?"

"Because I need to be connected to nature. That gadget is unnatural and not God's plan for me. When I do it the natural way, it heals my aching soul."

Stanley had truly heard it all. "That is out of the question, madam, you will use the toilet like everyone else."

"Over my dead body. This is my First Amendment right."

"Taking a shit anywhere you want doesn't count as freedom of speech," Stanley barked at her.

"Yes, it does."

"How? Spewing crap from your asshole ain't speech." Victoria was done being nice, "Look, you either move her or me out of this place 'cause I ain't taking this shit another day."

Stanley had had enough. "Yes. Woo, please move her royal majesty here to solitary and find Victoria another cellmate."

Gertrude struggled some more, "This ain't over, I know my rights."

As Stanley walked away, he looked down to the common area, observing the crowd of about thirty-five women. Few whites, the minority races, especially black and Hispanic, were prevalent. In groups or alone, they all looked deep in their own thoughts, each in their quiet haze. At the corner was a group of black girls beating up a Latina. Wardens Alicia Stone and Jake Jackson rushed in to stop the fight. While they were being broken up, Stanley's gaze moved and settled on Tana. At the same time, as if knowing someone was watching her, she turned her head straight in Stanley's direction, caught his eyes and returned an angry frown at him. She stared at him till he turned his gaze and walked away. He'd done the job long enough to not take these things personal, especially with the prisoners. If he was scheduled to die soon, who knew how he'd react himself?

***

No one else was out but them two. As they walked along the streets of Animmo, he noticed all the buildings looked the same as they walked in opposite direction from the stream across which he had first arrived. They crossed from *segments* into *regions* and into earlier *places*. Once again, he pondered how mixed-up time, or its absence felt. He knew they were going a long way, but it felt like they had only left his domain just a split second ago, whatever a split second meant there, same way it felt he crossed over into Animmo a split second ago, yet, both events still could have been an eternity ago, but did it matter? No.

He turned to Kester who only walked eyes forward.

"Care to say where we going?"

"Cool your horses, Seventh. You're with the Ice Man."

"I don't imagine that means anything down here."

Kester smiled.

"We'll see, bro."

"You always say that when you're up to no good."

Kester smiled again.

"Why you keep smiling? You gonna say something? We're dead. What could we possibly do for the governor? Besides, I'm sure you know there are rules to this place."

Kester stopped and faced him abruptly.

"Mr. Excruciatingly Prim and Proper, who just also happens to sell drugs by the way, what the actual fuck? Can you please drop the sanctimonious bullshit."

AJ just stared on at him.

Kester continued. "You know why *Oku Animmo* warns against manipulating death? Well, that's 'cause death can be manipulated, genius."

In Animmo, because time no longer exists and everything stands still, no one ever forgets anything, because time does not pass.

"You also know it says their path shall be with death for death to keep its form," AJ responded without hesitation.

"And what they gonna do, kill us again?"

"Well, it does say the dead do die, still."

"And what the fuck does that even mean?" Kester was done trying to convince him and walked on.

"Like I said, you have no choice. Follow me or Jessica and your mom will be joining you here soon."

He stopped and turned again to AJ to ensure his point was well driven home.

"And there ain't no family homes here bro, to each his fucking own."

He walked off again, briskly. AJ walked after him.

When they reached building 9 of the 22nd *segment* of the fifth *region* in 1998 *place*, AJ hit a wall. It was invisible. He put up his hands and felt around. It was impermeable, just like that wall when he first crossed over. Yet, Kester was still walking ahead, clearly oblivious to this.

"Ice!"

Kester stopped and turned.

"Oh, shit, this you?" he asked, laughing out lightly.

"What do you mean?" AJ wasn't sure how to respond as Kester walked back to him.

Kester gleaned the details from their current *situation*. "May 22, 1998."

"How do you know that?"

Kester responded by pointing him to the very building where he couldn't go past. "I see you haven't read all of *Oku Animmo.*"

"Bro, please explain." AJ was getting frustrated.

"In Animmo, you can't go back beyond the day and hour of your birth, kid!" Kester delivered proudly, as usual.

"Really. How much farther do you go?"

"Nineteen eighty-nine *place*, kid!"

"Okay, calm down, old man. So, I can't go any further, what do we do now?"

Kester stretched out his hand to take his. AJ pulled it away immediately, curious.

"Cool your horses, faggot, and gimme your hand."

AJ reached out and took it. Kester pulled him through that invisible barrier. It felt like he walked through a liquid shield that also passed through him, leaving him feeling slightly sick.

"Don't worry about that sick feeling. Its 'cause you ain't supposed to be here."

"So, all one needs is to hold someone who lived in that *place* to cross?"

"No!" Kester raised his shirt to reveal his frosty skin. Sunk into his navel by four sets of double extending needles, was a beetle shaped flat metal. He watched AJ closely as he examined it.

"What the hell is that?"

"It's called an *ezi*. If you got one, you could walk outside of your time of life."

"How did you get this?" AJ asked suspiciously.

"I'm the Ice Man, baby. Turns out that actually means something down here." He walked on and AJ followed.

When they arrived the 31st *segment* of the tenth *region*, Kester stopped.

"Now understand this, in there, you're with me alone and speak to me alone."

"Sure, but what's up?" AJ wondered if he should turn back.

"We are actually breaking rules so just don't make anyone uncomfortable."

"Oh!"

Inside, it held an average crowd, about twenty-five people in there. From their attires, one could guess what era or time they were from. An ancient Nubian-Egyptian, a middle-aged man in Nazi uniform, to a couple of black men in afro and bell bottom jeans and fitted shirts, a nun, knight from the dark ages, and many others from different times and past cultures.

Was that Fela? As usual, he was uncertain, but he didn't know of any other dead black musicians who walked around in their briefs. That was just for show, right. Although this would be his kind of spot, given its Shrine vibes. Many looked normal and AJ thought they must have died of natural causes or some non-physically altering ailments. Others clearly suffered violent deaths of various forms. As AJ observed them, an ancient Viking walked in, passed them and walked straight to the corner area in the back, speaking with an attendant. He had a shadowy hole through his neck and visible on both sides.

Kester gave polite nods to a few of them that knew him.

Kester leaned in to whisper, "the dead do die still, huh? These ones are here. They haven't died, still."

"What is this place?"

"It's called *Oluku*. It's like a brothel. For sexual pleasure and other vices."

"What?" AJ whispered, incredulous. "In Animmo, our senses are dead. To what end?"

"Time is no more but we keep our memories. Some like to re-live them. Pun intended." Kester followed with a chuckle.

"Why? They're dead. I felt my body and even my dick, I felt nothing."

Kester turned him around to watch the Viking at the bar area who had a bowl of gray-tinted blood. He dipped his open palms in the bowl and then walked over to take a human sized skin and wore it. The skin looked like one of those gender-neutral spirits he saw during his arrival.

Kester explained. "It's called an *ahu*. *A* body you wear and then you can see and feel the pleasures of the living. The alcohol or whatever substance they use and especially their sexual pleasure."

"So, they just choose people at random and what, experience them?"

"No don't be silly, kid. Only those who fuck with or generally use the gray one."

"Skooches."

"The kid is catching on."

AJ rolled his eyes. "So how do I come in?"

"Simple for a start. You'll come around and help deliver skooches to life."

"Skooches comes from here, in Animmo?"

"Bingo."

"How? What the fuck?"

Kester turned again and AJ followed his gaze, to the Viking's *ahu* as he intently watched a very advanced and exactly real life 3-D projection of a couple having sex. The couple he was watching looked like they were burning, but clearly not being consumed.

On the *ahu*, the Viking rubbed the genital region. Although the ahu had no noticeable or identifiable genital, the rubbing produced a ripple like many stones dropping into water, very slow moving but also having high amplitude, and all maintaining same height, even at their terminal points. As he continued to rub it, AJ watched in horror as he shuddered and from the genital area, at the wave elevations, he noticed a colorless liquid start to ooze out. It grew and finally filled up high above the crests of the waves and oozed to the floor, quickly settling into the consistency he was familiar with. He choked back a vomit.

"Reflex, kid. The dead don't puke," Kester teased.

AJ watched the skinned Viking stand up and go take off the *ahu*. He avoided eye contact with him as he walked out the door.

"That was beyond fucked up," he said clutching his stomach as the sickly feeling inside intensified.

"What? You pissed you been chugging some dead guy's nut? We all been cucking after all. Imagine that." Kester laughed out loud.

"For what it's worth, they're genderless," AJ quickly retorted.

"So, the ones you did were all squirt and not cum. Glad that makes you feel better."

As they both continued to watch, the Nazi uniformed man scooped up all the stuff into his mouth and swallowed.

"And that's how you collect skooches."

"Say again?" AJ demanded.

Kester pulled him to a corner and spoke in low tone.

"Listen, you were right, the dead do die, still. There are fucked up consequences for what you're about to be doing. You see, whatever you've got inside stays inside you and no one bothers you. Animmo only gets disturbed when what is inside is exposed. You transport skooches in your mouth, as a first option."

"Fuck no!" AJ blurted out, about to walk away.

Kester pulled him back and pushed him against the wall. "What's the problem, ain't it just squirt no more?" AJ lost that argument.

"By the way, you can't taste shit."

"Why in the mouth?"

"Cause of the *Ofuukus.*"

"The Ofuukus? Same Ofuukus?"

"The Ofuukus bro," Kester repeated sadly, slowly. "Some sinewy, one-legged mother fuckers, man. If you ever cross parts with those things," he put both hands on AJ's shoulders and lowered to hold eye level, "bro, you are fucking fucked."

"Then why go ahead?"

"Cause its manageable."

"What we keep concealed won't get us in trouble," AJ added, in realization.

"Which is why we move it in the mouth. You see, you're a fast learner," Kester responded gleefully.

"But wait now, you said we use the mouth as a first option. What's the second one?"

Kester paused and then sighed.

"Perfect segue. You, uhm, you swallow."

AJ had his vomit reflex again.

"You good?"

Now angry, he said, "Why the fuck we gotta swallow? No better options?"

"You might run into enforcers, and they might question you, as will most likely happen, then you gotta swallow it, bro, without hesitation. Don't ever think you can keep it in the corner of your mouth or think you can just smile, wave and walk away. If you're ever approached by an enforcer, you must speak up. Quickly swallow. You're gonna puke it out at the gate."

"Where's the gate?"

"Anywhere you want it to be. It's usually your domain."

"How?"

"I'll give you a chant. You recite it."

AJ heaved a sigh of relief.

"So, if I swallow and go past the officers, where's the Ofuuku danger?"

"At the gate."

His shoulders slumped again. "Fuck me. Come on. Does this get any better? But this is in my domain and what's hidden is concealed. How does the Ofuuku come in?"

"The chant literally opens a portal, a gate to life. And the Ofuukus are the guardians of Animmo. Not like Homeland Security or FBI shit. More like MOSSAD and KGB and CIA, all rolled into one and then dipped in some sinister, diabolical precision kief oil and then of course served with a glass of murder steroids. You don't ever wanna fuck with those guys, or better, you don't want them to fuck you 'cause if they fuck you, you're—"

"Fucked, I get it," AJ cut in.

Kester smiled with relish, enjoying the terror on AJ's face then continued.

"What happens when you meet the Ofuukus is what Oku Animmo means by 'for their path shall be with death for death to keep its form.' You read that yet?"

AJ nodded slowly, clearly terrified. Kester still enjoyed it.

"The only legal entry into Animmo is the one you came through. There ain't no exits. The gate the chant opens is illegal and once that happens, the *Ofuukus* sense it. And them brawny shadow, one-legged demons are fucking fast, bruh. You gotta do your chants quickly and be done. You don't ever wanna see those things, they're bleeding hideous, man. They look like Hades on crack, very malevolent, full of hate and vicious. See, Hitler and Bin Laden would be their bitch babies. Bottom line, do your chants fast and be done. Once the chant is done, keep your mouth open while the gate is open. A dog will lap it out of your mouth."

Another disgusting detail. AJ wondered if there was any use protesting again.

Kester quickly responded. "Like I said, you can't taste shit. Now the chant must be said in one breath. You cannot speak any words in between, that's the only way the gate opens."

"Okay. What's the chant?"

"When I recite it now, I'll break it in two by adding words in between, so we don't open a gate here, capishe?"

AJ nodded.

"So it goes, 'I plead the everlasting doors,' and add to it, 'may death be permanent, and this death be mine.' So, it's the full sentence I just made except the 'and add to it.' Is this making any sense? Again, it's 'I plead dot dot dot, may death be permanent and dot dot dot dot.' Now repeat it only in your mind, make sure you don't whisper shit. Alright?"

AJ repeated it in his mind, "I plead the everlasting doors, may death be permanent, and this death be mine." He nodded to Kester he had it.

"Good, you'll get a note as you're needed."

Outside, Kester pointed him to the direction of his domain. "Walk only in that direction." He looked him over one more time. "Well, bye kid. I'll see you now."

He walked off toward 1989 *place.*

"See you now." AJ turned and walked back.

***

AJ had been dead about a week. Sarah had not been to work nor generally functioned much since that day. Daily, her mood swung from sorrow to anger to numbness. Anger, directed at AJ, his father, Andrew, Jessica, the bastard that took her son, at God and at herself. She was also angry with the detective in her living room who was merely using her dead son as activity, knowing the case will never be resolved. Them poor folks were never priority where American justice was concerned. If he wasn't a cop, she'd ask him to leave.

Maleek could sense her frustration and anger and decided to tread lightly. "Ma'am, I understand what you must be going through, but it seems your son was involved in something way bigger than him. We're starting to see patterns around the city and young people are turning up dead. If there's anything else you possibly remember about that day, the men who were here or even any other information about Andrew that may help."

"You got any specific questions?" Jessica interjected.

Maleek took a quick run through his notes. "Yes. Are you familiar with the substance, skooches?"

"Nope," she said without any hesitation.

"Okay, you know what kind of drugs Andrew sold?"

Sarah frowned hard at Jessica who in turn paused, stole a quick glance at her mom and gathered herself before she continued.

"Mainly weed, and some party drugs. He sold mainly around the neighborhood and to SM students."

"SM?"

"Saint Matthew College," Jessica clarified.

"Ah, I see. What about people he ran the stuff with? You know or maybe remember any of them? He had another person he did business with?"

She thought for a bit. "Just Kester."

"Who's Kester?"

"Just know him as Kester. AJ sometimes called him Ice or Ice Man or whatever."

Maleek's lights went on.

"Ice? Man?"

"Yes"

"You know why he got that name?" He took more notes.

"Nope."

"You know how I can find this Ice guy? Know when they started working together?"

"Dunno. He's one of Reginald's boys." She caught herself too late.

"Jessica!" Sarah cut in.

Silence.

"What's going on?" Maleek inquired.

"It's nothing. Detective, that's all we got. Like I said, my daughter and I have told you everything we know."

"Mom, please..."

"Shut up!" Sarah cut her off.

"What is it?" Maleek asked.

Silence.

"Ma'am, please if you've got more information, we—"

Sarah cut him again. "I said we've told you everything we have to say. Good day to you, Detective."

Pause.

"Who's Reginald?" Maleek insisted.

Silence.

"Was Reginald the man that killed AJ?"

Silence. Maleek knew it was him, also further confirmed by the concerned looks on their faces. He took more notes.

"So, Reginald killed AJ. You remember any of the other guys who he was with that night?"

"Detective!" Sarah raised her voice.

Maleek in turn gave her a stare and returned his gaze to Jessica, who was both upset and uncertain. He sensed she wanted to talk.

"One final question?"

Sarah relaxed her shoulders a bit.

"This Kester, Ice person, Reginald's guy, any idea where I might find him?"

Jessica gave her mom a glance and reassured her.

"I don't know. AJ hadn't heard from him either. He said no one had seen him in almost a week."

"I see. Thanks." Maleek updated his note. "Thanks once again for your time. You still have my card?"

"Yes." Sarah answered as she opened the door for him. She banged it loudly behind him.

As Maleek walked away, he heard them starting to argue.

In his car, before driving off, he placed a call.

"Hey, Destiny, how's it going? Yeah, I'm good. Can you please run a search for me? The name I'm looking for is Kester. Yes, I only have a first name. He's also known as Ice Man. But people stopped seeing him about two weeks ago so can you please include morgue records as well, just in case. He should range from say, late-twenties to mid-thirties. Thanks."

4

A few press men and some ASCHA staff, were gathered in the viewing room. The podium set up for the governor was backing the execution chamber, seen through the transparent glass.

Stanley couldn't wait to be out of there. He knew the photo-op wasn't about justice but a show off opportunity.

Governor Tyson concluded his speech, "My administration will always take pride in the extent to which we have rehabilitated this annex of the Arizona State Correctional Holding facility, which of course could not have been successful without the diligence and foresight of the chief warden, Ms. Angela Blaine. I've also been fully briefed on the extent of preparation for the coming execution and as you all know, we will continue to support them in every way. Okay, I have to run so maybe one question each?"

"Governor, how much has your administration earmarked for these renovations and also, will the main site benefit as well?"

"Thanks for that. This was initiated mainly from our discretionary budget, which I'm glad to say we didn't have to exhaust. However, yes, the main site will also benefit but further renovations after this set will have to be planned into the following and subsequent cycles' budgets. Next?"

"Governor, seeing Tana Torres' last resort appeal has failed, can you say yet if you'll grant clemency?"

"On that, I'm not ready to give an answer. As you all know, while it remains in my power to grant clemency, I have to consider the crime committed, impact on the community, especially the family of the victims and such. So, in a nutshell, I'm still seeking counsel and of course in talks with the attorney general in weighing the best course of action. Once a decision is made, we'll release a statement."

He had no more time for questions, gestured by his glance at his wristwatch.

"Okay then, thanks everyone."

As the reporters and the rest of the staff members dispersed, Stanley paused a bit in case Angela needed him to continue shining on her behalf, but she threw him a look that dismissed him quickly as she guided the governor onward, followed closely by wardens Jackson and D'Agostin. Relieved, he walked away.

When he got to his office, Victoria, one of the inmates, was standing by his door, waiting impatiently like she didn't want to be found there.

"Can I help you?"

"Yes, Mr. Weppler," she responded nervously.

Stanley waited for her to state her case, but she just stood there, nervously.

"Okay? You gonna say something?"

"Uhm, please follow me?"

"What? Are you asking me a question? What do you mean follow you? Should you be here?"

Stanley was about to walk into his office when she gently blocked his way with her arm, her eyes were supplicating, hoping not to get into trouble.

"Mr. Weppler, I think you need to see this, sir. Can you please follow me?"

This had never happened to him before, and Victoria wasn't exactly one of the crazier ones. Maybe this was really important. Reluctantly, he followed her.

As they descended to the basement second floor, Stanley thought he may have made a mistake by following her. If she cried foul now, how would he defend himself? It would simply be her word against his. He kept going. At the landing ahead, she stopped and peeped and then walked stealthily behind a big pile of beddings, prison clothes and other supplies and motioned for him to do the same.

From their hiding place, they could see the governor, Angela, Wardens Jackson and D'Agostin with Tana and two other prisoners, Flavor and Galina, both in their mid-twenties.

If not for the unfortunate circumstances in her life, Galina could have been the typical Russian beauty.

Jackson and D'Agostin stood behind the girls while the governor and Angela inspected them. The girls all reacted differently to him. While Tana wore her regular vacant facial expression, Galina was scared and whimpered in front of the governor.

"This is a pretty one. Ensure she's made very presentable. Is she always this whiney?" Reginald asked.

"Don't worry about her, governor. She's easy to manage and we can bolden her up when its time," Angela responded confidently.

"Good, good. And what do we have here?" he asked as he moved on to Flavor, who was clearly defiant and ready for a fight. "Will you cause me any more problems?"

Flavor was silent and stared him straight in the eyes.

With a jovial hint he said, "You should behave, or I just might reconsider commuting your sentence."

She spat on his face.

Calmly and with grace, he reached into his pocket and grabbed a handkerchief to wipe his face. He then gave a quick glance to the wardens who grabbed her arms and restrained her. He stood in front of Tana to avoid getting kneed in the groin and then proceeded to force his hand into Flavor's underwear. She struggled to resist in vain. His finger went past the pubes and groped for the entrance. She kept her legs squeezed together and he scratched her hard, forcing them open. She resigned and kept them apart. He forced his fingers in, recklessly, ensuring it hurt, all while staring her straight in the eyes, also to ensure the insult was well understood. She only looked back at him defiantly, refusing to give him the satisfaction. While this went on, Tana looked on straight ahead as her eyes caught Stanley peeping at them. Her expression remained unchanged. The governor pulled out his hand and stuck his finger right under his nose and inhaled deeply.

"Ahh, the smell of resistance. These are the sweetest barriers to break, and you will be broken and when we're done, you will be tossed away like the trash you are."

He moved his gaze to Tana.

"Yes, the soon to be dead girl. Remember to keep your head low and our arrangement will be as discussed. Understood?"

Face still expressionless, she looked up into his eyes and said nothing, just staring into them. It made him uncomfortable. He stepped back a bit and observed her briefly.

"That'll be all. Angela?"

The governor walked away, with Angela behind him as the wardens directed the girls back to their cells.

In their hiding place, Stanley wanted to whisper a question to Victoria, but she motioned for him to stop. They had to leave first.

***

Maleek typed *skooches* into the browser. It returned "scooch." Not what he was looking for. He tried "skooches party drug." The first result entry was titled, "The Facts and Myths About Trending Party Drug, Skooches." It held no other information other than what he already knew. "New and unusual substance, chemical structure is still uncertain", "Some have wondered if its extra-terrestrial."

Next, he tried "Kester Ice Man Skooches." He quickly scrolled down the page, seeing no topic that related. In the middle of the page, he noticed the link titled "Spark Plug Plus – Your Easy Connect." It was an online bulletin page that anonymously posted contacts and interests in various drugs. One of the trending topics was *skooches*, still what Maleek had heard from Raquel earlier, and different questions and answers about experiments on a number of blood donors, experiences with twins, triplets, regular siblings, father and son, husband and wife. It even had people advertising their own blood sales. One of the advertised links was "Incest Blood." He refused to click it.

He ctrl+F'ed "Ice Man" and got a few hits, all saying the same thing, "Get that pure stuff. Experience the strong chill. Text only. Signed, Ice Man." He called the number, no answer.

Det. Chin Lee, "Destiny", walked in.

"Hey Shapiro, got a sec?"

"Hey, Destiny. Sure. Any hits?"

"We got a hit. Kester McKean. White male, thirty-four years old. Died almost two weeks ago."

She continued while Maleek schemed through the file.

"He had a few priors, misdemeanours, never really convicted of anything serious."

Maleek observed Kester's frozen images, the look in his frozen eyes resembled that of Tyler, the earlier dead kid. He turned the page and there was a picture of Kester with a black man in suit. Behind that were two profile and more defining pictures.

"Why is this picture here?"

"That is the current governor of Arizona, Reginald Tyson."

"Yes, of course I know who this is." Maleek had started to respond but stopped suddenly as his lights went on. "Reginald!"

"Yes. He's currently being investigated for, shit, drug trafficking, money laundry and murder, among others," Destiny answered.

"Fuck!"

"The Feds are all over this guy, just sniffing him. Got this quietly from a source within the core team, its being kept hush-hush 'cause it's a high-profile case," said Destiny.

"Yeah. Sure. Thanks."

Maleek racked his head for how to proceed. That was not the kind of twist he expected. He had to escalate this. He flipped back to the summary page and noted the head investigator was Detective Catherine Burke.

***

Stanley's head was light and spinning. He held onto the concrete beam steadily so not to fall over. All that information was all too much for one whole career, how much more for just one day. Did he wish he didn't know all this? Will he cower and do nothing? Fuck right or wrong, Angela alone, all by herself, was too much for him to handle, how much more the governor of the fucking state and whatever else apparatus he had at his disposal? Suddenly, it turns out ASCHA was an undercover sex and body/prisoner/criminal exchange ring, all aided and abetted by the chief warden herself under the auspices of the executive governor of Arizona. He wasn't sure what to do with all the information.

The girls had long stopped talking and just waited for his response. He was clearly in over his head. As his heart beat faster, he paused to wonder what the girls would say about him if he did nothing. Or was this a test, setup by Angela to test his loyalty? However, he knew they were telling the truth. Flavor's face said it all, and he also saw it all for himself. Was it finally time for his life to have some meaning?

"So, they basically drug Galina every time?"

"Yes," warden Woo spoke up. "I've seen it happen countless times."

"And you've done nothing?"

"Well, for same reason you're about to shit yourself, Weppler." Stanley knew she spoke the truth. "This shit is bigger than us and we need all the help we can get. So now you know. What you gonna do about it?"

"Why the fuck did I come to work today?" he thought.

***

Maleek nursed his ginger ale at the bar, slowly finishing off the rest of his sweet potato fries and the little ketchup he had to dab them in. While he rested his forehead on his open palm, he let his thoughts drift back to the new development in his case.

"The governor? What the fuck?!" He muttered.

Every cop would have loved an opportunity to solve a mega or career making case but, to take on the state governor, he needed resources.

Destiny returned from the bathroom and took a sip of her beer.

"Sup, soldier?"

Maleek chuckled pessimistically. "Soldier. Right."

She took a bit to observe him. "It's not like JPD ain't collaborated with the FBI before, you know."

"Yea, I know. Already got a time scheduled with Burke."

"Nice. Well, I'm sure you'll have it all figured out," Destiny encouraged.

"Ha. I better."

"Anyways, I didn't wanna spend much time here today. What do you say we go back to my place? We still have the final season of Golden Girls to finish. We could also watch Betty's SNL cold open. That babe still going strong at 102."

"Yup. To the strong ladies." Maleek raised his ginger ale and cheered.

Destiny laughed.

She raised her hand and signaled to the bar tender to close her tab.

***

His first collection was rather uneventful. The person who wore the *ahu* was a pretty, English girl, probably from the WWI era. No one was watching as he scooped the substance into his mouth. No witnesses, no shame, right? The enforcers were casual and about their business. He reached his domain when he reached his domain.

He paused for a bit and hesitated. He almost allowed himself think there might be a way out of it, but he remembered he was dead, his mom and Jessica were not but could be, if he knew the governor well. The *ezi* inserted into his navel felt uneasy.

"I plead the everlasting doors, may death be permanent, and this death be mine," he recited as casually as possible. Suddenly he felt the gentle gust of wind form around his face. He didn't need to force it, the substance moved easily from inside him to his mouth. The vomit brought no tears to his eyes, his stomach didn't clench, it simply poured up and gathered in his mouth.

***

Brazile and his dog, Zino, were returning from his walk that evening. They were at the building entrance when they both felt the sudden air pull and sprinted indoors.

The door closed, the substance gathered right there on the ground, surrounded by a gray mist. Zino ran straight in and gobbled it all up. The mist disappeared as soon as it was done. Moments later, it threw it up again, ready for packaging.

"That's a good boy. Who's a good boy?" Zino was rewarded with a scratch under the chin as his beetle-like *ezi*, hung onto his collar, dancing back and forth as it shook.

***

That was a quick and uneventful transaction, AJ thought. No Ofuukus in sight.

Suddenly, his building shook. He knew he heard a loud thud too, as if something heavy fell from the sky. Thud! He heard it again and the building shook even harder. Thud! Like a giant hopping on one foot. Thud! He knew it was getting closer because he was starting to increasingly feel its presence. Thud! The aura was ugly and unnerving, like a bad omen. Thud! He knew it was him, he had attracted the Ofuukus. Thud! He wondered if he should pray, but to whom? Thud! It was out there; he could hear its heavy breathing.

The dead didn't eat so he had no bowels to empty.

Suddenly, it landed on his building, not far from his very domain. This was followed by a loud, sharp scarring on the wall like an iron claw going through metal. The loudness and shriek were unnerving and sickening and for a moment, wished he was still alive so he could throw-up.

"The dead do die, still." He already knew it was true. He wondered what it felt like. Was this to be his turn? He felt the scratch screeching around his building, loud, grating on his very core. It took everything he had not to scream. The scratch stopped at his door. He felt paralyzed and then his life on earth flashed before his eyes all over again. He had no idea what whatever was out there looked like, but he knew it was truly evil, and it had come for him. What was it waiting for? He remembered Kester's words, "If you ever meet one of those things..."

He resigned himself to his fate, waiting for the second death.

Long silence.

Thud!

This thud landed not so close by. Thud. Was it retreating? He also felt the presence move away. Thud, like a faraway whisper, leaving you a last message, reminding you that you can be found, a warning.

He fell to the floor, in relief.

***

Catherine was on the phone when he knocked on the door of her office. She wasn't sure if she was supposed to know or remember him. She quickly ended her call and waved him in.

"Yes, how may I help you?" she asked politely but quickly.

"Detective Shapiro, we spoke on the phone."

"Ah, yes, you said you have some information on a case I'm working."

"More like more questions and little information," Maleek cautioned.

"So, what's up?" Catherine sat back on her chair.

"I'm investigating a murder that happened almost two weeks ago. The trails have led me to a street drug called *skooches,* which at the moment is starting to kill young kids, two of which I've personally encountered, and a suspect called Reginald who allegedly carried out the murder from two weeks ago and also possibly the kingpin for same street drug."

Maleek paused, waiting for her nudge to continue or at least an acknowledgement of the drug or Reginald. Her face stayed subtly inquisitive, same way it was when he started talking.

Catherine on the other hand tried to stay the alarm bells going off in her head, hoping this wasn't yet another leak in her case.

"How did you find out about this case?" She finally asked.

"Off the grape vine. Cops talk."

She seemed about to resign but he continued.

"Look, I know its high profile and much of the investigation is discrete, but I don't see this man acting with that much indiscretion at such a high profile as he is, he's starting to drop dead bodies. Something is up here and the sooner we get to the bottom of it, the better."

He paused for effect.

"Is there a question or request anywhere in there or you gonna give me the part two of the speech you've clearly rehearsed many times?"

He wasn't sure how to feel about that response. Although he did ponder if he just actually gave a performance or spoke from his heart. "Any information you can give me on the governor will help. If you've heard of this drug, skooches. Anything."

She considered him a bit before she continued. "This drug, Skooch?"

"Skooches," he repeated. "It's the only name for it we've got right now, to the best of my knowledge, there's been no official name for it yet."

"Aha. Skooches. I have never heard of. Although a contact at the DEA did inform me they've officially picked up on a new street drug connected to this. Perhaps you wanna reach out to them. For the main investigation, however, it's a federal case ongoing. So, you can file your report and refer them to the bureau. Capishe?"

Maleek wasn't sure how to proceed. What else did he expect to happen?

"Ah," he tried to speak but nothing else formed.

"So, I should be asking for whatever information you have that can assist us and also remind you to please keep these details, and anything else you discover, to yourself, except of course from us?" Catherine added.

"Same drug case is related to two ODs in my jurisdiction, so is the primary suspect to a murder in my jurisdiction. So regardless of the DEA or Feds, we too have a responsibility to our constituents. So, I'd really need more than just a side participation."

Catherine wondered if Jisike was just a boring county, and he needed some action, but you never say these things to other officers.

"I suppose you're joining the investigation then," Catherine managed.

"Exactly."

"You know the drill and the process. Will keep in touch as things unfold."

That was good enough for Maleek.

***

At Oluku, Kester obviously and deliberately ignored AJ's rage. He knew it was coming and had chosen to be unconcerned about it.

In the corner, on the opposite side of the viewing section, a group of about 6 people, clothed in Ahus were dancing, clearly ecstatic and spinning around. Their ears were covered with headset with life-like chords hanging from the ceiling. Whatever sounds they were listening to was not heard by the rest of the occupants who in turn were engaged in their own various conversations and activities.

In another corner of the bar, a different group of eight ahu wearers sat with weirdly constructed but subtle smiles on their genderless faces. In an aurora-like projection just above them, a group of exactly eight young people, high on skooches, were dancing in what looked like a college dorm room. Visible were bottles of liquor, water, and others.

AJ had quickly gotten used to it all and knew better than staring so as not to upset any of the customers. Kester stood beside him, bobbing to some imaginary tune in his head.

"You're not gonna ask me how it went?" AJ finally broke the ice.

"You're here, ain't ya? We ain't got participation trophies down here, bro!"

AJ's anger burned at his nonchalance.

"It knows where I stay. It came to my domain. It found me."

Kester remained silent.

"Yo!" AJ raised his voice enough to attract the attention of the others, as they turned around to observe. Kester cautioned him with a stern look and a shoosh. He pulled him outside.

Outside, Kester still seemed like he was struggling to find words.

"What happens now, Ice?"

Silence.

"If the Ofuukus can find one so easily then how long will this continue before the second death finds me?"

Kester finally sighed and responded. "You're right. Ya burnt!"

"So, what happens if I open the portal again?"

"Well, the kind Ofuuku won't just stop at the door. You'll surely see its face," Kester responded with his usual glee returning.

"I'm glad I contribute to your happy place. So does this mean I'm off the hook?"

"Nope." Kester responded with more glee. "As a matter of fact, you have many more deliveries to make."

"How am I supposed to make deliveries if I'm burnt? Does the second death take me to another section of Animmo where I'll continue to serve his royal madness?"

Kester genuinely chuckled at that. "Return to your domain. I'll bring you word now." He turned and walked away toward his domain. AJ walked after him, visibly upset and somewhat con-frontational.

"Your word ain't shit, bro. You'll give me an answer now."

"Isn't that what I just said?" Kester snapped back.

"Bullshit, Ice. And calm your bitch-ass down, you ain't got clout down here." He moved closer and stood right face to face with Kester.

"Get outta my face, bro," Kester repeated.

"Why don't you make me?"

In saying that, AJ wondered if fights ever did break out among the dead. What could they be fighting about?

While still standing close to him, Kester quickly lifted AJ's shirt and pulled the ezi from his frosty navel. Instantly, AJ felt an overwhelming sickness in his stomach that caused him great discomfort. He bent over, clutched his stomach and started wheezing, trying to throw up. He looked up at Kester who smiled at his anguish and mockingly waved him away. AJ ran toward his domain as quickly as he could. When he passed building 9 of the 22nd *segment* of the fifth *region* in 1998 place, he felt immediate relief, then stopped running and bent over, as if catching his breath.

***

The office was typical for a governor, luxurious mahogany desk with pictures of his family resting on top. They looked truly happy. The one on the right side of the desk was of his Caucasian red-haired wife and three bi-racial sons.

Reginald sat on his very expensive leather chair, on the phone.

"What you must understand is there's no going back. The ball is already rolling and it's a one chance opportunity, boy. There will be no do-overs."

He listened for a while, his face a mix of determination and anger.

"Yes, I'm aware. The bodies showing up now is just the beginning and if all go according to plan, the FBI's case and whatever evidence they've got against me will be irrelevant. We stay on course. Is that clear?"

After a bit, he hung up the phone.

***

His thoughts were all over the place. Michelle was in her usual spot on the sofa, still with one leg curled up, remote in hand, Jerry Springer on.

Stanley realized for the first time in a while, she was not the center of his attention, at least during his dinner time. He ate his bland spaghetti dinner in deep contemplation. He thought about quitting his job and moving on with his life but to where? He had neither the resources nor the impetus to start all over again. Besides, the house was in his name and had too much of his equity tied into it. He wasn't about to leave it all for Michelle.

Tana Torres, the other girls, Angela Blaine, Governor Tyson. He remembered the look on Mindy Woo's face when she called him out during the staircase meeting. He wasn't sure if to consider it the end of his miserable life or an opportunity for some adventure. He thought about calling 911, but then to tell them what? The governor is running a sex trafficking and prisoner swap ring?

When he came to, he raised his head casually and noticed Michelle had been observing him. While distracted, he had started scrapping the fork along the whole length of the plate rim, making a continuous scraping sound. He stopped. He wasn't enjoying the food anyway, so he dumped the rest into the trash and took it out.

He decided for the time being, all he would do was wait, observe, try to alleviate the girls' plight where he could, possibly gather evidence but in all, he would have to wait.

The distracted thoughts followed him from his man-cave to the bathroom. There, he couldn't have his usual routine. This time around, instead of seeing his problems and Angela's face, he kept on seeing Tana, weeping Galina, and the governor. All their faces kept him from crossing over the arrival threshold. He finally gave up, hoping he wouldn't have a sleepless night.

***

He watched Zino lap up the skooches and just as quickly, threw it up into a clean container beside it, while the mist disappeared. It then ran into his arms for its reward scratch while licking his face. As he scratched, he brought Zino in closer to himself while he drifted away and the sound of the dangling ezi faded into the background of his thoughts.

"How much longer?" Brazile weighed his plans, or better still, his interpretation of the plan, and all the resulting moves he'd set in place. Who was he kidding? Would it not be bigger than them all? Had he done enough to guarantee his survival when it was all over? Getting in trouble with the police and ending up back in prison was the least of his worries.

"For their path shall be with death for death to keep its form." He'd heard those words before and knew enough to not doubt them.

His phone buzzed, snapping him out of his mind travel.

"Come outside," he noted in his phone's summary, from Dibia.

He stood up and threw off the light blanket he had on him, revealing the extensive scars from wounds that looked like claw marks. They covered him from his neck all the way down to his feet. His entire backside was covered in claw marks. He quickly threw on a pair of jeans and t-shirt, threw three concealed jars into his backpack and went outside, shutting Zino indoors.

***

Just outside his door, he saw Dibia's black SUV approach. Brazile crossed over to the other side of the road and the car pulled up just beside him. He walked behind the car and got in on the left back seat.

From the backpack, he brought out the jars and carefully placed them into a cooler beside Dibia, a mysterious, skinny old white man who looked like he was born to be an evil man's assistant. In turn, Dibia handed him a sealed envelope. He placed same in his backpack and made to exit the car but paused.

"Where's Kester? Haven't seen him in a bit."

Dibia glanced him a "shut up and fuck off" look.

It was well understood. He opened the door and left.

5

Tana's abuela had warned her often about the love trap. "People are not always what they present themselves to be," she would chide. "It seems to be the way nature has designed it, but you must do the work to get more clarity on people's intentions, or at least ensure outcomes are in your best interest. That part is primarily your responsibility. If you don't pay it attention, the universe will punish you, my girl."

Her abuela spoke very little English though. With her three grandchildren, at sixty, Tana being about eight then and her younger brothers, about five and four, Rosa had crossed the border illegally. Her daughter, Tana's mother, had died of a mysterious ailment along their way to the border. The children were getting desperate and dangerously malnourished. She had no other choice but to dig a shallow grave somewhere in a bush and bury her there.

They finally made it to a relative's place in Prescott, Arizona and the rest was history. The children quickly got acclimated to the community and learned fast street English, but Rosa only got enough English to survive communications needed for her daily chores. Even then, the words flowed better in Spanish when she said them.

"La gente no siempre es lo que aparenta ser. Parece que así lo ha diseñado la naturaleza, pero debes hacer el trabajo para entender mejor las intenciones de las personas, o al menos asegurarte de que los resultados sean en tu mejor interés. Esa parte es principalmente tu responsabilidad. Si no le prestas atención, el universo te castigará, chica."

Tana had met and cautiously, eventually started dating Victor, a Chinese-Mexican mixed boy from their neighborhood. She had waited months before going all the way with him. He was sweet and patient and even eventually got her abuela's approval. Not like she needed her granny's approval to date, but Victor was so sweet even Rosa seemed taken by him and welcomed him to the family. She was on a roll and things were starting to look up, just turned 18, had an amazing boyfriend, whom her granny loved, and also just bagged her GED.

She knew Victor sold weed. It was what many poor kids did, and it hurt no one so, why not? Although, she had made Victor promise not to let her granny find out about it because she was scared she wouldn't understand. Her granny had seen too much suffering and pain from drugs that she only had one opinion about it.

Sometimes they drove around together while he did his deliveries. It gave them a chance to spend more quality time together, talk, laugh and sometimes, when it was dark enough and the coast was clear, they would have passionate sex in the car.

The weather had changed for Victor after he told her excitedly about a new connect he'd gotten and was gonna become more of a wholesaler and make more profit.

"What about the law, Victor, and the two-ounce rule?"

"Don't worry bout it, baby. I got it all sorted. My connect's connect is a powerful man and he's got the popo in his pocket too," Victor expressed with way too much confidence. In a later conversation, she had heard his name, Reginald Tyson, the state attorney general. She recognized the corruption in government but hey, at least her boyfriend would be safe.

He was not, at least not for long. One of his consignments got stolen from his car while he stopped briefly for a drink with some friends. It was worth over thirteen grand and knowing Reginald, a pound of flesh will always have market value. In exchange for his life, he was asked to donate someone for entrapment. Reginald had heard about Tana, and had asked specifically for her.

On the night it happened, they had caught an early dinner together at a local fried chicken place. She knew he was not himself, it was clear, but she assumed it was him just being his sulky self. Tana reached into his plate to take some of his fries, he hesitated and shot her a glance that surprised her. She wondered if something more than the fight was what upset him. He moved his hands to the side and let her take some, his face turned away. Usually, he would reach in and take some of hers too. He didn't and his face remained blank. It was getting ridiculous. It had to be another girl. Was this how boys moved? Why didn't he take some of her coleslaw? It was their thing. Sure, she also did it with her other friends too, but this was signature for them.

The day they started it, his choice of words had left her giggling.

"Do you mind if I take some of your fries?" She had asked cautiously, not sure whether he was one of them easily eeked out people.

He lit up.

"Sure. I'm glad you asked. And I want some of your coleslaw too. I would really love to eat your coleslaw." He winked at her.

She smiled and turned her face away, embarrassed.

"I'm sorry, did I say something?" he asked with an obvious fake obliviousness on his face.

"Oh, shut up!" she teased. "Sure, have some of my coleslaw." She smiled again.

He winked at her again, most seductively.

He reached into his own plate and arranged some fries, lined up and pointing toward her.

"You can have some more of my fries too. See how they're pointing at you, like they dying to poke at you."

She smiled shyly again and took some.

"With me, you don't gotta ask," he encouraged.

"Yeah, not everybody likes it, you know."

"I know. That's why I said, to you," pointing at her, "with me, you don't gotta ask. In fact, I'll tell you what, let's make it a tradition between you and me. Our special thing. Let's make it a duty to always eat each other's thing." He stared her straight in the eyes, "You eat mine, I eat yours." He winked at her again.

She burst out laughing.

Later that day was the first time they went all the way.

That was then, even up till very recently. But today was more unusual. He continued to eat steadily without giving her a glance. His phone on the table buzzed and he reached for it speedily.

"I knew it, it's another girl," she thought.

Victor focused on the phone intently for a few seconds, then locked the screen and put the phone in his pocket and for a while, just stared at his plate.

He finally took a deep breath, let it out, and suddenly turned his gaze to her and smiled.

"Can I have some of yours too?" He smiled reassuringly.

She wasn't sure how to read it and why his mood changed suddenly. Maybe it was a new deal he got or maybe he got some money.

"Sure. You don't gotta ask, right?"

He smiled in return as they finished their meal.

They had a final delivery for the day. On their way, he apologized for his earlier behavior.

"Just that I've had some mad stress of late, you know."

"Well, please try not to take it out on me. I'm your girl. Instead, you should talk to me about it. You know I got you."

"I know, babe. I got you too." He reached in and caressed her thighs gently.

It was about 6:45 pm when they pulled into the spot, at the back of a local diner. They'd been there many times before. Victor said he used to work there. In fact, he mentioned that the chefs only cooked with the expired stuff. They got the products cheaper and made more profit that way. She had promised herself never to eat there.

He got a text on his phone and read it.

"Shit."

"What?" Tana followed.

"He's about ten minutes late."

"Oh."

They stayed in silence for a bit.

"You know, since we got some time," he winked at her.

She smiled and leaned in for a kiss. They had a quickie. This time instead of pulling out since he wasn't strapped, he released inside her.

"Did you just nut inside me? Why did you do that?" She lightly pushed him away, in protest.

"I'm sorry, baby, I got carried away. You know I love you so much."

She was not happy. It wasn't the pregnancy risk she feared but she hated taking the morning after pills. It always made her sick. She was pissed at him for making her have to go through that. As they dressed, the text came in.

"Hey, he's here. Can you please just help me drop it off? I gotta trash stuff out with one of my dealers. It's important. Please?"

"Sure." She knew the drill. They had done this before. It'll take a quick five minutes.

At the door, she did the knock, a specific pattern of knock. A guy in restaurant clothes and head cover opened. She knew her way and went quickly to the chef's office. There, she met their usual contact and a new guy she hadn't seen before. There were always new guys.

She handed over the merch, took the money, and suddenly felt a cold metal slap on her wrist. It was the new guy, and he did it the moment her hand touched the cash.

For much longer than a moment, she refused to believe her eyes. It was Victor's deal; he knew the AG of the state. Were they fucking with her? If they weren't and this was really an undercover cop, was he new? Didn't he know they knew the AG? Was he not in his pocket too?

"You are under arrest for distribution of illegal and poisonous substances. You have the right to remain silent. Anything you say…"

The rest trailed off. She tried hard to calm her spinning head. When they reached outside, Victor would call his Reginald, and all this would be sorted out. She thought about the story she'd tell her friends when she got out. She didn't say anything to the cops, there was no need to spill and let out Victor's deal by mentioning Reginald. Victor will handle it.

Outside, Victor was gone. That was the first time it registered that Victor might have screwed her. With her hands still cuffed to her back, she bent over and threw up. The arresting officer let her and assisted with her hair.

***

She had stopped crying. She'd been punched in the stomach by the biggest and most masculine woman she'd ever met, in the cell where they were locked up. She'd dared her to cry again. So, she sobbed silently, the tears a constant stream on her face. Victor was her first love, and the love had been sweet. The pain she felt all through her being was overwhelming. It made no sense how love could betray her in such an aggressive manner. She switched between sobbing for being locked up and for Victor's betrayal. Finally, she stopped crying and went to sleep.

She got no phone calls. She begged and screamed and even threatened them with a lawsuit.

"You and I both know you ain't nobody and your family ain't shit and can't afford a lawyer. You wanna keep acting like a bitch? Maybe you'd like to taste some solitary confinement, that ought to wake you up," a guard told her, as a matter of fact.

She was also refused visitor requests. Neither her brothers nor grandmother came to see her. She worried and her heart broke for her abuela and what the pain of not knowing would do to her.

They held her for three months before they finally allowed her a phone call.

She couldn't hold back the tears as she heard her granny scream in horror and relief. She wailed inconsolably as if receiving her child back from the dead.

"Dios te bendiga mi amor. ¿Estás bien?"

It was her go to phrase when she'd not seen you in a while. "God bless you, my love, are you well?"

She was not. Victor had told them she got arrested but he didn't know why, and then warned them not to bother him.

After another one week, she finally got her first visitor, her lawyer, a public defender.

"I'm sure you're well."

She knew right away that was a rhetorical statement. There was no way he was concerned; besides, his face didn't even try to hide his indifference. She ignored him. He continued as if her response was not needed.

"My name is Michael Jackson."

The moment he said that, her eyebrows knitted up in surprise. He got that a lot. "I'm from the office of the county public defender and I will be taking your case."

"Aah, okay? Thanks?" She wondered if she should allow herself to have some hope.

"Mmhhmm." He said and observed her curiously for a bit. "Look, the case against you isn't looking good."

"That was fast," she thought.

He continued, "You were caught in possession of over a kilogram of marijuana and same package contained two kilos of fentanyl tainted cocaine and one kilo of meth, also fentanyl tainted."

That part surprised her. She didn't know Victor dealt coke or meth.

"A similar batch, also delivered by you, was traced to a fentanyl poisoning that killed three teens in the area.

"Okay, now you're just making shit up," Tana blurted out. "I delivered some weed for my boyfriend. That's all I did. If you say you really work for the state, why not bring the AG in here, let's talk."

Michael stared her straight in the eyes, in long silence, clearly warning her to choose her next words carefully.

"Is there something you'd like to say about the AG?" he challenged, with a smile.

The message was clear, and her anger quickly dissipated. "No."

"Oh, no, please, by all means, speak your mind. I'll make sure the justice department takes it up. Speak, I encourage it," he seemed to mockingly insist.

She knew he was luring her. His face was nowhere reassuring. Instead, it said, "snitches get stitches, or better, die."

"Nope. I'm good."

"Good girl," he replied. "Now, where was I? You were caught with a ton of drugs. And your drugs killed people. Now, while the state of Arizona has recreational tolerance for marijuana, distribution without a license, as you have done, still remains a crime."

She tried to speak, but he cut her off with a raised finger. She let him finish.

"In addition, distribution of dangerous substances is also a crime. And, layered on it will be at least four counts of manslaughter. That'll get you 30 to life, depending on how lenient the judge decides to be."

"But I didn't do anything. Don't I get a say in all this?"

"No, you don't," he stated as a matter of fact.

"Why not? This is still America, ain't it?" Tana clapped back.

"Of course, it is. And in America, what you say you did or didn't do don't mean shit. The law works by evidence and currently," he looked through his pages quickly and making his face to show how hopeless the situation was, "it looks like they're all pointing in your direction."

Tana could tell something was off about this man. He did not sound or act like her own advocate. Was this how all public defenders behaved?

"I want another lawyer." She finally let out.

He was incredulous at first, then smiled at her audacity and then laughed at her, lowly and clearly with derision.

"How long have you been here? Four months? Do you think the public defender's office will grant such an ungrateful request and send you, a bloody undocumented coon like yourself, a lawyer of your choosing?" He paused and let it sink in. "Besides, with the outcry on all the fentanyl deaths, the state could also go after your family and have them deported. The drug was sold by an undocumented immigrant. The righteous wing would want a sacrifice, and hearing your abuela and brothers have been deported would be soothing for the public."

Tana was speechless for a full minute.

"How are you my lawyer?" she asked, almost in tears.

Michael responded with satisfaction. "Yes, that's me, the angel who's come to save you. Now, imagine what the devil looks like."

Tana sighed resignedly, "Okay, so what do you want me to do?"

"Look, this case is stacked against you, mad, and will be impossible to win. Even with an expensive and highly experienced legal team, with the evidence against you, basically, you're still fucked. So, I would ask you to just cut a deal and plead guilty."

"But I'm innocent!" Tana let out in muffled frustration, the tears flowing from her eyes.

He observed her for a moment before responding.

"Did you deliver the drugs or not?"

He was right.

"My boyfriend, Victor. He set me up."

"Well, that is truly heartbreaking, isn't it? Still, pleading not guilty on account of love will not fly with the judge. You delivered drugs that killed people."

"They were not mine. They were Victor's."

"Your Victor already gave a statement. Says he knows nothing about anything. Says he dropped you off there because he was just doing you a favor, as his girlfriend. Both deliveries were made by you and it's your face on all the surveillance cameras. It's a slam dunk case, my dear."

She sobbed hopelessly, the pain eating away at her. He waited patiently and let her cry.

Finally, she let out, "so, what should I do, just go plead guilty to manslaughter?"

He paused, hesitating as if he was contemplating turning things around for her.

"There is another option."

"What is that?" she asked, hope rising in her again.

"There is a way to salvage some things. We can make this go away and get the AG to drop the case."

Reginald Tyson, of course. The hope left her immediately. What would he make her do, sell drugs too?

He continued, "You confess to another case, and this goes away."

"That sounds stupid. Why would I do that? Or will this other crime not send me to prison?"

"Oh, you are most likely to do time as well," he stated almost cheerfully.

"So, what the fuck, man?"

"You still get to do prison time but we, they, they will leave your abuela and brothers alone."

Once again, he paused to let it sink, watching her puzzled.

"In addition, if you take the deal, we might even add something on top of that. We could provide your folks with some monthly stipends. You know, help abuela meet her needs. She's been really sick of late, hasn't she?"

"Are you really a lawyer?" She couldn't help it.

He chuckled.

"I believe that's what it says on my card." He reached into his pocket and checked, then extended it to her, "See, there it says, public defender."

He gave her a carefree smile. She shook her head at him.

Suddenly, he closed his briefcase and stood up.

"Let me summarize this. You have two choices here. On one hand, we have enough to screw up your entire life and have you locked up for a long time and also, fuck your entire family over. And we will do it. On the other hand, you could confess to another crime, stand a chance of doing time and even if you do, your family will be taken care of. The choice is yours. I'll give you time to think about it."

He exited, leaving her speechless.

They gave her three more weeks to think about it. In that time, they let her family visit, who in turn, all had troubles to report. ICE had somehow started to focus on the entire family, and they were starting to panic. Her granny was inconsolable during her visit and looked more frail than ever.

After the third week, the lawyer returned. She took the deal.

On her way to the court for her arraignment, she thought about Abuela's words and cried once again. Thoughts of Victor made her cry some more. One part was losing a love like that, or what it had seemed like. The betrayal was the second part and to think of it, he actually gave her a final fuck before fucking her over. Ain't life the ultimate bitch?

She, alone, stood in court that hot morning while the judge read out the charges, aggravated mass murder that resulted in the death of thirteen people, including five children. She'd never even held a gun.

The judge had called out at her a third time and hit the gavel to snap her out of her incredulous drifting. Jackson, her lawyer for a little while had forgotten to act neutral, and the subtle amusement she noted on his face when she snapped out her trance told her that her fate was sealed.

"I'm sorry, your Honor?"

"On 13 counts of murder in the first degree, how do you plead?" the judge barked at her.

"What?" Tana was hazy and struggling to compose herself. She leaned over on the desk to calm the sick feeling in her stomach."

Michael finally spoke up, "Your Honor, may I have fifteen minutes to confer with my client?"

"Denied!" The judge barked again. Even Michael was surprised.

He turned to Tana and shrugged, resignedly. He leaned him and reminded her, "Think of your family."

"Miss Torres! On thirteen counts of first-degree murder, how do you plead?!"

The tears fell down her face as she let out, "Guilty," lowly, and muffled by the lump in her throat.

"Please repeat that, Miss Torres, and louder," the judge ordered.

"Guilty," she repeated louder.

"On the charge of..."

As the judge continued to read the charges, she trailed off once again, sobbing. She remembered when her mother was buried on the road, something in her had told her that her mother had made the ultimate sacrifice for them and that somehow, the universe would take that as a seed and let the lines fall for them in pleasant places. It didn't happen. Her mother had been buried on the roadside for nothing.

Despite her trailing off, she was present enough to respond with "guilty," after each charge was read.

The trial was smooth, and she was handed the death penalty. She was eighteen years old.

6

AJ lifted his shirt and inserted the metal ezi into his navel. He closed his eyes and focused on his mom and Jessica for a bit, before exiting his domain.

When he reached the edge of P1998-R5-S22-B9, his body felt like he'd walked into a light forcefield, like walking through, and submerged, in a pool of water, only the far-less viscous kind. He didn't only go through it, but it went through him as well.

At Oluku, the skooches were made by an ahu wearing old man who clearly had died in some auto-crash. He swallowed up the substance immediately when he scooped it up. His way had been full of enforcers, and he was certain he would be stopped going back to his domain.

On his way, AJ wondered how he would describe Animmo to the living. How desperately inadequate words would be, compared to the true nature of the universe. How would he explain the enforcers, their general nature, with no distinguishing features, yet somehow, each unique in their own way; or the nature of time and the fact that everything that could ever happen has already happened? How would it be, telling the living that our current existence is a mere snapshot of a matter already finished? Will they understand that all possible roads will be taken? Are they aware that every path will be followed; every stone, overturned; every life, lived?

However, his thoughts were interrupted with the second transport he was about to attempt. In the eternal moment it took to reach his domain, his mom, Jessica and Reginald never left his thoughts. He wondered if they'll still get hurt if he experienced the second death. But Kester seemed sure of the cold ahu he dropped off.

"I guess I'll find out."

Inside, he held out the cold ahu. The ahu's face looked peaceful. It was an Emirati man in his early twenties. He sighed and put it on. Slipping into it felt like being covered in someone else's skin, like every inch of his skin being covered with the insides of someone else's flesh. In a way too, he could feel the young man's presence. He could sense his person inside his cold ahu enough to feel like they'd been acquainted.

He proceeded to say his chant, "I plead the everlasting doors, may death be permanent, and this death be mine."

The wind came, pulled it out of him and it was quickly lapped up. When the mist disappeared, he paused, stood still, and waited for the heavy thud. Silence. No Ofuukus in sight. He sighed in relief and took it off.

"Does this mean even Kester's own cold ahu is right here in Animmo?" He made a mental note to ask him when next he saw him. Of course, mainly to upset him.

***

"A series of bizarre cases of drug overdose are occurring across the states of Arizona and Nevada. These users have been reported to die suddenly by freezing. Yes, you heard that right. One overdoses on the drug by freezing to death. This drug, currently known by its street name, Skooches, is said to have left the authorities baffled as they don't understand either its chemical composition or its origins. There are rumors it might even be extra-terrestrial."

The scene changed from the newscaster to a footage of a young couple, one on top the other, in the missionary style, being carried out on a stretcher covered in a giant cloth. The arms of the couple were partly visible from beneath the sheet and their hands look like man-made ice sculptures, as if frozen to near absolute zero.

The shot changed to a young girl speaking with a blurred face, as the reporter noted her request for anonymity.

"The thing be like, if it really good, you know, it give you the strong chill. You feel it deep inside and it feel good too, you know. That's what I heard, though, me not use it before. But they say if you done do too much, the chill come too strong and you freeze like that, you know."

The newscaster continued, "There's still no official statement from the DEA and no one really seems to know where this thing comes from or how it's made. The PPD and state attorney general both released statements condemning the distribution of such a deadly substance, and both tried to assure the public that adequate resources are being mobilized to ensure this is nipped in the bud.

They also encouraged parents to have conversations with their children about this and general use of illicit drugs. Back to you."

Stanley finished dressing, turned off the TV, and left the room.

***

"Is the entire tree not inside of the seed?

Yet, does the seed itself not come from the tree?

Does one have boast over the other?

For the one comes from the other, and the other must go to the one.

Should they two not fellowship in their shared existence?

For to live is to die, and to die is to have lived!"

-Oku Animmo

"The living cry about death.

'Death is bad', they lament.

For neither letters nor messages can be delivered,

Nor exchange nor embrace; nor love nor kindness.

For they all shall be swallowed up into that singular eternal mo-ment."

-Oku Animmo.

Once again, AJ reminded himself that he will know all there is to know, but then again, in the eternal moment, he had known it. He headed out to Oluku for another delivery.

***

In the eternal moment that AJ fellowshipped with the *abikus*, he also recalled the eternal moment he had fellowshipped with them before, in that one eternal moment, but before life, before he became Andrew Jackson, when he was but pure energy, a mere seed of consciousness, an instance of the eternal source, just before he would be flung at a moment of conception; he knew them.

Like a single photon travelling the universe and illuminating any object in its path, each instance of the eternal source dances back and forth in a joyful rhythm, as if in a celebration of life or a snapshot of the chaotic gyration after which the universe patterns itself. Each instance that is flung at conception pretty much acts the same way, but not the *abikus*. Their essence was of a different shade, as if the kind of light they produced would be colored differently. He knew what they were about.

While the intricate meaning of life and its grand purpose are impossible to properly express or even grasp, especially within the limitations of the third dimension, it is true, however, that the fundamental and eternal driving force of every living thing is to survive. In the eternal moment that they're all flung at conception, it is normally their desire to be born and live a long and fruitful human life; but not the abikus. They did not live long and fruitful lives and neither did they plan nor intend to. They were a result of the same eternal source but somehow, they ended up in some kind of loop that made them live short and miserable lives, repeatedly, and in the process, brought much grief to their parents who sometimes went bankrupt, trying to keep their only child alive. Unfortunately, once the seed was marked, the bearer also became marked and was trapped in a cycle of giving birth to one abiku after the other. Same soul, coming back in a different body with each iteration. It was basically giving birth to the same person, again and again. This would usually continue until the couple gave up attempting childbearing or the marriage ended due to the suffering they caused. The dead called them "the returners."

"He probably died around eight years old.," AJ thought as he walked into Adank's domain. Unlike the rest of Animmo, abikus had a subtle transparent hue to them, as if they were just starting to fade away. Adank's appearance, however, was notably more transparent than others, as he had already returned, again.

"How many times you gone back?" AJ asked politely.

Adank thought for a bit as he paused for clarity.

"To the same parents." AJ clarified.

"Oh, on my third trip. The second time was really long. Some-times, I thought, maybe I might actually stay. Poor guys. I always felt sorry for them."

***

Troy, the movie, was fresh in the cinemas and Luca was taking Chiara to go see it. It was the week just before their wedding. He had graduated first and was waiting for her to graduate as well, as her parents insisted, before getting married. They were also devout

Christians, about the only few left in Lauterbrunnen, a small town of about three thousand people in Bern, Switzerland.

He too was a Brad Pitt fan but when scenes of him in valor came up, she shrieked weirdly like a possessed fan. In the scene with the captured Trojan girl, he noticed Chiara tense and bite down on her lip, hard, as Achilles raised the girl's skirt and had his way with her. In that very moment, he was glad Mr. Pitt was far away, and the fact Achilles himself was just a movie character. It was a feeling that quickly passed. He was sure of their lives together and a bright future.

They made it to their wedding day, untouched, keeping their sanctity vows to one another, and their friends and community knew they both got married as virgins.

"How was it?" his friends later asked him about sex on his wedding night.

The smile on Luca's face said it all. They didn't need any further response, and all burst out laughing.

"It was eye opening." Luca finally found the words.

"Ich wette, es war so," one of them replied in Swiss-German for "I bet it was," as they burst out laughing again.

He was glad he waited. And to be honest, he admitted they'd been going at it every night since, sometimes multiple times a day.

Their first child, Nina, was born to Luca and Chiara Sutter the following year. However, the bundle of joy that she brought with her turned sour on the day of her first birthday celebration.

Her tongue started swelling after she was given a bite of her own birthday cake. As the evening wound down, Chiara noticed her mouth no longer closed and her breathing started to struggle due to the swollen tongue. They had to rush her to the emergency room.

"Yes, it's possible the cake could have triggered an allergy, it is of course not unlikely, but we just have to run some tests to be sure exactly what we're dealing with. In the meantime, we'll need to observe her closely over the night.

A night quickly turned into three months. Many tests were run with inconclusive results, and she had crises frequently that required intervention. By the third month, she had seemed to stabilize, and the doctors were convinced she could be sent home but to be under careful supervision.

Chiara had to quit her job to nurse the child full time. Around her fourth birthday, she had been reasonably stable for well over eighteen months straight, with some minor ailments in between, and her parents were starting to have some hope again. On the night of her birthday, it was triggered again after she ate something she was already used to eating and her tongue swelled up again. She stayed admitted for another three weeks and suddenly stabilized. Once again, the doctors were sure she was safe going back home, and her vitals were much more encouraging than ever before.

That evening in her hospital ward, Luca was gathering her things while Chiara played with her, making faces and smiling while little Nina laughed heartily. Right in Chiara's arms, she suddenly stopped laughing and got very quiet for about 15 seconds while looking Chiara straight in the eyes. Chiara made more faces, but she remained silent.

"Luca?"

Luca dropped what he was holding and came closer to them. He caressed Nina's face and smiled at her. They both watched her intently, wondering. Chiara thought maybe she was quietly wetting herself, like she did sometimes. She looked around her and saw she was dry.

"Hoi Engel, alles klar?" Luca asked in Swiss-German for "Hey angel, you alright?"

Nina remained very quiet then suddenly, she convulsed and died right in their arms, all in less than thirty seconds.

She was playful and laughing, then stopped, convulsed and died.

The image of the tiny box at the funeral wouldn't leave Chiara's head. She saw it everywhere she turned, in every small box in the house and every store she entered. Fearing losing everything, Luca finally forced a conversation to try pull them out of their misery. He demanded to keep her in their memory but, move on with life.

After they wiped their tears and sorted their conversation, they made love dutifully as a deliberate step to move on. Soon after that, she got pregnant again.

Adank Simon Sutter was born a healthy and robust little boy. He wore his mom out with his incessant need to feed.

"Thank God his only problem is that he eats a lot," Chiara would say, reminding herself to count her blessings. The little boy slept good too, on average, slept better than most infants and through the night. The only thing that worried Luca was that he and Chiara had been trying to conceive again for over two years without success, even while Nina was still alive. The doctors even told them there was nothing to worry about.

"I rebuke you in the name of Jesus!" Chiara found herself muttering occasionally as Adank's first birthday approached and she tried to ignore the anxiety building from Nina's experience. It came and passed without incident.

By his fifth birthday, his parents had already forgotten about Nina's trauma and were comforted by Adank's increase in grace and strength. However, as the celebration was winding down, while Luca was hanging out on the front porch with his friends, Chiara rushed out and pulled him aside.

"Adank's tongue is swelling up, and he has a fever too."

They stared at each other in silence, Luca battling to hold himself together while Chiara's eyes were already welled up with tears. Luca had to stand strong on his faith.

"Why are you crying?" he demanded.

"I don't want to go through this again."

He held her closely to himself and admonished her gently.

"My love, affliction shall not rise a second time. This is a lie of the devil, and we must hold onto our faith."

Chiara held onto his word desperately. It had to be true. She needed it to be true.

"What if we, you or I, have some genetic thing we need to test? What if its genetic or something?" Chiara asked.

Luca thought for a bit. "Yes, we should talk to the doctor about that but even so, Adank is much stronger than Nina. We have nothing to worry about."

"It's brain cancer," the doctor said.

Luca got angry immediately, at nothing in particular, or maybe he was trying to not let himself believe he was angry at God.

"How bad is it?" Chiara asked, fighting back tears.

"That's the weird thing. We know it's there, unfortunately, it's in a delicate spot we're afraid to operate, so we will have to monitor it to see its potential for malignancy. For now, it's best to wait, watch and hope for the best. Any physical intervention now will be unnecessarily risky."

So, they watched and waited. Adank continued to live and grow, but no longer with grace. He became stunted in height and features.

They continued to try to have more kids but couldn't.

Luca and Chiara had just made love, on that early morning of Adank's 13th birthday. Chiara had gone to his room to kiss him happy birthday and start to make ready for final birthday party prepping. She found him cold. The coroner said he had died at least five hours before he was found.

* * *

AJ and Adank sat in silence for a bit. Both, saddened by the story.

"She was already pregnant with me again before she even realized the old me had died."

"So, you basically went back immediately?" AJ added.

"Yup. I, or better, Elias, my would have been baby brother, was born exactly nine months after I died.

I'd hate to think of what's going on up there right now, but unfortunately, I know.

They both sighed.

"Anyways, life will present itself how it wills." Adank broke the silence. "Here you go." He handed AJ a fresh cold ahu.

"Where is the other one you used?"

"Returned to Kester," AJ replied.

"Good. Don't know if he said why but please don't use for more than three transports. Its power could wear off and the Ofuukus start to smell us in them. Okay?"

AJ nodded.

***

"Calm it, bitch, or I'll calm you." Warden Jackson's stern warning to Galina was well received. She responded by willing herself to deliberately swallow her giggles. The alcohol plus happy drugs cocktail she was given wore on too strongly, but she'd been punched in the stomach by Warden Jackson before, so she knew enough not to call his bluff.

Tana was well made up in a red, tightly fitted dress that split up at the knees and flowed to the ankle. Her hair or wig was full in volume and her make-up was bold to behold, not leaving out the bright red lipstick. She looked like a desperate housewife from the eighties, trapped in an abusive marriage to a millionaire. Her eyes were big and bright that night but still remained lifeless deep within. She felt like someone stuck in a costume on its way to go put on a performance for a group of stupid but dangerous little boys. She quickly stamped out the cigarette she was smoking and entered the front passenger seat of the black suburban.

Seated behind her, Flavor was calm but aloof, about as dead inside as the rest of them, while Galina had a slight fake smile plastered on her face that just vaguely covered the terror beneath it. The SUV drove along the winding road within a private estate close to Aztec. It had rained earlier that day, and an unexpected calm came over the region. Arizona, that day, was generally cool.

The first time she came to that mansion, she had allowed herself to get carried away, for just a bit. The green landscape, beautiful flowers in the well-maintained gardens and the calm and quiet of the place made her mind travel, to dreamy places, and made her think of when a good future still looked possible, before all her innocence disappeared. But she had eventually entered the house and understood another reason why a book should not be judged by the cover.

As she walked into the mansion today, she was well aware what she was walking into and thanked God for the drugs. They certainly helped, especially since she had no choice.

Dibia opened the door. Dibia would remind one of Alfred Pennyworth, if Batman was an evil villain. Tana already believed Dibia was one of those men who were predestined to do evil and had no choice about it, like a vessel made specifically for dishonor.

He smiled diabolically at the girls and directed them inside. As they walked in, all the despair on their faces, like magic, faded off and transformed into genuine looking cheerful smiles, like a committee of grateful housewives who'd come to honor their husbands for all they had done for them. It wasn't just the drugs, they'd suffered terrible punishments from the wardens before, and even from the governor himself for not being convincing enough. They had been in these situations enough to know the script. Act like a guest, even pretend to be a lady of substance. Let them chase you a little, then succumb to their advances. Make them feel like alpha men. The girls were in character, smiling heartily and cheerfully like obedient housewives from the '60s, laughing when they sensed the idiots needed their egos boosted.

Maha Pinto, an Indian businessman who looked just like the Penguin played by Danny DeVito, sat on a red leather single that was clearly too big for him. From that chair, he glared straight at Galina, with the kind of smile only an evil, brooding clown should wear. He made her quite uncomfortable despite all the drugs in her system that were meant to keep her calm.

The men stood around and whispered to one another while they glared menacingly at the girls. Tana, Galina, and Flavor sat still in their assigned seats but, of course, smiled heartily and convincingly. Their chairs sort of backed each other, forming a triangle, and facing the guests. Four servers stood on each corner of the wall ready to respond to calls. They were all plain faced, all vacant expressions.

Derrick Obiojor, a German aristocrat, had his eyes on Tana while he and Governor Tyson conversed.

"We had to keep the admittance much tighter. If it passes a certain number, it no longer makes sense anymore, yes?" Derrick asked.

"Of course, Derrick," Reginald encouraged. "However, the results we're seeing are not as we expected. Events are culminating much quicker than we planned, and we must be ready."

"I see. And his majesty?" Derrick asked.

"He's been distracted with new responsibilities. I thought of letting him enjoy his new playground for a bit before we call him. But I suppose it's time we did. Ofuuku reports are getting to us. We must move quickly before judgement comes. Everyone must be ready."

"I agree." Derrick nodded. "So let the shift begin."

Reginald nodded.

"How much more do we need to collect?"

"We'll be more than provided for," Reginald assured.

They both returned their gaze to the girls. Around the room, all the men glared at the girls while they whispered their conversations.

Maha Pinto had asked for Galina to be moved directly in front of him, and then still continued his intense stare, resting his hand on this cane and brooding. Galina's drug cocktail was not able to withstand the effect. She quickly got uncomfortable and started sobbing.

"Can you stop that? Why do you just stare like that? What is wrong with you?" Her present Russian accent fought through her sobs. The other girls fought to keep their composure because they knew. Galina had broken the rule. She was done, bad.

The skooches was administered to her intravenously while they restrained her. Held down and in tears, she wondered if she would come out of it alive, if these were her last moments, her last experience of consciousness. She sobbed, and with her eyes, smiled goodbyes to Tana and Flavor, who in turn, remained fiercely in character, desperately afraid for their own lives and clung to the smiles on their faces.

She was still at first, then her eyes began to move, like she had seen something and then she stared out far into nothing, watching a scene unfold that she alone could see. It quickly turned into excitement, like she was watching a fascinating spectacle. Her smile was like of a child beholding the most beautiful place in the world, it was light and sweet and without malice or guile.

As she saw it, the single source of light that beamed came out of nowhere and hit all manner of obstacles in every direction, as it travelled in a zig-zag manner. Every obstacle the light hit morphed into a different animated shape. Each animated shape would get up and run. They too would run into other obstacles and one another, and the collisions would result in other animated objects of other shapes. Meanwhile, the main light source still continued to hit different obstacles in its zig-zag fashion and create other animated shapes.

She suddenly saw herself in a room, observing herself as a third person, with Pinto, still crying. The room was suddenly covered in mirrors, every wall, even the floor and the ceiling became mirrors.

They showed reflections of one another and reflections of the reflections. In one of the reflections, she saw herself, yet again, in the same room with Pinto, but she wasn't crying. She looked around to the previous room she just saw and noticed that version of her was still sobbing. She stood up, wiped her tears, and looked in a different direction, it was herself also, same room and same face. While she stared intently at that version of herself, her face began to change and switch expressions and moods, as if in different situations of life. The background also began to change to different scenes. Finally, it settled on one of her, in the arms of a handsome lover who held her in his arms and kissed her.

Everyone else watched her reactions while she experienced the trance high, all except Tana and Flavor, who remained in character.

In Galina's trance, once again, that zig-zag light beam hit something and broke into different pieces, all travelling in different directions. She sighed heartily and continued her smile, eyes lost in a beautiful trance. She understood. It was clear. It was all crystal clear.

On the outside, the old men brought out razor blades and cut her all over her body as the effects kicked in. While her trip happened, they helped themselves to her razor wounds and drank her oozing blood, like a pack of vampires, right until she began to freeze over.

They screamed and howled at each other like animals.

Reginald raised his hands, "gentlemen, it is time to usher in the new age. Let the shift begin."

"Let the shift begin!" They all responded. "Let the shift begin."

Flavor and Tana sobbed quietly, the celebration of their hosts keeping them from being noticed.

*****

Animmo has a wasteland. A space where some mysterious "garbage" gets dumped. The dead simply called it "wasteland." Unlike one's domain in Animmo, wasteland came with a feeling of desolation. For every bit of the eternal moment spent there, the dead experienced the pain and emotional anguish of the living, hopelessness, depression, fear, anxiety, self-loathing, worthlessness. It made the dead uncomfortable, even in their death. However, every soul in Animmo has already visited it in an eternal moment. It is a part of Animmo that the dead must have already experienced, and for those who cared to look for anything specific, they may just find what they were looking for there.

The Nazi soldier walked by, eyes glancing back and forth, not walking straight but seeming to stagger like a depressed drunk, weighed down by guilt. He spotted it and quickly staggered over. Lying there was Galina's cold ahu, a replica of what her frozen body would have looked like. He picked up the skin, looked it over and folded the head part to narrow it. He then opened his mouth as wide as he could and pushed the ahu into his mouth, gently guiding it till he swallowed the entire thing. After he swallowed, he clutched his tummy and bent over, sobbing with a deep groan. The dead do cry, but the dead shed no tears.

***

Ebuka and Linda were the first couple Maleek ever dated. He'd always kind of preferred men but, his taste in men was severely restricted and picky. Maleek occasionally dated gay men, but he always preferred them straight. In fact, he preferred to bed straight men who currently had girlfriends. After seeing the struggles of meeting straight guys, he had to recalibrate his sexual preferences to be more accommodating of women, that way, he could kill two birds with one stone. Dating couples was the answer, and it turned out Jisike had a vibrant underground community of swingers. Not just ones that fucked other couples or those that brought in girls to their beds, there were those who sought out men to bring into their beds too.

He officially began to identify as bisexual and for the last two years had only gone to bed with couples, or one of the partners, as long as the other partner gave their blessings. It felt good and also amused him when a lady's husband would come drop her off for a dick appointment. What was this world turning into?

He was still in touch with Ebuka and Linda, who remained his favorite couple. Their main dynamic was initially, Linda having both of them to herself, but after a while, the line between the men began to blur and, the accidental friendly fires became much more targeted as time progressed. It worked for them as there was no awkwardness. Outside of their regular routine, Maleek and Ebuka also began linking up for matters they felt might disturb Linda, so they were best handled without her, but with her blessings, of course.

The trio met up at the local Pakistani restaurant occasionally to gorge on very spicy food. The kind that required a part two of the experience when you sat on the toilet. They bonded over the heat, intense spices, and runny noses.

Ebuka and Linda had a good relationship. Theirs was his best example for an open marriage. They'd met when they worked together at a law firm in Phoenix. Of the options or possible paths they discussed for the relationship, they agreed to amend their sexual terms and conditions as it best suited them and see how it went. Well, so far, so good.

When he read *Men are From Mars, Women Are from Venus,* he totally held its notions as some form of gospel because Maleek sometimes wondered if he didn't really see women as aliens, or maybe a different specie; one he couldn't understand. He always felt color blind to a woman's sexuality. He definitely knew when a woman was beautiful but to him, a woman was only as attractive as the man she was sleeping with and as he experienced more couples, he got more understanding of how to bag them. Linda was pretty, but his arousal for her would not be possible without Ebuka right there with them.

They hadn't played in months. It was about time.

His phone buzzed.

"Hey, Destiny," dabbing his runny nose with a paper napkin.

They had found Galina's frozen body. She was dumped in Jisike.

"Hey, guys, I gotta run. Something came up."

"Isn't that your default state?" Ebuka quipped.

"Ah ha, very funny," Maleek responded as they all stood for their goodbyes.

"Linda, enjoy your trip," he hugged and kissed her on the lips. He also reached in and kissed Ebuka on the lips. "And you, see you Saturday."

***

Stanley stood mouth agape in his bedroom, partially dressed. His dirty socks and shoes not yet worn.

On TV, it was the morning news. The body of a young woman had been found, frozen to death by Exit 35, between Aztec and Yuma. They showed two photos of her, side by side. One was her mugshot, where she looked human, and the other, an image of her frozen face, a deep freeze too unreal. Beneath her pictures was her name, Galina Vasiliev. He sat back on the bed, in total shock.

A crew in hazmat suits and special gloves carried Galina, still in her dress, onto a stretcher and covered her with a large blanket.

"An unknown person had called 911 about a dead body on the side of the road. The paramedics say they had to call in support when they arrived and discovered what they were dealing with. Mike?"

Back to the anchor in the studio. "Thank you, Stacy. What do we currently know about this latest victim and why so remotely?"

"Yes, Mike. Details are still being verified. Although we did receive a tip-off that this victim was an inmate of the ASHCA, at Yuma, but how or why she ended up here, especially clad in the attire she was discovered in, remains a mystery. So far at our various news desks, and also reaching out to our police contacts, we haven't received any news of inmate escapes. However, that is still being followed up with the chief warden's office. Mike?"

"Thank you, Stacy. Stacy Velasquez reporting live from Yuma."

Stanley staggered to his car and remained lightheaded his entire drive to work.

Thinking about it, and honestly, he wished this thing would just go away quietly. As much as he would love to do something right, these were certainly powers beyond him. What was he supposed to do to the head warden or the governor of the fucking state? If the police couldn't deal with it, why should it be his problem? Galina's frozen face flashed his mind and startled him.

***

At his desk, his head raced. The truth was that his only viable option was to turn his back. He thought about leaving again, and once again, remembered he had neither the infrastructure nor even the savings to quit his job.

Staff were summoned for an emergency meeting.

At the staff room, no one seemed to be able to look the other in the eyes. Wardens Jackson and D'Agostin looked slightly defiant, stone faced, trying very hard to fit in with the rest of the humans while some of the others seemed to be aware of their individual culpability resulting from their silence, despite knowing the truth.

Both Stanley and Mindy could see some others knew what was going on, but there was a collective code of silence, not one born out of loyalty but fear, fear of the consequences of challenging the powers that be.

Angela walked in, putting on her own version of a sad straight face.

"Morning, everyone. As you all would have heard by now, one of our inmates, Miss Galina Vasiliev, successfully escaped from the prison walls yesterday." Across the room were various shades of eye rolls and disbelief. Only Jackson and D'Agostin nodded in agreement.

"Given how smooth and untraced her escape was, there are suspicions that she might have had help. So, we will be launching an internal investigation, and we will get to the bottom of this. This institution is a model of uprightness, and I will not tolerate the stain to our name."

Stanley and Mindy couldn't help but exchange incredulous looks.

"Lastly, and as a reminder, all communication with the police or media on this matter is to be handled solely by me. I repeat, I alone speak to the police or press on this matter. I hope that is clearly understood as doing otherwise would be an aggressive violation of our policies and we will have zero tolerance." She looked around, making sure it was well received.

Stanley wondered if the police would come snooping. ASCHA was a state prison, so city or county police would not have jurisdiction.

"If this is a state police matter, then the case is as good as closed," he thought. There was going to be no way out of it.

***

"For to what shall we liken Animmo?

To what shall be compared, the descent to the nether lands?

Examine the center point of a clock, does it not connect to every point on the circumference?

Can you not trace your way to any point in time?

From eternity past to eternity future, does it not all sink into that great eternal moment?

Let the living concern themselves with the past and the future; and even traversing to and fro between them.

The great eternal moment. The beginning to, and the end, all at once.

The great eternal moment, presented to you, you who have received the gift of the fourth dimension.

Should the living not envy you, oh death and the dead, for the great eternal moment?"

-Oku Animmo.

***

Stanley and Michelle, in their eight years of marriage, and the six in which they had been practically estranged, had developed a kind of routine, one with assigned roles and responsibilities that kept them each in their own corner yet still around each other, like how two celestial bodies maintain gravitational pull on each other without touching. They could have been long divorced but theirs was more of a stalemate gone on for way too long.

They met while Stanley was completing his post grad at Blinn. Michelle's father owned a popular diner in Brenham, and she happened to have been waitressing that first day they met. She was pretty, forward, and quite talkative. She also had what he thought, at that time, was a sparkling smile. It wasn't a love at first sight thing, he simply thought she was pretty. He was in a flirting mood, so he left his number on the receipt. She called shortly after.

On their first date, he took her to a local trade fair, her suggestion. It was mainly local artisans from the neighboring towns showcasing their wares. It was also an annual opportunity to mingle and possibly meet new people. The fair structures were set in the middle of the broad street for about a length of five city blocks. They were lean too, enough to leave some space for customers to walk by on both sides of it.

Michelle was truly a talker. As they strolled on one side of the stalls, she had already talked for five straight minutes about every single subject imaginable, jumping from one topic to the next in a matter of seconds.

"How you liking Brenham so far? This a cool place?" Michelle asked.

Stanley tried to give a regular polite response, but Michelle continued.

"Maybe you don't think it's cool, I'm sure. It's just a small town, right? Not a big city like Phoenix. I love Phoenix and big cities. Lots of funs stuff to do. Once, we had this amazing ice cream at the cinema out there. You like ice cream? They're so yummy. Vanilla and strawberry flavors are my favorite. Desserts in big cities are just pure evil. I almost died the day I tried the Turkish delight. Have you been to Turkey?"

"No, I haven't," Stanley responded.

She continued, still, "Neither have I. I haven't been anywhere, really." She laughed out loud. "Travelling must be so much fun, seeing new places. Just sit on the train somewhere, reading a nice novel. Do you enjoy novels? I've read a few. Great stories. But they take time and also, that was when I realized I might have needed reading glasses. Ha, I remember when I first got my glasses, I looked just like my math teacher from ninth grade, Mrs. Spencer. You remember your ninth-grade teachers? I remember all mine. I have good memory. How's your memory?" She stopped again and looked up at him.

He looked down at her, wondering what response to give her. But she continued immediately, again.

"Some remember better than others, right? It's the important things that count. Like you, you look very responsible, I'm sure you're smart and focused. Anything catching your fancy? Lots of nice things to eat here. Come on, let's go sit over there, finally get some time to talk."

She led him to a bar.

The sex started immediately. She was nice and made for good company. Occasionally, he would go down to her restaurant and leave her a nice tip when he knew she'd be there. On one of his visits, she introduced him to the owner of the restaurant, her father.

He was supposed to be playing it cool, have a nice girl to warm his bed during his last months at Blinn. He had planned to finish and leave Brenham after. He would move on with his life and Michelle and the memory of her would sail into the sunset of his past. Then, she announced she was pregnant, which surprised him. He'd had a complicated medical history, and his doctor had informed him that his chances of having a kid would be next to zero, if not absolutely impossible. So, she shouldn't have been pregnant, at least not by him. But she thought she was, informed her family and the welcome he was given kind of spoke for itself. He didn't know how to look the man in his eyes and tell him, "I know your daughter is pregnant but I'm not sure it's mine and even if it were, I still don't want to marry her." So, he went ahead and made their courtship official.

Her tummy had well bulged by their wedding day. He never really fell in love with her and didn't believe she loved him either. He was merely a good prospect in a small town, she was pregnant, and her father approved of him. He had also shown him the kind of kindness that made him decide not to contest the paternity of the child. So, he went along. They got married, and he used his years of savings, took out a loan and got some contribution from his folks to make a down payment for their house at Jisike.

Michelle had a still birth. For the next couple of years, they kept trying until Michelle insisted they go see a doctor.

"I don't understand your hesitation," she had said again and again. "Is there something wrong with you? Something you're not telling me?"

"It's fine, let's go to the doctor."

The outcome was just as Stanley had suspected. He was sterile and there was no way he could get anyone pregnant. Michelle seemed to have forgotten about her pregnancy when she went into a fit of rage at the doctor's office after Stanley admitted to knowing he had problems.

"Why didn't you tell me? Why would you keep such from me, what kind of a person are you?"

"Well, you did get pregnant, didn't you?" Stanley barked back.

She froze and for a moment, the "oh-oh" showed up on her face. Stanley's suspicion was confirmed.

He continued, "I'm sorry but I thought maybe it was a miracle. Maybe I wasn't sterile after all. I thought, 'Great, I'm actually gonna have kids? Awesome.'"

Michelle searched her head for a way to respond but clearly, she had gotten a man to marry her with another guy's pregnancy.

Her family took her side.

To salvage the situation, he added he was fine with adoption, but who were they kidding? They never really loved each other and never really developed any real rapport. Everything fell apart quickly, but in a silent and malicious way. Silent treatments led to distance, which killed their already mundane sex life, which killed their relationship as a whole. After a while, they stopped talking entirely but neither wanted to let go, especially of the house and of claim to it. They maintained the same bedroom but slept with other people. They slept in the same bed sometimes but never spoke again. Neither wanted to call a truce or throw in the towel. She couldn't get pregnant outside because he would know the child was not his and didn't want to be a divorcee either. Whenever they could, they would find ways to torment each other. One of hers was the tampon tantrums and he too, found his own ways of getting under her skin whenever he had the chance. Make no contact but find ways to grate on each other's nerves from a distance.

Stanley's recent pre-occupation with the ASCHA drama had left him distracted. He hadn't even noticed it was that time of the month again and once, even took out the trash without seeing the used tampon in the bin. In her opinion, he couldn't fail her that much, as a husband, and still get to live his life peacefully. Peace in that house, especially his peace, would ruin her rhythm, and she wasn't about to let that happen. From time to time, she would do things to push him to get physical with her, and hit her, so she could call the cops. He knew this and avoided her. This time around, he was not paying attention.

He became distracted during dinner and had started running the fork around the rim of the plate that made such an annoying continuous shrieky ring. She had tried to ignore it and ignore him. Even when she turned up the volume on the TV, it was still impossible. When she finally glanced at him, she saw he was absent-minded, in his own world. He looked worried, and at first, she recognized his right to worry, but still, how dare he have a private worry and be absent minded? That was like taking a vacation. He had to stay and own his share of their mutual misery.

She walked behind him while he remained distracted and scratched his neck, deep. He let out a high-pitched scream, like a kid, and jumped around, throwing his fist up in the air, ready to confront whatever it was. Her face was set right in the path of his fist, clearly praying he would hit her. He'd known she could be that diabolical but her dedication to it, to this, getting him arrested, still surprised him. He almost screamed at her but didn't want to break his streak of silence too so, he chewed down hard on his teeth and forced back the angry lump in his throat. He stared her straight in the eyes, waiting for her to say something, but she didn't either. He simply shook his head, moved the plate to the sink and stormed toward the door, briefly mentally assessing how bad it'll be being locked up for a while, if only to enjoy the relish of actually hitting her.

On opening the front door, he was startled again to find two people standing there.

"Oh, hi there."

"You better not be Jehovah's!"

"Stanley Weppler, right? Agent Burke, FBI," She raised her badge. "This is Detective Shapiro, with JPD." Maleek showed his badge as well.

Stanley's head froze. He stood, silent.

"We were wondering if we could have a word with you?", Catherine noted.

***

They were already in the man-cave before Catherine realized she forgot to come up with a strategy to approach this civilian. They weren't even sure where his loyalties lay. As Stanley tried to contain himself and not show he was freaking out, as he himself wasn't sure where their loyalties were, Catherine couldn't help but wonder if they were literally about to blow their entire case to a snitch, or worse, a loyal employee of the governor himself. Stanley, on his own part, kept replaying Angela's speech a couple of days prior about speaking to cops or the media. There was no way this so-called FBI agent, and whatever the Shapiro guy was supposed to be, were not a plant. Angela was doing house cleaning, and this was definitely a mouse trap.

He took them to his man-cave because, if they were to have that talk, he couldn't let Michelle hear it. He was suspicious of her to the point of superstition.

He opened the fridge and took out for himself a light beer, opened it and took a seat. Maleek and Catherine's expressions showed that they expected him to have offered them a drink at least, even if they would have said no. Stanley didn't care.

Apart from the center table upon which rested a pack of cards, a couple of plastic water bottles with some water in each, and the ash tray with some cigarette butts; there was only one other low stool. He didn't offer them a seat. Maleek glanced at it and motioned for Catherine to take it. She did.

After some initial and inevitable awkward silence, Catherine gave it a go.

"Mr. Weppler, thank you for seeing us."

Silence. She continued.

"Mr. Weppler, how long have you been an employee of AS-CHA?"

"What is the reason for these questions? Like I already said, all inquiries regarding anything about anything go to the management. Do you not know where their office is? ASCHA is quite a popular place, you know."

Catherine and Maleek exchanged quick glances; Stanley noticed.

"Mindy? Your colleague, Warden Woo?" Maleek entered. As he mentioned her name, Stanley visibly became a bit extra alert, he didn't have much of a poker face either.

Maleek continued, "Warden Woo, yeah, she gave us permission to mention her name to you. She said to say, 'staircase,' does that ring a bell?"

If Mindy would drop her name, Stanley thought, surely, she was on board with this and trusted them.

"But what if...," he started to think but stopped himself from that analysis and chose instead to take the plunge.

"You spoke to Mindy? About what?"

"Some shenanigans that have been going on, forced prostitution that got Galina, one of your former inmates, killed," Catherine offered.

Stanley countered. "That doesn't say anything. I heard that on the news, I mean Galina's death. You could have deduced your conclusion by some other means. How do I really know Mindy spoke to you?"

"Given how guarded and, honestly, freaked out you are, even though you've tried hard to hide it, we can tell you know some shit's been going on and you're clearly scared to talk about it too," Maleek stated.

Stanley tried to weigh Maleek's words, if he gave himself away truly.

"Look," Maleek continued, "we've got kids dropping dead from a drug in circulation, same thing's been linked to Galina the dead inmate and is somehow connected to your workplace and the governor. At this point, we're not sure who else is involved but we really need your help."

Catherine added, "Also, I can assure you that you will be given whatever federal protection that will be necessary to keep you and your wife safe."

Stanley realized that as he's been fearing for his safety these past few days, it hadn't occurred to him to remember his wife. Now that this agent said it, he wondered, if the governor found out about him, would kill his wife, maybe as a warning. He decided to relish the thought for a few more seconds. Anyway, if he let himself think too much about it, he'd never decide.

"Yes," he said quickly before allowing himself to consider changing his mind.

"Yes, what?" Catherine inquired.

"Yes, something is going on," Stanley said quickly again. His heart rate increased, he started breathing heavily and felt a weird chill in his stomach. The first time he felt that kind of chill in the stomach was when he had finally stood up to a bully in the ninth grade. The guy had been significantly bigger than him and he was sure he would get murdered by the much bigger kid, but he had just given standing up for himself a try. He did end up with a black eye but that wasn't the point, he was feeling that chill again. The chill that was his alarm bell, the symptom that flushed his body when it overflowed with adrenalin. He wondered what a black eye from a corrupt and murderous governor would look like. Again, he hoped that if it came to that, they'd kill Michelle instead, just to teach him a lesson.

"What exactly do you mean?" Catherine inquired further.

Stanley sighed and allowed himself to wonder if it wasn't too late to take it all back but continued. "I found out just a couple of weeks ago myself and I'd been thinking about a way to approach this without sounding crazy." Then he recounted the events witnessed at the staircase.

Racketeering had been the central word for Catherine. What Weppler just described could also be included under that umbrella, but now with diabolical layers. She prayed the case wouldn't become a white elephant project or spiral into a sea of meaningless and unexplainable accounts and hearsays.

"Are you able to help us convince the girls to give statements?" Maleek asked.

"I don't know. I could certainly find a way to run it by them. But Angela has eyes everywhere and if my interactions with the inmates are more than usual, boom, red flags."

Catherine and Maleek sighed. "Yeah, we know," he added. "Like Agent Burke said, you will be given adequate support and protection. This is becoming way bigger than all of us here and any help you give will be greatly appreciated."

"I'll see what I can find out."

They both dropped their business cards.

7

A t ASCHA, it was a uniform "no" from the girls.

"It's too fucking early, man! You ran off and told the first person you saw? What the fuck is wrong with you, man?" Flavor barked at him, briefly forgetting her place.

"Hey, watch it!" Stanley barked back.

Flavor realized herself and kept quiet. Tana still remained silent.

Stanley turned to Tana, "Ms. Torres, anything?"

Tana gave him her usual vacant face and shrugged. Stanley sighed, resignedly.

"Look," Stanley tried to reassure them, "I understand you have your reasons to not trust them, but they've been investigating the governor for a long time. They assured me."

"Aww, they did?" Warden Woo responded while the rest rolled their eyes.

Stanley sighed. "All I'm saying is just think about it and if you have demands to make you feel more comfortable, I could relay back to them. But I'm just as powerless on this matter as you are. So, we gotta venture out and involve someone with actual power to at least do something, and that most definitely cannot be me."

Silence. Flavor and Tana's faces showed nothing. Mindy clearly understood.

"What if they were to find a way to bug you guys, maybe like with tiny microphones or cameras?"

Both Mindy and Flavor started laughing, even Tana shook her head, as they all walked out of his office.

***

Maleek was in the middle of his lunch. He stood working the vending machine for a soda while chewing on his sandwich. His phone rang.

"Hello."

"Hello, Detective Shapiro?" the voice on the phone said.

"Yes, this is he."

"This is officer Craig," slight pause while Maleek racked his head to remember.

She continued, "if you remember from couple of weeks ago when Tyler Patrise OD'd on skooches, with Raquel?"

"Oh, yes, hi, Officer Craig, what's going on?"

"So, while responding to a non-related incident, we came across a homeless man found with a huge amount of skooches. The responding officers are of course handling it, but I thought you might wanna know."

"Wow. Thanks for calling. Is he currently still being held?"

"Yes, he is." Officer Craig responded.

"Please keep him there. I'll be right over. What precinct?"

He quickly grabbed his soda and walked off.

***

Detective Burke was already standing behind the glass wall when Maleek entered the interrogation room, holding a file.

"Mr. Delroy Foster," he called out as he walked in.

Silence.

Maleek sat down and opened his file. For some moments, the two men just observed each other silently. Maleek's initial thoughts were, "what's a homeless man got to do with this?"

"Mr. Delroy Foster, is it okay if I call you Delroy?"

"No, officer. You may call me Mr. Foster," Delroy shot back.

"Of course, Mr. Foster. I'm Detective Maleek Shapiro, with the JPD."

"And how can I help you, Maleek?"

Maleek was at first surprised but dismissed him with a light giggle. He refused to be offended by that.

"You were found in possession of over three pounds of the substance, skooches."

Silence.

"Can you tell me what you were doing with it, and also how you got it?"

"That's nunya business," he said, defiantly.

"Oh, is that right? How so?"

"First of all, I don't know nothing about no skooches. What your officers found coulda been hair gel or some shit. You just looking for reasons to fuck a brother."

"I assure you, we're not. We're just trying to get controlled substances off the streets."

"Then why am I here? What you asking me about, Maleek?"

"You don't see anything you did wrong with this stuff you were carrying?"

"Where there is no law, there is no transgression!" Delroy stated with the eloquence of an olden day's politician. "Show me any law or statute that proves this to be a controlled substance."

Maleek was surprised at his sudden eloquence.

"Why are you homeless, by the way?"

"That a crime too? You see, you ain't got nothing, boy. Controlled substance. Give me a fucking break. You can't even name it, can you? Show me the law!"

Maleek took a bit to assess him, as Delroy's face took a victory lap.

"Okay here's the thing. You were found in possession of a large quantity of a deadly substance, substance that has killed countless people around the state and beyond. So even if we're not able to charge you with possession of a 'controlled substance'," he did in air quotes, "we could possibly still hit you with various counts of manslaughter. And the fact that you have refused to cooperate with investigations will make them voluntary and aggravated. And also, in the best interest of public safety, I'm at liberty to seize your stuff and also get a judge to sign a whole range of warrants on your ass."

The victory smile was wiped off Delroy's face.

"You feel me, Mr. Foster?"

He remained silent.

Maleek continued, "You got something to say or should this," emphasizing it, "'boy', find other legal ways to truly fuck you over?"

Delroy sighed.

"Yeah. It's skooches but I ain't done nothing wrong."

"I'm listening."

"Cos I never gave or sold none that shit to nobody."

"So, all that for you, alone?"

"I'm allowed to use it ain't I? Where there's no...."

Maleek cut him off, "Yeah, yeah, no law, no transgression. I get it."

"I never sold shit. I ain't taking no fall for shit I didn't do."

"It's stuff that's killing people. There's no known regular or practical use for it and it's in enough quantity to be presumed for distribution. The probable causes are stacking up here, pal. What do you expect us to do with all that?"

In the silence that followed, Maleek noticed the pendant on his neck. A flat, beetle-shaped metal. He thought nothing of it.

"I'm waiting, Mr. Foster."

"I use it but I'm very well controlled. I won't die, if that's what you're worried about."

Maleek would've liked to state as a matter of fact that his welfare meant nothing to him but let it slide for the sake of the session.

"Also, Mr. Foster, whoever you bought it from is distributing a deadly substance, and we could also charge you as an accessory to every charge that person is faced with, including the ones you're already charged with."

"I didn't buy it."

"So, what, it just magically appears in your little skoochy bank?"

"Yeah, sorta."

Maleek looked pissed.

"That's it. You've made your choice. Enjoy prison. Or maybe that's what you been gunning for, so you'll finally have some regular meal and a place to sleep. Congrats, it's gonna work." He stood up to leave.

As he headed to the door, Catherine walked in and motioned for Maleek to pause.

"Mr. Foster, I'm Detective Burke, with the FBI.

That certainly got his attention.

"I'll cut to the chase," Catherine continued, "I've been standing out there listening to your conversation. I'm just in here to let you know that this stuff that was found in your possession has caught the eye of not just Jisike police, but the DEA and the FBI, together with all the deaths connected to it." She leaned in to face him, "So even after Detective Shapiro and the JPD are done fucking you, the FBI will take our turn, fucking you, and when we're done, we'll hand you over to the DEA. You'll be fucked at the city, state, and federal levels."

The message was well received.

"Now, would you like to try again," she encouraged, "or maybe you'd prefer to try your luck with a public defender and see what they can do for you."

Delroy sighed again and sat up. He motioned for Maleek to take a sit.

"That stuff is shit ya'll don't understand. And the shit kinda gets crazier."

"How?" Maleek followed.

"I wasn't fooling when I said it just appears."

"Where, in your piggy bank?"

"No. I know how to find it."

He knew he still wasn't making sense to them and could sense their growing frustration.

"Where does it come from?" Catherine ordered.

"Honestly, I don't know, I just know where to find it."

"Where do you find it?!" Her frustration was still visible.

Delroy clutched his pendant gently.

"I can take you there. We could go now if you're ready. But first, I want my dog back."

***

"In the SUV, Maleek sat beside Delroy in the back while Catherine sat in the front passenger seat beside the driver.

"There he is," Delroy said, clutching his pendant again with his left hand and cradling his tiny dog with the other.

They followed his gaze to see Brazile walking back toward home. They watched him open and disappear behind his gate.

"His name is Brazile. I come snooping around sometimes and I find it. Sometimes I don't."

"And you said you don't know where it comes from."

"Yup. I just find it."

"This gotta be bullshit. I'll get a warrant for both you and him. You're gonna be seeing a whole lot more of us and given your homelessness status and the fact that you got nothing holding you back here, and therefore, a flight risk, I could have a judge hold you indefinitely or at least make you wear an ankle monitor around," Catherine added.

"I'm telling you the truth."

"The hell you are," Maleek said.

"Look, this shit ain't like nothing you know. Don't fuck around."

"Fuck around? Let's go back to the station," Catherine ordered the driver.

"Wait. I can prove it."

Catherine looked back at him, waiting.

"Why don't one of you, you know those in authority, try it out, so you know what you're dealing with?"

"No!" Catherine stated.

Delroy turned to Maleek and challenged him with his eyes. "With experience, comes understanding."

"Thanks, Prof.," Catherine returned.

"I also have another way," Delroy added.

He looked at his dog and rubbed the corner of its eye, in the tear duck corner, with his finger, then raised it and pointed it at Catherine.

"Why not try this first and then lemme know if you still think I'm fulla shit."

"What's that?"

"Gunk from my dog's eye. I'll rub it in yours."

She laughed out loud at first, "You got to be joking and really trying my patience."

"It ain't gonna screw up your eyes or anything, it'll just give you some perspective. Seriously, you can take me back to the station, lock me up, get one of your boys to follow me around, whatever, I don't care. But if you really serious about knowing what the hell is going on, then you do this, or you leave me the fuck alone. You got no right to fuck with my life if you ain't serious about the truth."

"So, tell us this truth."

"No, sir, I already sound crazy enough as it is," he said, turning to Maleek. "You do the damn skooches and you, take this and have an experience for yourself."

Maleek and Catherine exchanged glances.

Her face showed she was considering it, as she gazed intently on his outstretched finger.

He stretched forth and rubbed it in Catherine's left eye corner. He repeated the process and rubbed it in the right.

"Do what I say, detective, but I guess that'll be easier said than done, eh?"

"What do you mean?" Maleek asked.

"I mean, if she sees anything out of the ordinary, don't stare. If it pokes at you, don't blink." He finished with a sinister smile.

***

Elias was going through a bout of high fever. His mom held him while he cried, trying her best to comfort him.

Luca opened the results from Elias' latest round of tests. He read through it, slowly, and sighed, shaking his head.

"What is it?" Chiara asked, as she gently rocked Elias.

"Nothing. It's nothing. They found nothing, yet again." Luca responded, his voice breaking.

They both sat silent for a while.

"Maybe it's a good thing. We don't have to be upset his test results are coming back fine, right?" Chiara asked.

"There's nothing too unfortunate about maybe having a condition or disorder. Just that if we find it, maybe we can handle it, before it kills our child, for the third time."

Chiara blocked out his last response completely. She couldn't stand to hear it.

***

Ebuka had Nightcrawler on repeat, Maleek's choice. Something about the beat took him into moods that quickly helped him untangle the thoughts of the day. It was soothing too. It was his pre-planned date with Ebuka. Linda had gone away on a work trip and of course, they had her blessings.

He had gone ahead and decided to try some of the skooches according to Delroy's instructions and convinced himself that truly, as someone investigating the drug, it was best to try it himself. Ebuka had gotten a full disclosure and was excited to try it as well.

It had the consistency of a thick hair lotion, dull gray in color. According to Delroy's instruction, Ebuka scooped a tablespoon full into a glass, poured a little hot water from a kettle, mixed it to a lighter consistency and added about half a glass of water and stirred. Satisfied, he took a small tube of blood and mixed it in. The color of the drink changed from dull gray to a deeply gray tinted red. He walked back to the bed to join Maleek, both men in their boxer shorts.

"You sure you wanna do this?" Ebuka cautioned.

"You scared you might lose your shit?" Maleek laughed at him. "Don't worry, I'll watch out for you, so Amadioha doesn't strike me," saying "Amadioha" with an exaggerated Nigerian accent.

"Right," Ebuka returned with a light chuckle, looking back at him.

They both bobbed their heads to the beats, still holding eye contact, openly, freely but mentally letting each other know what was about to happen. Their fingers touched and locked, still holding each other's gaze, both terribly aching for each other. The pain of delayed gratification was always a high for him and he intended to bless Ebuka with the month-old nut.

Finally, Maleek lowered his left leg to lie flat on the bed, further revealing his bulge. Ebuka stared down at it. He looked up back at Maleek with an expressionless face while his eyes screamed hunger. They liked to do that. Just stare at each other endlessly, soaking in their lust for each other. Maleek finally reached in and pulled it out through the flap. Ebuka held it, firmly. As it throbbed, pulsating in his hand, he raised back his eyes to lock with Maleek again and held it for minutes while puffing his weed. Maleek was not a smoker. Maleek then used his hand to caress Ebuka's face first, then gently guided his head lower. Ebuka throated him immediately, he shuddered.

Of their many foreplay routines, they liked their 69 sessions the best as they were both big fans. Both lengthy and girthy, sometimes they spent fifteen to twenty minutes just orally cleaning each other's pipes. After, Maleek laid Ebuka faced down and went to work, using his tongue to assess the sensitivity of those nerve endings.

When they finally got ready, Ebuka lubed up extra, adding to the wetness already there from Maleek's tonguing.

The rest went like this. They each held their own glass, cheered, and downed them. Ebuka laid on his back, Maleek lubed up, inserted, and then turned off the lights. It was absolutely pitch black, the way he liked it. It helped his mind travel. The high came quickly, however, it made for a rather smooth take off. Shortly after, he paused suddenly and almost pulled out because he thought he was about to release but, he steadied and continued. After a short while, it seemed like the room began to brighten, even in the pitch darkness. He looked down at Ebuka, who's face he could make out clearly, like an infra-red night camera. Their bodies began to relax and felt like they were melting into each other as Ebuka spread his legs wider apart and grabbed Maleek's ass to pull him in deeper. Maleek stopped thrusting and looked down at Ebuka again for a bit, now they both could see each other clearly, they could see it all, the clarity, the unpretentious and raw animal desire that was present. While they held that gaze, Ebuka squeezed his anal muscles against Maleek's dick very tightly, nudging him to continue. He knew it always drove him crazy. Maleek leaned in and kissed him deeply, then began to give slow but purposeful, deep thrusts. Each pump was like an assignment, a mission. Not just the need to satisfy but as if a higher calling, a duty. As they continued to melt into each other, the line between top and bottom began to fade. It didn't matter. His dick was no longer just a part of him but, became him. The friction between him and Ebuka's insides didn't just result in pleasure but also came with messages, as if could be interpreted like Morse Code or machine language. Ebuka's legs remained spread apart, high up in the air. In that space, there was no ego, no misgivings; nothing mattered. With that spark, he raised his legs even higher as Maleek continued thrusting and his hands reached down to choke him gently. His balls began to warm up and the heat spread down to his legs, his toes, and to all over his body. He felt the heat all over Ebuka as well. The heat turned up and it seemed they caught fire, a gray colored flame, burning bright but gentle. They both could see it.

As the burning continued, they felt a presence, and then more of them as the nothingness in the room began to take shape. Their spectators, who were men of old, men of past times, surrounded them, watching, as if in deliberation about their sex. Maleek and Ebuka understood that their actions were pleasing to them. The smoke from their burning bodies ascended and pleased their watchers. Maleek felt one with his dick and with each thrust, it felt like every part of his body was inside Ebuka.

He didn't need to alert him. They were both one and were both ready. Ebuka pulled him to a stop, holding him still, deep inside. Suddenly, Maleek's whole life actually flashed before him, he gasped for breath and they both screamed out loud as he emptied all of himself into Ebuka, while Ebuka sprayed his face with the most violent facial he'd ever experienced, both with such a force that it seemed the semen fled from them, while also experiencing every single split second that combined to make up the full duration of their ejaculations. Like a microscope zooming into an organism, they particularly understood every single split second of it. What followed was the longest and most intense post-nut euphoria they'd ever felt. It lingered on and on, the images of the watchers also lingered. Finally, they began to fade away and the room darkened once more.

In the dark, lying there cuddling, they both began to shiver as their teeth chattered violently. After the initial shock of it, as they started to stabilize, they reached out and held each other tightly. Their shivers calmed as they drifted off to sleep.

***

In Animmo, the dead had watched the show. AJ had come to Oluku for yet another delivery. In the entertainment corner, a crowd of those who cared had gathered to watch, some wearing ahus, some not. In the centre, was a projected image of two men, clearly Maleek and Ebuka, in the doggy style, going at it. They were on fire, a fire that burned but didn't consume. Of the watchers, for those who wore ahus, some of their genital regions showed ripple effects. Of those not wearing the ahus, Kester turned his gaze to AJ and gave him a wicked smile.

***

Catherine stood in front of the bathroom mirror and observed herself.

"No work today. Zone out, babe, you deserve it," she thought.

She closed her eyes and inhaled and exhaled deeply, trying to clear her mind. She kept her eyes closed for a few seconds.

When she opened, there was a tall person, with Catherine well below the shoulder, dressed in business attire with a very male edge to it. It was chic, but quite man-ish. For a split second, she looked up and it was an androgynous looking person, with the face of a ten-year-old, like the prank those kids tried to pull off in The Little Rascals. The make-up was also quite goth but still didn't help to swing the gender appearance in any direction. She had already looked away before the look was returned. She remembered she had to show her ID at the door before entering and it wasn't Halloween either.

As she turned from the mirror to walk out, three women, one tiny, one really tall and one of average height but massively obese, ran into one stall, shut the door quickly, and immediately let out rather explosive farting sounds that also synchronized between all three and formed a nice rhythm as well, like a note from a song she'd heard before. She held her laugh till she got out the door.

The inside part of the bar was lightly occupied with guests having their drinks. Ahead of her, in her path, was a group of three couples seated at a round table. One of the men's forks dropped, with a piece of food in it. As he reached down to pick it up, an old man standing next to a nearby table rushed over and licked the fork vigorously as he picked it up. The man holding the fork acted like it wasn't a bother. The old man also bent over and licked the man all over his lips, yet the man acted unbothered and just continued what he was doing. Catherine observed it as it happened in her line of sight but tried not to be rude.

"It's got to be some freaky festival I'm probably not aware of," she justified to herself.

Outside, she sat on her chair, opposite her husband. It was their wedding anniversary.

"Hey, Chuck, is there a festival going on in town?"

"How do you mean?"

She thought of it for a bit and decided to let it go.

"Just some weird people I saw inside just now." She responded.

"I bet. Come on, its downtown Jisike, isn't this where the crazies come to play?"

They both chuckled lightly when a waiter returned with their drinks.

As they clicked their glasses and took sips, she noticed across, over Chuck's shoulder, a man dressed in a kimono walk up to a table, open his garment, and urinate into a man's glass of red wine, as he casually positioned his hand, listening to his companion talk. The man in kimono finished and cleaned the tip of his dick on the glass rim. He proceeded to mix the drink with his fingers and taste it. The man holding the glass then drank from it, like nothing had happened.

"What the fuck?!" Catherine said out loud, jaw dropped and unable to look away. The man in the kimono looked over at her and their eyes met. His eyes narrowed as he looked back at her.

"I think she can see us!" the kimono man said calmly.

Suddenly, some people, scattered within the crowd, including those in the inner part of the bar, the Little Rascals looking person and the weird trio in the bathroom all paused in unison, while every other person carried on. Then they all turned around to her. In shock, she looked around at all of them, individually, as they stared back at her.

"You okay, sweety?" Chuck asked.

No response. She was consumed by what she was seeing.

Chuck looked around himself but saw nothing.

Kimono man walked up to Catherine and made to poke his fingers in her eyes.

She blinked.

All their faces expressed alarm, and suddenly, a punch landed on her. From all over the bar, they all came running, punching her one after the other.

"Jesus, honey, what is it?" Chuck asked, confused and alarmed. He went in to hold her, but a punch landed on him and knocked him away from her. The other guests all stood and surrounded her, many holding their phones, recording. The tall one with a baby face delivered the last one she remembered, knocking her out.

***

In the shower the next day, Maleek noticed the slight bump in his pubic region. The image of the dead Tyler's flashed his mind. He also remembered Raquel's words, "Tyler used to say each time he nutted, it felt like a divine messenger came and took the cum out of him. It was forceful too. Sometimes he could feel pain in that area for days." At this point it didn't matter, Maleek knew he'd do it again, but he'll have to keep it discrete and just with Ebuka.

While he dressed up, his phone rang.

"Hey, Jake, what's up?"

"What?"

"What? Hold on."

He turned on the TV. The news was on. On it was Catherine Burke, roughed up clothes, bloodied face, first on the floor, then seen raised from the ground and seeming to throw herself around, as others stood around taking videos. Her face was badly bruised, jerking around like she was being hit by invisible forces and with each jerk, a new bloodied bruise appeared on her face.

"The surreal images you're seeing, many who were at the scene swear they all witnessed personally and described it just as its being shown. A woman identified as Detective Catherine Burke, and get this, an FBI officer, is being described to have suddenly gone hysterical. They say at first, they thought she was crazy but as you can see here, she also looks badly beaten. As a matter of fact, by the time the paramedics arrived, she was already unconscious."

"What do you think happened here today?" Stacey asked, stretching the microphone to an eyewitness.

The eyewitness looked incredulous. "Oh, boy, that was the craziest [bleep] I ever saw. It started suddenly. I mean, this chic was sitting down with her man, I guess, and suddenly, she fell off her chair and hit the floor. At first, I thought she fell like by accident, or maybe had one of those crazy sneezes, you know, but no. She started screaming and throwing her hands all over, like she was being beaten by an invisible mob."

Shot shows Catherine punch the air weakly while seeming to be taking more invisible hits. When the shot returned to the eyewitness, some faces from the mob were suddenly beside and all around him, looking curiously at him and at the reporter. Neither he nor the reporter acted like they were seeing anything unusual. On the screen, as Maleek watched, only the eyewitness showed as well.

As the broadcast continued, Governor Tyson, Brazile, the old men from the club, and Delroy were all watching, Delroy, at a bodega. He shook his head.

"Thank you, Stacey. Stacey Velasquez reporting from downtown Jisike. When we come back, Governor Tyson on whether or not he will grant clemency regarding the fast approaching scheduled execution of death row inmate, Tana Torres."

***

In the hospital, Catherine was awake but covered in bandage, both legs suspended in the air. She was badly broken and visibly shaken. Her eyes were teared up and disbelieving.

"Did you see the video yet?" Maleek asked.

She nodded faintly, as the tears rolled down her face.

"You think this had anything to do with what Delroy did?"

Catherine's glance back at him was clearly scared. Unknown to Maleek, the baby-faced giant, the weird trio, kimono man and a floating arm holding a dagger all hovered close to her as she lay, all knowing she could see them, staring back at her, as if daring her to say something.

They sat in silence, Maleek just looking at her at intervals, unable to wrap his head around it all.

Finally, he let out, "I'll go find Delroy Foster and talk to him. Also, Tana Torres's barely got three days, I'm not sure what else she's got to lose."

***

"The third man.

To the first man, is but a line, a mere shadow of the second.

To the second man, a trace, a sketch, a mere shadow of the third.

So then, shall the third man not also be a mere shadow of the fourth?

As above, so beneath.

The second man is made of the first, as the third is made of the second.

So, also, is the fourth man made of the third.

Each man, made from infinitely multiple combinations of the lower instances.

Each man, able to control and manipulate its own differentiating attribute, which the lower ones do not have.

As above, so beneath.

If then, time is the prerogative of only the fourth man, shall he not then see all the infinitely multiple instances of the third?

Shall the fourth man not manipulate time just as easily?

Shall the fourth man, with every observation of the third, not see all possible permutations?

As above, so beneath.

The first is part of the second yet cannot comprehend it.

The second is part of the third yet cannot comprehend it.

Likewise, the third man is part of the fourth and will not comprehend it.

Same way, the first man is part of the fourth because he is a part of the second which is a part of the third; and also, will not comprehend it.

As above, so beneath.

An exit from the first allows stepping to the second.

An exit from the second allows stepping to the third.

As his breath ceases, so shall the third man step to the fourth.

As above, so beneath.

Rejoice, ye who are dead, for the great eternal moment.

Rejoice, for the gift of the fourth plane."

-Oku Animmo.

AJ lowered the book and pondered.

***

At Oluku, AJ sat at the bar. It was the usual average capacity. People talked in pairs, threes and so on.

In one of the entertainment corners, there was an old African woman from the late 19th century in a loud but solemn performance of a song. As she sang, AJ felt she was narrating her side of a story. The soul of man has one universal language.

"What will kill Gese's child for me? Let a giant falling object kill Gese's child. Look, a giant falling object killed Gese's child."

It sounded like a rhyme from an ancient folklore. AJ noted that with each verse, she incremented the casualties, like someone always ending up with an extra loose end while trying to clean up a mess.

"What will destroy the object for me? Let fire destroy the object. Look, fire has destroyed the object that killed Gese's child."

By the end of her song, the final verse went, "Death killed the hunter that killed the elephant that drank the water that quenched the fire that burnt the object that killed Gese's child."

As she walked away, AJ wondered if that was indeed her story or if she was just reliving an old play rhyme but, he had a strong sense that hers was the original version. That could not possibly be a nursery rhyme with all the deaths involved.

The source of the next skooches for delivery put on the ahu and walked toward a projection of an already going session.

***

Delroy was holding his little puppy close, petting and kissing it while he held a grocery bag in the other hand. By the time he saw Maleek, it was too late. Startled, he looked around, as if contemplating a run.

"Ah ah, don't even think about it," stressing "Mr. Delroy Foster."

"What the fuck you want, Officer Maleek?"

"So, its officer now. Oooh, progress."

"How can I help you?" he raised his voice, demanding.

"What you say we go somewhere quiet for a talk?" Maleek said, clearly faking the niceness.

"Nope. I am good right here."

Maleek wasn't asking. He grabbed him by the shirt and pushed him toward a back alley while the puppy barked. In the back,

Delroy put the dog down and watched it run off into a small shed in the corner.

"Start talking!" Maleek demanded.

"About what, exactly? You got a question for me?"

"What the fuck happened to Agent Burke?"

"Ah, I see. Yeah, that. We all saw it on TV, didn't we? Strange," Delroy said, mocking.

"Don't fuck with me."

"Or what? Delroy challenged. "You'll arrest me? Over what charges?"

"What did you do? Maleek demanded.

"Who? Me? Oh, God, I hope you're joking. Officer, if you really think I'm invisible, maybe you wanna cut this out right now before people think you cray cray."

Maleek accepted the need to calm himself and looked around to make sure no one was watching.

"What the fuck happened to her then?"

"I told her not to stare, I told her not to blink."

"Stare? Blink?" Maleek was clearly confused and exasperated. "You put something in her eyes, what was that about?"

"I simply opened her eyes, baby. And she saw."

It had started to come together for Maleek, but he refused to believe it because, it was all supposed to be mumbo jumbo nonsense. Ghosts didn't exist.

Maleek sighed. "What did she see?"

"The spaces in-between and the spaces unseen. It depends, I don't know."

"Please dumb this down for me," Maleek pleaded.

Delroy walked closer to Maleek. Unknown to him a winged cat with the eyes and nose of a human floated just behind him, unseen to Maleek.

With a wide smile, as if longing to educate the ignorant police officer, "I know it's confusing. It's the way of man to not know. The simpler things are, the better it soothes our ignorant ego. 'Apex specie,' what a laugh." He chuckled, in pity, shaking his head.

"What did she see? What spaces are you talking about?" Maleek reminded, letting his head fall in frustration.

"I don't know, bro. Perhaps other dimensions, perhaps other universes, if those two are different. All I know is that there's really no vacuum in nature. Everything and every space are occupied."

As he spoke, the floating man-faced cat disappeared, still unseen to both.

"You saying, the stuff you put in her eyes made her see things or beings from other dimensions?"

"Spaces," Delroy corrected. "We ain't sure. But all I know is that reality is individual to each one. And there's many entities on this planet we don't see. 'Cause we don't need to see them. We couldn't, even if we tried. And they don't take lightly to being discovered."

Maleek thought for a bit, incredulous and muttered, "Don't stare, don't blink."

"Exactly," he whispered in response.

"How did they find her?"

"Find who? Are you even listening to me?" Delroy got irritated with Maleek. "They don't need to find you," he continued. "They're where they are and do as they please and go where they choose. Do you think the realms need your permission for anything?"

"So, they're everywhere?" Maleek sought to clarify.

Delroy smiled again. "What? You think you're standing in that space all by yourself? Nah, bro, you ain't. You're in and part of a multitude of entities, in dimensions you cannot see that are layered upon each other. Mister, you are merely a physical manifestation of the resultant effect of many forces and energy streams. You, sir, are a perspective of consciousness."

"So that's a yes."

"Oh, boy, officer. Layers and layers of it all. Every space is used by everyone. Everything is a part of something else, something bigger. It never ends. But then, how would you know? We all know nothing." Unknown to Delroy, the man-faced floating cat was back and with it, a multitude of all manner of creatures that would be disturbing to behold. A pair of floating eyes, an alligator standing upright, floating giant baby diapers, dripping and sagging with wet faeces, an exact copy of Delroy himself but with a different eye color, much bigger, and well dressed; all standing out of his eye shot.

Maleek saw how all what he explained would make sense but still refused to believe the experience.

"What the fuck?" was all Maleek could say.

Delroy smiled further before proceeding, "Imagine a single cell in your body wondering, 'Hmm, are we the only cell in the universe'." He paused to let it sink in. "In fact, you want me to let you in on a secret?"

He suddenly felt a breeze behind him, he turned and saw the cat and then, all the others became visible, surrounding them. Suddenly, the cat lunged at him with a fierce bite to the face. He screamed out loud. All the others joined in and started hitting.

Maleek looked confused as Delroy continued to scream and thrash himself around, like he'd seen Catherine do on TV. He reached for his gun but clearly had nothing to point it at.

Before his very eyes, Delroy was lifted in the air, held at the neck by an invisible hand.

As Delroy gasped from the choking and his legs dangled helplessly, he looked into the eyes of the man whose face was exactly his own, but was definitely not him, nor related to him in any way. His eyes were filled with a life force he didn't recognize and looked like they were on fire. His pupils were empty in the center, like an incomplete 3D printing. The hollow center wasn't circular either, but jagged, like a missing piece of Lego or puzzle.

Delroy gasped out a cry before the strangler snapped his neck.

His lifeless body was thrown at Maleek, who fell under its weight, sending him crashing forcefully to the ground.

While Maleek struggled to push Delroy's lifeless body off him, the strangler walked to Maleek, knelt on the ground beside him, and lowered his face down to look Maleek straight in the eyes, their faces very close, as if almost touching.

Maleek continued to struggle, visibly frightened and confused but obviously oblivious to the entity in front of him. Satisfied, they all vanished.

Finally out, Maleek sat on the ground, a bit away from the body, seemingly spaced out and dazed by what he just saw. He took a bit to finally recover before he reached for his phone and called it in.

***

It wasn't the usual mid-day buzz at ASCHA's common area. Some administrative personnel were sometimes around the premises, along with the wardens who were always a presence to deter unwanted behaviors. That day was quieter. There was a hush in the air, one that had begun to settle in a few days prior. Tana was about to be executed, literally in forty-eight hours from then and it was her last day to walk around before she'd be locked in solitary, in preparation for her execution. There were quiet whispers as inmates around talked to each other while shooting her quiet glances with mixed emotions.

As he rested against the railing on the top floor, looking down into the common area, Stanley stared down directly at Tana, as he still pondered any way he could help the situation or even just escape it. He couldn't shake the sense that something bad was about to happen, even beyond Tana's pending execution.

Lejandro sat quietly in the corner, observing Stanley. As he followed his gaze to Tana, she just happened to look up and notice Stanley looking back at her. Her usually vacant face wasn't as deliberately absent, for just a moment. Something about her gaze back at Stanley seemed to carry an understanding of camaraderie, as if energy exchanged between them. Stanley gave her a subtle but noticeable nod and she nodded back, fleeting, and quick, but noticeable. Tana had broken character. That nod wasn't meaningless and Lejandro noticed.

***

A small crowd, most with their phones out and recording, stood around the perimeter while some officers and other first responders did their thing. A crew zipped up Delroy's body in a body bag and loaded it into the ambulance.

Detective Chin Lee, "Destiny," stood watching the security footage, clearly showing Delroy lifted into the air by an invisible force, his neck snap while still floating in the air until his lifeless body is flung at Maleek, aggressively knocking him to the ground. Lee was incredulous, together with the officers standing around her. She looked up at Maleek, who was seated quietly in an open ambulance, being attended by a medic. Maleek was totally spaced out, as the medic quietly examined him, shining a torch into his eyes and asking him questions. His confusion was vivid.

She replayed the clip. It showed Maleek initially shoving Delroy to the corner, the conversation, and then suddenly, Delroy turned back and started screaming, got beat up, lifted into the air, clearly by the neck and clearly by an invisible but tangible force. She saw

Delroy's legs dangle, his neck snapped and then flung at Maleek. The viral video with Detective Burke flashed her mind.

"I have truly seen it all," she muttered.

For a bit, she and the other officers just exchanged looks, each one clearly confused and concerned.

She walked up to Maleek.

"Hey, Maleek."

Maleek pulled out of his trance slowly. "Hey, Destiny."

"You alright?"

"I'll survive, I guess." Maleek responded lazily, still holding a hint of bewilderment in his eyes.

"Glad to hear that. Look, I know talking is not what you wanna be doing now but can you say what the hell I just watched on that security footage?"

Maleek wondered what he was supposed to say or how he was to say it.

"Just as you saw it, that's just how I saw it. I have no other answers." At least they all saw it on video. He would not be certified crazy.

"What were you and him talking about before that thing took over?"

"I had questions about what happened to Agent Burke."

"It was same thing, wasn't it?" Destiny's worry showed on her face. Was this a new thing they had to deal with?

Maleek nodded. This clearly terrified the medic and other officer standing close by.

"Do you know what it was?"

Maleek thought, "Yes, I do. It's an entity from another dimension that attacks you when they realize you can see them." But of course, he knew better. "No, I don't."

He stood up slowly and walked to the little shed in the corner, knelt lazily and whistled for the dog. It barked and ran over. Maleek picked it up.

"Destiny, if you don't mind, I'd like to go home now and rest. I'll talk to you later if you have more questions, but the rest are matters of my own investigation. Cool?"

"You keeping the dog?" she asked.

"Yup. Figured I give him a home for now."

8

Mindy had slipped Stanley a note that Tana was ready to talk, just before she was placed in solitary that evening. If anything was going to happen, they needed to act fast. Stanley first, honestly still allowed himself to think if it was in his best interest. Tana would die the next day, the investigation was likely to go nowhere and even if the FBI took it seriously, the governor wasn't just gonna standby and let things slide. If he was as diabolical as he believed him to be, was it not then a suicide mission?

He stopped by a Ghanian restaurant for some jollof rice and spicey goat meat. It had been a while and wanted to spoil himself, since his actions were about to throw his world to shit.

"That'd be to go, yes?" The attendant at the counter asked.

"Yes." Stanley answered instinctively. "You know what, I'll have that to stay." It was time to change the routine. "Maybe that'll put a crack in the matrix," he thought.

The dish did not disappoint, the more elongated rice grains and a zesty spice, just the way he liked it. He'd never admitted to his Nigerian friends, but his vote was for the Ghanian jollof.

Having eaten to his full, he took the final gulp of drink, burped and sighed.

In his car, he got out his cell phone and called.

"Hi, Officer? Shapiro?"

"Yes, this is Detective Shapiro with Jisike PD."

"Yes, hi Detective. Yeah, so I kinda saw what happened to your FBI colleague on TV. Is she alright?"

"Who's speaking?"

"Oh, shit. My bad. Its Stanley Weppler, with ASCHA. You and the FBI lady had come by my place?"

"Ah, yeah, she'll be fine. Thanks for asking. How may I help you today?"

"I don't know if you know but Tana Torres, the inmate, is supposed to be executed tomorrow, if the governor doesn't grant clemency, not like we expect him to."

"Yes, I know."

"Well, Tana is ready to talk. I told her I'll let you know but I'm not sure if there's anything you can do between now and then. So here I am, telling you."

Maleek was still clearly shaken, and the fatigue showed in his voice. "Thanks for letting me know. But hey, any idea why she didn't do this sooner?"

"Not sure, really, but my guess is she had a deal with the governor and he was supposed to grant her clemency."

"Damn. Okay, thanks. I'll take it from here. Something might be possible."

"Thanks," Stanley said and hung up.

When he got home, as he walked to the front door, a car pulled to a stop in front of the house. He made ready to walk closer to the car to find out who it was but just then, Michelle barged out the door, dressed in a short skirt, and high heels, and walked straight to the car without a glance at Stanley. However, Stanley quickly recognized all that storming was to ensure he saw her going out on a date.

"Wow." He wondered if that was a sign of things to come. He quickly ran through his head if there was anyone he wanted to give the gist. It was a good thing he ate out instead of coming home as usual, he thought and wondered if he truly threw a wrench in the matrix.

To be sure, that night, he only showered, for the first time in a while. He also slept in their bed, after changing the sheets, sprawling out carefreely. Michelle would have to choose the couch or the spare room when she got back.

He slept good.

***

He hadn't woken up in their bed in recent months. Instinctively, he had wondered why just for more than a second. Then he remembered, Jezebel had gone out.

He got out of bed and walked to the living room, expecting to see her sleeping there but she wasn't. She wasn't in the guest room either.

"I'll be damned," he muttered after chuckling.

He turned on the TV. The news was on, with Tana Torres mug-shot close-up. The ribbon scrolling past at the bottom read, "No clemency!"

For a bit, he just stared at the TV, picking up a few key words from the news cast as it went on, "hate group", "domestic terrorism", "mass murder", "thirteen dead, including five children". No one had actually expected the governor to grant clemency but still, tucked away somewhere in the deep corners of their hearts was a glimmer of hope that somehow, he would, especially with what he had said when he first watched them from beneath the stairs. Now he didn't and now they knew. He felt for her.

All the way to work, he couldn't think of anything else. He even forgot to turn on the radio and instead, drove in total silence.

The press vans and many more cars than usual were parked around. He found his own reserved space and parked.

Inside, some press crew stood around talking and engaged in different activities. Some of the wardens were dressed in their more immaculate uniforms, special for the day.

Angela Blaine casually walked by, decked out in her best office outfit to date. Her make up was impeccably done and her hair was clearly freshly done too. She even had had a facial. "The bitch prepared for a red carpet," Stanley thought.

Just as he sat down at his desk, Mindy Woo knocked hurriedly, entered and shut the door. It wasn't until then he even remembered to wonder if the cop was able to set something up.

"Hey, Mindy. And yeah, did you—"

Mindy raised a finger to cut him off. He stopped.

"Did you see my video message?"

Stanley also hadn't remembered to check his phone since he woke up. He reached for it. She had sent him a video on WhatsApp. He downloaded it.

She continued, "The cop couldn't make it down or secure a warrant. So, he called me last night to record a video confession from Tana. I've sent it to him as well. It's the best we could do."

Stanley nodded and sighed. "So, here we are."

"Yup, here we are," she replied and stood. As she was standing, Lejandro opened the door without knocking and entered quickly, which startled her slightly.

"Hey, bro, what's happening?" He turned to Mindy, "Hey there, Woo, didn't mean to startle you." He chuckled. "Hope I didn't walk in on something unholy." He chuckled again.

Clearly, neither Stanley nor Mindy was amused.

Mindy simply ignored him and walked out. Lejandro couldn't care less. He smiled back at her with some disdain as she left.

"Hey bro. How you doing?"

"I'm good, bro," Stanley replied, rather blandly. "How you doing?"

"Good, good." His eyes darted around quickly, in a snoopy manner, as if intended to not be noticed. Stanley noticed.

"Yeah?" Stanley prodded.

"Yeah, so, Angela said to tell you to be seated on time."

Stanley frowned for a bit then picked up his intercom. The tone was on. The phone was working. He hung up.

"Yes, Lejandro. I plan on being there, and on time too. Is there a lateness issue with me that I haven't been notified of? And it's not even for another forty-five minutes, so why you reminding me already?"

"I know your phone works, bro. Take it easy. Me just a messenger. Let's keep the drama for Angela, eh?"

Stanley let out a wide fake smile. Lejandro was clearly displeased by it and just walked out.

***

She had already politely asked the priest to leave.

"I know you're feeling abandoned, my child, but this is not the hour to harden your heart against the Lord our God."

"The Lord your God can eat my shit!" she stated calmly but clearly.

The priest was appalled. "What did you say?" he demanded.

She looked him straight in the eyes and repeated, much louder but still calm, "I said, the Lord your God can choke on my caca! Somebody, shout hallelujah!"

"May the Lord have mercy on your soul," the priest said and started walking out.

"Wait," she quickly said.

As he turned around to her, he was surprised to see her fall on her knees and clasp her hands together in prayer form. He sighed in relief.

"What is it? Repentance is never out of reach, but only while you're still alive. The Lord our God is merciful."

Her face looked contrite for the first time and as if her voice had choked up with tears she said, "Father, would you please ask the Lord our God to take his mercy and shove it up his heavenly ass."

He shook his head and banged on the door.

"Guards!"

The door quickly opened, and he stormed out.

Many people do more terrible things. All she did was fall for the wrong guy. Whatever God dealt her this life and expected more from her was surely not worthy of her worship.

"I'll take my chances in hell," she muttered.

Earlier, Warden Soro had hung up a clock high up on her wall. He smiled at her when he did it too. He hung it there to torture her and take his final swipe at her before she died. It was clearly custom made because it ticked very loudly, with an exaggerated ring to it as if some weird sound effect had been added. Each ticking second grated on her nerves like a spike, like the voice of death, calling out ahead to her from a distance, telling her it was coming, and it was coming only to get her. Tick. Tock. Bang. Bang. Her abuela would hear of it. Tick. Tock. Bang. Bang. As it progressed, she started missing the tick tock rhythm. It seemed to start blending into each other, as she wished it'll hurry up and finish, so she'll rest, but at same time, she wanted to will it to slow down, perhaps indefinitely. Who would ever want to die? The ticks and tocks and bangs flowed into each other. As loud as it was, she couldn't tell each apart anymore. Her life flashed before her eyes, again.

She feared for her imminent death, yet she ached for it all to be over. Why should she be afraid of death? Had life given her any reasons to cling on? Perhaps they were doing her a favor. In that moment, she comforted herself again that she had given herself an honest self-assessment and still didn't see why any of her choices should have resulted in the life she experienced. "Such is life," she thought. "Sometimes, it doesn't work out as planned. Bow out. It's enough."

***

She had hardened sufficiently throughout the process, until she once again thought of her granny. That poor woman had had a hard life and capped it off by burying her own daughter on the roadside while fleeing from trouble back home. Her granddaughter's execution was surely to send her to her grave. Maybe that too would be welcome. Wouldn't she deserve the rest? The total fuckery of a life they all got wasn't worth clinging onto.

Through the glass partition, she saw the cameras flash, the people who came to watch, all seated.

At the last minute, Stanley came in and publicly signed his portion of the standards assertion. Then Angela Blaine signed it.

After the lethal stuff was injected into her and she got the first hint of drowsiness, she noticed the governor, and seated just behind him was Victor, her Victor, looking back at her with a total blank face. She shook her head at him before she slowly closed her eyes and faded away.

About a whole minute after her head slumped, the doctor came in and examined her. He then signaled and certified her dead.

Tana had been their first execution in over nine years. For the rest of the day, ASCHA remained quiet as if everyone was in sober contemplation, each thinking about life.

In her corner, Mindy cried quietly, alone, beneath the stairs.

Stanley called out sick and went home early.

***

Maleek drove with the windows down. The high AC plus wind mix gave the different kind of cool just perfect for that hot Arizona day. He turned up the radio volume to counter the disturbance from the breeze and let his thoughts drift, wondering when or if Catherine would recover enough to re-join the case, or if this would be yet another case to go cold on his watch.

The music on the radio was interrupted to announce the breaking news of Tana Torres' death. The newscaster further repeated her crimes and her family's illegal status before noting again the number of deaths she caused. After he asked the listeners to stay tuned, a song started playing, "Life" by Des'ree.

He had called Jessica and her mom earlier and demanded they stay home.

When he got there, he pulled out a clear picture of Governor Reginald Tyson and showed it to them, as all three stood facing each other.

"Ms. Sarah, Ms. Jessica, is the man in this picture, Governor Reginald Tyson, the man that shot your brother, your son, Andrew Jackson?"

"Yes," they both replied.

"Are you willing to testify to this in court?"

"Yes."

He thanked and let them know he'd keep in touch and left.

He had earlier assured them on the phone that their identities would be kept secret and by the time it made it to court, they would be placed in witness protection, if needed.

***

"Fuck it and fuck them all," she had said after shaking her head at Victor and closed her eyes to zone out the death activities around her. Within her, she felt a widening departure from all the chaos. She knew it worked.

As she opened her eyes, she stopped. She had found herself walking, in a multitude of people of all races, all walking in same direction, now walking past her, no pushing whatsoever. She understood immediately where she was. She had died. The ride was a lot smoother than she imagined. Death was truly close by, as close as the next breath you take. It happened like a movie, simply fading from one scene to the next.

In that eternal moment, she remembered her anxieties and pain from life, but only in its very simplistic and basic form. She remembered them but no longer had even the capacity to feel them. All the pain was gone.

***

"Our love began with a gag.

A tease in a mailbox became real.

Passion blossomed despite the raging war.

I so loved you and knew you more than I ever did anyone.

I learnt self-intimacy with thoughts of you. I felt you in and around me.

I gave you my heart, yet we'd never met.

I accepted marriage when you asked me.

You spoke of your visit, and I yearned, waiting.

Alas! Your life was cut short in the war.

Now I am empty, never to be filled.

Goodbye, soldier of my heart, for I truly loved you."

-Oku Animmo {Martha's heart}.

"For form is no more, without death, an end of what gives it form.

For to take away death is to be formless.

So shall be the fate of those who would seek to manipulate death and the dead.

For their path shall be with death for death to keep its form.

Be warned, for death is for the living but the dead do die, still.

To each, an Ofuuku; everyone, with an Ofuuku."

-Oku Animmo.

"It is wise to fear death, for it gives wisdom to the heart.

Yet, it is foolish to fear death, for the dwelling is meaningless.

Is he not a fool who pursues eternity in the flesh?

Is the fear of departure not as foolish as the fear of being born?

Hasten, for the time is short, yet be of good cheer, for it completes your life."

-Oku Animmo.

***

The governor's car and escort vehicle pulled into a stop at the parking curve in front of the FBI office. As Reginald walked up the stairs, flanked by his security and lawyers, he stone-faced walked past the passersby and bystanders that recognized him, ignoring all the "hey governor" calls shouted his way. The few that tried to approach were duly shooed off by the scowls of the security men.

"Damn, what an ass hole," a few let out after he went inside.

***

Tana wiped her tears once more, as she looked lost in thought.

"It's been a nightmare since that day. I went out with my boyfriend and boom, I'm gonna be executed tomorrow, for shit I know nothing about."

A clearly disguised voice asked her, "So, Miss Torres, to be clear, and to summarize, you're accusing the current governor, Reginald Tyson, of drug trafficking, prisoner/body swapping, human and sex trafficking?"

Tana said, "Yes."

"You also said for the past three years at least, the governor had made you prostitute yourself to a ring of his contacts?"

"Yes," she repeated.

"Finally, you're also saying the governor is responsible for many deaths, including that of your former co-inmate, Galina Vasiliev?"

"Yes."

"Thank you, Tana."

The video went dead.

The light turned back on. Seated at the table were Reginald and his primary lawyer, Tracy Menendez, a stout old woman, and Michael Jackson.

Agent Bill Blitz, the regional Bureau chief, sat across the table from them, together with Catherine Burke, who was still clearly bruised (she had insisted on looking the governor in the eyes), and Maleek Shapiro.

Reginald's countenance was dead still, aggressively blank.

"Governor," Blitz started, "thank you for coming here today. We understand how difficult this must have been, given your schedule."

Silence.

"Governor, as I'm almost certain you're already aware, the FBI has been carrying out an investigation regarding some of your business dealings for a while."

"You and a whole lot of others," Reginald replied, and took a straight and mean look at Maleek, as if they were supposed to be sharing a secret. "So, how can I help you today?"

"Of the various items being investigated, the one primarily of concern is murder and sex trafficking, using the ASCHA inmates. Mr. Governor, do you have a response to the accusations levelled by Ms. Torres?"

"It's all nonsense."

"Do you deny having a hand in Galina Vasiliev's death?" Burke shot back.

Reginald gave her a stare for a few seconds before replying. "Didn't I see you on TV? They said you lost your mind. Blitz, come on, I've shown you due deference by coming here. If you must level accusations against me, you better have concrete evidence beyond useless conjectures built upon an investigation led by a clearly crazy person."

He turned back to Catherine, "Have you even recovered? Why are you here?"

"Are you the primary source of the street drug named 'skooches'?" Catherine demanded.

The governor's smile at all of them was clear to tell them he knew they all knew he was responsible, just that hunches and personal beliefs don't play in court.

"I've given you my answer. If you don't have anything concrete to drive this meeting, that would be such a shame. I'm also aware you did a raid on my private property upstate. I hope you found what you were looking for."

More silence.

Blitz carried on, "Governor, an inmate that was just executed accused you of among other things, sex trafficking. Another inmate's body, dead from an apparent overdose on this same skooches you're allegedly connected to, was found strangely and conveniently between the route from ASCHA to same private property."

He pulled out a picture of him clearly giving instructions to Kester McKean. Then he dropped another picture of Kester's dead body in the skooches overdose deep freeze.

"This young man, Kester McKean, who we had understood to be once one of your numerous assistants, was also found dead, from same situation."

Silence.

"Governor, we're willing to cut some deals in exchange for a lot of cooperation from you."

"Is my client under arrest?" Tracy demanded.

"No, Ms. Menendez, we're hoping your client will cooperate with us in closing this investigation," Blitz offered.

"Well, he already answered your questions. If we're done here, the governor has to get back to the business of working for the people of Arizona."

"I have a question," Maleek added, turning to Michael. "You were Tana Torres' public defender during her trial, while the governor was attorney general, right?"

"Yes, a different time," Michael responded.

"Quite convenient if I might say. Same case your office prosecuted her for while you were her defense attorney?" Maleek said.

"Detective Shapiro, is it? See, if you think what you just described constitutes a smoking gun, please go ahead and make your move, I dare you. Let's see how far you go with your pile of circumstantial evidence," Michael stated confidently.

"I guess we're done here," Tracy said. "Mr. Governor, I believe we're good to go."

Reginald fingered her a halt.

"This street drug thing, skooches? Yes, I've had my attorney general looking into it and following several leads. Detective Shapiro, is it a lie that you bought some of this same street drug yourself?"

Catherine and Maleek exchanged glances.

"Ah," Reginald continued, "it seems even agent Burke was also involved. Did you take some of it too? Is that why you lost your mind?"

Maleek thought about denying and calling his bluff, but it was clear he knew something. Did he have anything to worry about?

"It was purely for investigative reasons," Maleek added, not sure how believable he sounded.

"Sure, it was." Reginald turned to Blitz, "Your agents now go about taking illicit drugs?"

"What is he talking about?" Blitz asked, turning to Catherine.

"We had gone down a path where we felt it may have been helpful to better understand how the drug affected people."

"Did you both take the stuff?" Blitz asked.

"No. Just me," Maleek quickly offered.

"And how was this investigative experience?" Reginald mocked.

The subtle shame in Maleek's eyes betrayed him.

"Is there a point to this?" Maleek demanded.

"Oh, yes. From what we found out, it seemed Shapiro here got carried away with his investigations."

Maleek himself had no idea where the governor was heading. Now he was sure he had to be bluffing.

"Detective Shapiro, is it a lie that after you obtained the substance, you, as a matter of fact, used it to engage in sexual intercourse with a male partner of yours?"

Maleek's eyes bulged and completely gave him away. How could he possibly have known that? Was Ebuka a mole?

Blitz only just had to ask for statement reasons, "Shapiro, is this true?"

"That's bullshit. It was given to me by one of the suspects we picked up, but I didn't use it." He didn't think that lie through, but how else would they know?

Michael responded, "from what we gathered, whenever the abusers of this drug used it for sex, they experienced a permanent forward extension in the pelvic region. It's quite unique and undeniable. If we're lying, then submit yourself to a physical exam, by a trained medical staff, of course, not by one of your many male lovers." Michael mocked him with his smirk.

Maleek knew he was screwed, and they knew it was true.

"So, let me get this straight," Michael continued, "you've presented a case led by Agent Burke, who clearly has mental issues, and Jisike PD officer who is already addicted to the very same shit he's trying to investigate? Blitz, you're the chief here. I hope you got your house in order."

Blitz was pissed.

***

She had lost two children, back-to-back. Elias was just under four years old. He didn't show any signs of anything out of place but both she and Luca had become broken. They did their best for Elias and loved him, and with as much devotion as possible, but she couldn't help wondering if it wasn't all in vain, yet again. Even if he crossed the age of five, who was to say six or seven wouldn't be it?

Their grief took a toll on their relationship too. It was in their grief from Adank's death that they found out Chiara was pregnant again and for that, Elias' birth was received with cautious thanksgiving, exactly nine months after Adank passed away.

"It's like we only get pregnant when our child dies," Chiara blurted out one day. Luca had been thinking about it too but refused to let the thought take hold, so he scolded her instead.

"Sweety, please! You don't know what you're talking about."

"You can't tell me it hasn't occurred to you either." Chiara shot back.

"Hold on to your profession of faith. You're walking in doubt."

"I'm walking in doubt. Okay. How about your faith, isn't it strong enough to hold us both?"

Luca ignored her.

"Affliction shall not rise..."

"Well, it already did rise a second time," Chiara cut in. "In case you lost count, Nina died and then Adank was the second time."

Luca paused but had no come back. He kept walking.

"Nothing to say?"

"And what do you want me to do?!" Luca snapped.

"We need to branch out and look for solutions. Get to the bottom of this. I cannot do this waiting game any longer. Its driving me crazy."

Luca had nothing else to say. He stormed out.

One Saturday afternoon, while Chiara did some chores, she entered Elias' room to drop off his laundry and found him sleeping, his eyes closed but he was giggling and moving playfully. She smiled. Kids sometimes had some interesting dreams.

"Where are you guys?" he said in his almost four-year-old voice.

Chiara stopped to observe him. Yes, he muttered stuff in his sleep sometimes but the words he just spoke were too specific; rather crisp too. She waited and watched to see if he'd repeat it.

"Nina?" Elias mouthed, still sleeping.

She froze. Did she hear him right? "Don't be silly," she thought.

"Adan?" he called out again.

The folded laundry fell from her hands and her hand clasped her mouth shut to muffle her cries and then ran out of his room.

"There's no way you heard right," Luca scolded her. He felt her grief had started to mess with her head.

Still sobbing, "I know what I heard. He first said, 'Where are you guys?', and then 'Nina' and shortly followed by 'Adan'. Yes, he didn't sound the 'k', but he said Nina and Adank."

"That's impossible," was all Luca could think.

While Elias played with his toy set later that evening, they both sat down to play with him.

"Hey, buddy," Luca broached carefully.

"Hey, daddy."

"Say, did my little man enjoy his nap today?"

He responded with a big, child-like nod and smile.

"That's great. Did you have any dreams?"

He nodded again.

"Really? Wanna tell Mommy and Daddy about your dream?"

He nodded again. "We ate ice cream, and had fun, and we did hide and seek."

"We? Really? You and whom?"

"Nina and Adan," he said and casually went back to his playing.

They both stared at each other. They had no pictures of either of them hanging anywhere and both knew the other didn't tell him. He turned back to the kid.

"How do you know about Adank and Nina, buddy? Did Mommy tell you about them?" He gave Chiara an accusing look, which hurt her.

Elias giggled. "I see them in my dream."

"Who are Adank and Nina?" Luca asked with a very plastic smile. His mind was spinning but he wanted to still soothe the kid.

Elias just laughed.

"Really, buddy. Can you tell me about Adank and Nina?"

"Meeee! Before and before," Elias responded cheerfully.

"Huh?" Luca reached in his pocket and pulled a picture of Adank from his phone and showed it to him.

"Adan!" Elias said gleefully, upon seeing it.

"Sweety, who's Adank?" Chiara asked, unable to help the tears.

"Meeeeeee. I am Adan. I am Nina. And when I die again, I'll be back!" Elias repeated that rather cheerfully.

Those words were too clear and crisp for a four-year-old, no matter how quickly developing the child was. He couldn't conclude on the "sick joke" idea he wanted to brand it because no one had had any meaningful access to their child, let alone to plant such a heinous idea in his mind. As absurd as it all was, somehow it made perfect sense to them. It sounded like some voodoo shit, but it was happening. They'd not yet introduced Elias to the knowledge of his earlier deceased siblings. He was way too young.

They believed him. Was it possible the spirits of his siblings were contacting him? But no, he said something else, "Me. I am Adank. I am Nina. And when I die again, I'll be back." Such a string of words didn't fall into place by accident.

As Elias looked back at them again, still smiling, they both stopped seeing him as their baby, but possibly an entity that had plagued their family. In that very instant, he ceased to be their adorable little Elias. They felt cursed.

***

When Christof, Luca's dad, arrived with Pastor Oseyi, they found Chiara seated outside, eyes bulged from hours of crying. Luca had also seen them and come outside.

The three men stood around Chiara, who was seated on a stool. She looked like she had witnessed a personal calamity. On the phone, Luca had described exactly what they heard but Christof had to come down to see for himself.

"So why are we sitting out here?" Pastor Oseyi asked.

"That's not my child in there." Chiara dared to speak out. "I can't bring myself to see him the same way again." She looked up at them, eyes wide with confusion and anger, "He said it. Luca asked him, who are Nina and Adank? And he said, 'Me. I am Adank. I am Nina and when I die, I'll be back again."

"My goodness," pastor Oseyi said.

"I understand how alarming that sounds but this is just a toddler, sometimes their minds interpret things in crazy ways and many of them think they see things." Christof said. "I know I saw things growing up too that I thought were real."

Chiara hoped desperately that was the case but no, there was no fooling anyone. She knew he wasn't being silly. She felt it too.

"It's true. What he's saying is true." Chiara remained adamant.

"Honey, that's absurd," Christof opposed gently.

"Dad. Actually, and yes, maybe she doesn't know fully well what she's saying, but neither do I, and it's not nothing. There's something up with our child. What he said doesn't feel ordinary, besides, we keep trying to get pregnant but only succeed when a child has died."

"Twice doesn't make a pattern and this one hasn't died and will not die. Please have some faith in your maker." Christof cautioned sternly. "Besides, are you saying your child is what, reincarnating? That's silly."

"Dad, for the five years Nina was alive we tried very hard to get pregnant but couldn't till after she died. In the thirteen years Adank lived, we tried continuously, even going to several doctors, including trying fertility clinics, still nothing. But suddenly Adank dies and boom, we're pregnant. He said it, 'It's me. I'm Adank. I am Nina, and when I die, I'll be back.' Dad, it's not nothing."

They all pondered in silence.

"Pastor Oseyi, what do you think?" Chiara asked.

"I certainly do not believe in reincarnation. The scriptures are clear on what happens to the soul of man after death. However, and I don't have many details on it, but I've heard of things like this in my many travels, preaching. The last one I saw was in a town in west Africa."

"Really, what about?" she asked.

"Many believe they're myths, but I met even Evangelical Christians who believed they had experienced it. Parents whose children kept dying young, usually after a protracted illness. They say it's same child coming back again and again." He thought for a bit, "Ah yes, 'Abeekoos' the called them."

"How do you spell that?" Luca asked, getting out his phone.

"I'm not sure. But the last town I remember hearing of it was in Nigeria. You might find some details online. Maybe check under Yoruba mythology."

***

It was clear as day. The examining physician had felt the protrusion and shaved off that region of Maleek's pubic hair, after much protest, for documentary evidence. The protrusion appeared in the picture clearly.

He was suspended without pay, effective immediately.

By the time he made it to his desk to clear out his stuff, he met his entire department staring at him, in much judgement, some visibly disgusted and shaking their heads.

"Fuck y'all," he muttered.

Destiny kept her head down initially but glanced up, with some concern on her face, and gave him a quick slight nod as he walked out. He appreciated it.

***

As he drove to work that morning, Stanley's phone beeped. When he picked it up, it was a text from Mindy.

"Something's up in the office about that Tana case. Watch yourself, bro," it read.

He still had to go to work, his current life situation offered him no other choices.

When he walked into the conference room, of the officers standing around, Angela Blaine and Wardens D'Agostin and Soro turned to stare directly at him, whispering to each other and turning to glance at him. They wanted him to know they knew he was involved. He'd seen the governor in his base state, he knew of the dead bodies and other things they were capable of. He felt that heat rise up in his stomach and his legs started to feel cold. He wanted to vomit and run to the bathroom at the same time but knew it was all nerves so forced himself to sit down and focus on getting calm.

The others, noticing the looks, also turned to look at him.

Mindy Woo was not there. "Hey, where are you?" he texted her.

When Angela took the podium, she went straight to the point. "We found out that certain individuals snuck a recording device into Tana Torres' cell and conspired with her to tell heinous lies against the governor and this great institution." She smiled wickedly. "We know who they are. The investigation is already concluded."

She looked straight at Stanley, "Mindy Woo has already been terminated, her appointment, that is, and for her other accomplice, we would give them a long rope with which to hang themselves."

She saw that her statement made some of her staff uncomfortable and tried to walk it back some.

"We will see if they change their ways and abide by the code of conduct of ASCHA. But like I said, we will be watching and find the best ways to address this betrayal of our core values."

After the meeting, in his office, he tried Mindy's number for the umpteenth time, and it still went to voicemail. He checked his social media. Her account was disabled. He hoped she was at least not dead. He remembered Angela's tone. "God, I hope she's alright," he whispered, trembling in his seat. Could they have hurt her? Instead, he hoped she had run away but then, if she had run away, what was she running from? Was he fucked already?

Across his savings and investment apps he had roughly fifteen thousand dollars. If he had to run away, maybe he could also draw down on his 401k and pay the price later. He also had the equity on his house but that was too illiquid and therefore, not a short-term running away solution. He admitted to himself running away would be really hard and wished he didn't have to, but from what he had seen and knew of the governor and Angela and co., he was sure his safety was not guaranteed.

"Maybe I should call the cop again when I get home," he thought.

On his way back from the hospital ward, through the common area, he noticed Flavor, seated in a corner, visibly tense, her face and lips swollen. As Stanley saw her, his face clearly inquired what could have happened. He attempted to go closer to ask but she gave him a stern look to back off and quickly glanced to see if Soro was watching. He was. Stanley looked up and saw Soro too and backed off. Soro smiled pitifully at Stanley and shook his head.

He stopped by a drive thru for a burger and fries dinner and ate in traffic. With a casual glance at his rear-view mirror, he noticed Victor, the same man he'd seen with the governor the day Tana was executed. As if Victor knew he was watching him, he seemed to stare straight at him by looking straight at his image in the mirror.

The car followed him for three turns and went another direction by the fourth turn. He then drove around a little bit before heading home.

When he walked indoors, he was too zoned out to notice his wife. He dropped off his work stuff and went into the room to change. He called Detective Shapiro. It rang for a bit, then cut and went to voicemail.

"Hey, uhm, Detective Shapiro, this is Stanley from ASCHA. Stuff is going down and I could really use your help right now. Please call me?" He called out his number before hanging up.

As he sat on the bed, wondering what direction to go, he turned on the TV and Bill Maher's show was on.

"New Rules, the phrase 'do not crap where you eat' should probably be extended to say, 'Do not snort the drugs you're investigating." As the audience laughed, he first paused then continued, "Yes, this man here, Detective Maleek Shapiro with the Jisike PD in Arizona" Maleek's picture showed, "who has been investigating the governor of that state for trafficking the street drug named skooches, was found to have been taking the drug himself and guess what, been laying pipes in men's backyards with it. A fact they confirmed this because he too had the protrusion, a usual tell-tale for men who've been boinking under its influence. And get this, while he was being questioned, he said he had done it as part of the investigation. Okay, Detective Pelvic Bone." As the crowd laughed, he waited for them to finish. "I guess by the time you solve this case, you'd need an entire hip replacement."

The audience burst out laughing again.

While Bill continued, puzzled, Stanley picked up his phone and searched "Maleek Shapiro, Jisike PD." It was confirmed. Detective Maleek Shapiro had been taken off the case and suspended without pay, indefinitely.

"I'm fucked."

He walked to his window and glanced out. Parked right by his window was Victor. He parked right under the streetlight, as if deliberately trying to be seen. In the moment Stanley looked outside, the light from the room caught Victor's attention and he looked straight back at him and held the gaze.

"Oh, God, I am fucked," he repeated.

When Michelle entered the room and saw him seated by the window, visibly shaken, she wondered what could be going on? Was he upset she went on a date? She started to smile at his pain but noticed her presence in the room didn't raise his feathers, he remained deep in thought and his hand was tightly clung to the curtain. It was something else.

She walked to the window and looked down. The person in the car turned again and looked straight at her. Was he in trouble? She didn't know him to gamble. Nothing she knew about his life was exciting enough to have some guy doing a stakeout outside their house. She wondered if she should go to her father's house for the time being. She would have asked but she too remained committed to their silent treatment, so she took a change of clothing and went to the guest room.

***

Jessica was standing on their terrace, talking to her friend downstairs.

"Devonte will be there too," her friend below said.

"And what that got to do with me? I ain't looking out for no Devonte," Jessica stated.

"Mmhmm, and dogs don't bark. Girl, tell me what I don't already know," her friend countered.

Then both girls started laughing. Her friend stopped laughing first, as she noticed Sarah come out the door. Jessica turned around to see her too.

"Hey, Mom."

"Who's Devonte?" she asked, clearly angry.

"He's no one." Jessica replied, recognizing her mom's salty mood.

"Come inside, now!" Sarah demanded and walked back into the house, leaving the door open.

Jessica followed and shut it behind her.

Inside, Sarah looked at her with disgust.

"Mom, what is it?"

"Who's Devonte?"

"Mom, he's just a boy from the neighborhood. Mrs. Henderson's son. You've met him."

"I don't know no Devonte Henderson and your legs better not be knowing him too."

"Mom, please don't start. Don't!"

"Don't start what? You children are out of control, always acting like you wish. If your brother had been a bit more responsible, maybe he'd still be here today."

Jessica recognized her mom's pain and kept quiet, mentally assessing if she'd given her enough time to grieve and when it would be okay to start talking back at her. But she barked back, a little.

"Mom, you called me?"

Sarah gave her one more dirty look and picked up the remote. On the TV, she had paused a news broadcast. She pressed play.

The broadcast read "...on the street drug named skooches, the Jisike Police Detective Maleek Shapiro, who had been investigating the case, was reported to have been caught with evidence, abusing the substance, and using it for sexual activities. The Jisike Police Department has also confirmed his immediate suspension without pay. As to the impact on the case against the governor, given the embarrassment it has caused the JPD, it's unclear how the case will shape up going forward, or if the department would even still want to continue the investigation."

She paused it and turned to a stunned Jessica.

"I warned you to keep your mouth shut but nooooo, you had to blab to the officer. If the governor comes for us, who will protect us now, Jessica? What we gonna do?"

Jessica had nothing to say.

***

"If the living knew the truth of death, would they fear it?

The newborn cries while those that care rejoice.

So shall the departed rejoice while those that care cry.

Does the arrival of the pendulum swing not mean a departure from the other side?

The fourth. The eternal moment. The eternal clarity."

-Oku Animmo.

As AJ turned the page to continue reading, he heard a knock on his door.

When he opened, he saw Kester and standing beside him was Tana Torres.

"Seventh, meet Tana Torres. Tana, this is Andrew Jackson, AJ for short, aka Seventh."

"Reginald?" He asked as the trio stood in his domain.

"Yessir. Who else but the governor?" Kester joked.

"So, what's up?"

"We all got Reginald Tyson in common, don't we?"

"Yes?"

"Well, isn't it about time we showed that fucker the way to Animmo? I got a plan."

***

Stanley woke up in the middle of the night, still seated on the ground near the curtain but in a more slouched position. He was already standing up to go pee when he remembered he was being watched. He looked out the window and Victor was standing on the street, just beside the car, right under the street light, hands in his pocket and staring straight into his bedroom window, looking at him, as if he knew he'd be awake at that very moment. Startled, he dropped quickly to the ground, spraining his ankle in the process.

"Fuck," he cursed under his breath. As he took time to steady his mind from the pain, he managed to crawl to the wall and turned off the light, then crawled for the remote and turned off the tv. He stood up and walked, bent over, to the bathroom to pee. In the bathroom, he checked the time, it was 2:17 am. This kind of dedication had to be diabolical. "This is domestic terrorism," he made a mental note to self. When he finished, he closed the toilet seat and sat on it. He knew calling 911 would be useless. He decided to take only few critical essentials and one change of clothing in a backpack in the morning. He would find a way to skip town and maybe get a hotel room for a bit before figuring out next steps.

***

Maleek had watched the Bill Maher episode, but not on TV, he'd gotten the video link from Destiny. His mom, a devout West African Muslim, never actually accepted him for his lifestyle and had once told him he would end up in hell, even here on earth, if he continued in his unholy ways. How his folks would be justified. He imagined the satisfaction on his mother's face for being proved right.

The house was quiet. There was zero appetite for anything. He just lay on the couch, looking up to the ceiling and staring. He'd always taken pride in his house and taste in furnishing and always considered himself an elegant minimalist, taking pride in the few objects in his space which were also well thought out and well placed, but, in that moment, he couldn't have been more absent from that space.

"Detective Pelvic Bone." He had cringed when he first heard it, and as he just thought about it again. He reached down in his pants and felt the protrusion and sighed, but still wished he could have the experience soon. He sighed again.

There was a knock on his door.

When Maleek opened, his face looked dejected and somewhat unfriendly. He felt his pain.

"Hey, stranger," Ebuka said in a low but reassuring voice.

"Hey." Maleek's response was flat and unwelcoming. He didn't make way to suggest coming in.

"Can I come in?"

Maleek stepped aside and he entered and shut the door behind him. He observed him with some pity while Maleek wore a defiant straight but still unfriendly face, as if trying to be strong. Ebuka reached in to hug him, but he pulled back. Ebuka understood.

"Hey. How you holding up?"

"Seriously?" Maleek asked.

"Huh? I mean how you holding up? I saw the news. Are you alright?"

"Do I look alright?" Maleek stance became a bit more confrontational, but Ebuka still had no reasons to be concerned.

"I imagine not," Ebuka responded. "I'm sorry, silly question. I'm sure you're not. I saw the stuff on the news and came to check on you. You weren't picking my calls. I got a bit worried."

"Gee, thanks, bro. You're too kind."

Ebuka wasn't sure how to proceed from there. "Uhm, okay, so, I just came to see that you're good. I'll let you be now. Please reach out if you need anything, okay? I mean it."

"Who are you?" Maleek blurted out.

"Huh?" Ebuka returned.

"Who the fuck are you, bro? What's your name and I mean, your real name?"

"Have you been drinking?" Ebuka asked.

Maleek immediately swung at him and knocked him to the ground. Ebuka's shock quickly recovered, and he jumped up as he saw Maleek coming back again and posed to defend himself. Maleek tried to swing at him again, but he dodged it and hit him instead, knocking Maleek off his feet.

"You fucking stupid? Mother fucker?!" Ebuka asked.

"Who the hell are you?"

"Swing at me again and I'll fuck you up, officer. You ain't on uniform, bitch!"

"Who did you tell?" Maleek screamed at him.

"About what? Wait, you think I told on you? Why the fuck would I do that?"

"Who else would it be?"

"I don't know, maybe the other boys you been fucking? You think I was done fucking you and then what, called who, the press? Look, bro, I get you going through a lot, but don't you ever fucking do that again. I swear, I don't care if you got a badge on you, I will fuck you up."

Maleek looked confused and angry.

"I've only done that shit once, and with just you. How could they have known?"

Ebuka instinctively looked around his place. "I don't know, officer, perhaps your place is bugged? Wasn't that your first thought?"

Maleek's eyes darted like it actually just occurred to him. Ebuka shook his head. "To think I've been worried about you. I guess stupid's as stupid does."

"Hey, look," Maleek said, trying to reach out to him.

"Oh, fuck off," he shoved his hand away and walked out the door, slamming it behind him.

Maleek stared at his door for a little bit then turned around to observe his apartment, suspiciously.

He went into his storeroom and got a flashlight. He turned off all the light in the house and turned on the flashlight. With its blue colored light, he spent hours combing through the length and breadth of his apartment, then twice more each for the living room and bedroom. He found nothing.

He got out his laptop and phones and typed in certain codes in both to scan the devices. He found nothing.

He poured himself a drink and continued to mope, totally exhausted. Nothing else was new in the apartment, except the dog. The dog!

He walked to the little corner with its makeshift bed, where it slept and picked it up, shushing and stroking it gently it as it growled and barked some. He examined the pendant closely. It was beetle shaped but nothing about it else seemed suspicious except why Delroy and his pet wore similar pendants. As he stared at the dog, his eyes settled on its eyes too, the tear duct corner. As he continued to stare, the image of Catherine on TV and Delroy flashed his mind. "Don't blink, don't stare." He remembered the warning. "I'm already screwed," he reminded himself.

He placed the dog gently on its bed, turned it around and then rubbed his fingers on the corner of the dog's eye. He rubbed it into his left eye and repeated the same for the right.

He got an extra glass of whiskey and sat in bed, waiting to see something. He drifted off.

***

Maleek wasn't sure how long he'd been awake, just lying in the dark, or when he even turned on the music. A dark melancholic cello tune played way too loud for that time of the night. He felt around the bed for his phone to turn it down. As he clicked on his phone, the light from it making him squint, he observed it for a bit, swiping down and checking around when he didn't first see the music app running. He checked all active apps, and confirmed the music wasn't coming from his phone. The room was still pitch black, his TV was still off, so it didn't come from there either. In his slight confusion, he still retained his certainty that the music was coming from within his apartment. His building was noted to be quite soundproof. You hardly heard the neighbors unless someone or something was being way too loud and if his was that loud, he was concerned the neighbors would complain. The cello number stopped playing. It started playing again, repeating the exact same number.

"Alright, Beethoven," he muttered as he forced himself to rise and reach for the light switch on the wall beside his bed.

In his bedroom, everything seemed normal, same as he remembered. The music, which was still very present, had to be coming from the living room. He held his breath and walked out there.

There, he saw, as real as his own self, a girl of about fifteen, seated on a stool, with a cello between her legs, eyes closed, diligently running the bow across the strings. It had to be a dream. Who would break into his apartment in the middle of the night to play cello? A girl for that matter, a teenage girl. He stood there at the room door, watching her play. She was dressed in jeans and a shirt. He noticed a backpack beside her on the floor. As he watched, a woman walked from the kitchen area with a freshly packed meal and proceeded to put it in the girl's backpack.

Then he heard movement behind him and turned around. Standing in front of him was himself, a different version of him. That version of him was dressed in suit and tie, his police badge and gun well holstered in place. In the instant he saw him, that version of him walked right through him to the kitchen to grab a cup of coffee that was already made, and then headed out the door.

In the corner of his eyes, in the living room, he noticed an old man he'd never seen before, sitting on a sofa he didn't recognize, watching TV, which he just then noticed was on.

Then he heard more sounds coming from his room. As he walked back in there, he saw himself again, just out of the shower, towel wrapped around his waist, his work clothes for the day laying on the bed. While that version of him continued with his dressing up, he heard another sound in the bathroom. He walked in there, went to the shower curtain, and opened it. In there was, yet again, another version of himself. That showering version of him didn't react but as he stared at himself showering, the showering Maleek suddenly stopped and looked around in the general direction of the observing Maleek, as if he felt a presence. It was at that moment he remembered, the dog, the goo and that this experience was not a dream. He quickly closed the shower curtain instinctively and tried to stabilize his breath. Then he remembered the words again, "Don't stare, don't blink."

"But why are these ones not seeing me?" he wondered. He also remembered the night with Ebuka after they'd taken the skooches. Were those truly entities from other dimensions watching them?

As he turned back from his showering self, he saw yet another version of himself sitting on the toilet, phone in hand, scrolling through social media. While he stared straight, carefully observing that version of him on the toilet, the toilet him kept his phone on the stack of toilet papers close by, wiped his ass and walked into the same shower, yet after that toilet him stood up, still another version of him remained seated on the toilet.

As he made it back out through his room and into the living room, suddenly the house was filled with various versions of himself in different stages of readying for work, him still laying down, the cello player, her mother, the old man on the couch, and a couple of others, all in various activities.

Then he got terribly startled and tried to catch himself as suddenly, all the walls around him and the floor disappeared. The whole building disappeared. He saw himself standing exactly where he was, but high up in the air, as if his apartment building didn't exist. He quickly calmed himself and remained standing. He closed his eyes to focus his mind, using thoughts of Catherine Burke and Delroy. Don't stare, don't blink.

With his eyes still closed, he sensed someone standing close to him, breathing heavily. Maleek opened his eyes, with his eyes looking down. He decided whatever got those two would not get him. He could already see what it was from the corner of his eyes.

He turned around and picked up the remote control to turn on the TV. The mouth with glaring fangs continued to follow him, its hot breath remaining in his face as he tried desperately to act normal. He tuned to the morning news, trying to continue his morning activity without attracting any attention, however late, since fangs was already following him around.

He deliberately looked through the fangs to the espresso machine on the kitchen counter, all in a bid to prove he couldn't see anything. He walked right through the fangs to the kitchen and started making himself a cup.

The fangs made some indiscernible sound and suddenly, all the various versions of him, the girl, still playing her cello, her mother, the old man on the couch, and all the other faces he had seen; all in the multiple activities all filled his apartment at the same time. Looking at it, it would have been impossible for even a cat to walk through the room with the multitude of occupants, yet each one walked freely like they were all, each, alone in the space. The cello sound complicated matters too. With the various instances of the girl at various points of the rendition, the melody became disjointed, like an orchestra of chaos. It literally drove him crazy, so he had to struggle not to scream at her. Deciding none of it was real, at least, in his own dimension or timeline, he worked with his original mental image of the apartment and carried on with his morning like nothing was out of place.

As he sat on the toilet, with his phone in hand and scrolling through social media, a large man dragged himself from the room into the bathroom, standing in front of him. Determined to get a good look, Maleek leaned back on the toilet to raise his gaze to the general upper area. He observed this entity, not directly, but through the general range of his vision. The man towered over him, about 6' 7", at least 400 pounds, open pot belly, filthy pants and shoes; and he smelled like he'd been homeless for all of eternity. The man then sat exactly where he was sitting, as if through him, and also started taking a shit. Maleek felt the man's general essence, in a slightly tangible way, however, he especially felt the man's shit passing through his own ass. The feeling reverberated into his stomach which made him so sick he threw up a little, from his empty stomach, though he caught the vomit and swallowed it up. He was desperate to show the fangs he couldn't see anything. After what felt like forever, he managed to once again, calm the sick feeling in his stomach, wiped and went into the shower. The fangs stood at the door and watched him enter the shower and close the curtain, without joining him.

Maleek realized keeping a knowledge of them permanently in his mind would help him get quickly accustomed to them. It would help him not get startled. "How long was this supposed to last?" he thought, and realized he didn't find out. So, he focused his mind on them and worked hard to rationalize them into a comfortable reality. "They're always here, they've always been here. You've just not been seeing them," he thought.

He lathered some shampoo into his hair and closed his eyes to wash it off. As he opened his eyes, a giant, ugly black spider with bright red patches swung directly at him. Without thinking, he lunged backward, slipping in the process, and hitting his head, hard, on the bath floor. He passed out.

The fangs floated just above him for like a minute before floating away.

***

Brazile had also served Reginald in some capacity years prior. He then got in trouble and went to jail for a few years and continued to serve Reginald since his release, still trying to pay off some debt. As everyone knew, with Reginald, a pound of flesh always had market value.

Reginald agreed to cut him some slack since he just got out of jail and transition him to doing tasks with zero police risk.

"And by the way, get yourself a dog, a nice pup," Reginald had said. So, he went to a local shelter and got himself a dog. He named it Milo, after his favorite pet lizard in high school. Reginald seemed to like the name and officially signed him on with a pair of beetle shaped pendants, one for him and one for Milo.

The first few collections had gone smoothly as expected. On about the fifth collection, in his then basement room he was renting, Milo had just run into the mist coming up from the ground when suddenly an evil presence filled the place. Milo shrieked suddenly, then whimpered loudly as it was flung violently against the wall and died instantly. Brazile stood terrified, as he saw the unfortunate soul from the great beyond that was transporting the skooches scream out in terror, while a swipe of claws went zig-zag across in the mist. From within the mist, he saw it, not clearly at first, but he knew it was looking at him. Those hateful eyes, full of anger, sunken deep in their sockets, like a being with zero percent body fat, gray, sinewy and dry. It emerged almost fully out of the mist, standing on its one leg, breathing heavy, teeth gnashing, an embodiment of hate. As he was overcome with this demonic ugliness that stood before him, Brazile couldn't help but notice that this entity had his own face, like looking into a mirror and seeing the basest and most depraved and evil version of your own soul. It raised its claws and reached for him. Luckily, he lived in a small room and the door which led straight into the sunlight was close by. However, it wasn't close enough and before he could leap out the door, the entity's hands landed on his back, clawing into him and holding him back a bit. It tore him from his neck, mutilating his back and tore all the way down to the feet. By the time he made it outside, he lost consciousness immediately, bleeding profusely from his back and causing screams from the passers-by.

He still sensed the entity's presence sometimes when he and Zino did collections. Now he could sense the end was coming.

***

When Stanley woke up, it was past 9 am. His alarm had rung earlier, and he turned it off. He was not calling in sick, he was turning his back on his life and running away for a while. From the side of the window, he peeped downstairs and saw Victor was no longer there. The street was back to life and a few cars drove by occasionally.

From his tiny safe, he grabbed his passport, he checked the profile page, it was long expired. He also took the seven hundred dollars in crisp five dollar notes he had saved. He took his laptop, a couple of shirts and jeans, a few sanitary essentials, and headed out the door.

As he started the car, he had first opened his map app to enter an address but realized he'd not finalized on where to go. He decided to hit the road and see where he ends up. He ended up in a bed and breakfast in Agua Caliente, thirty miles east of Yuma, for no justifiable reason.

9

They were all assembled in Nina's domain; AJ, Kester, Tana, Adank, and Nina. AJ noted the resemblance between Adank and Nina.

"So, who are these guys you know?" AJ asked.

"My former skooches connect, Brazile. I also know the cop, Maleek Shapiro. He's done skooches too," Kester said.

"I also heard that name, the Shapiro cop, through the counsellor at our jail, Stanley Weppler." Tana added.

"Okay. You got a plan?" AJ asked.

"Simple and short," Kester said, "Reginald is too powerful. If we're to deal this man a blow, we gonna have to do it right."

"What you thinking?" Tana asked.

"We gotta let the Ofuukus loose on him. We gotta find a way to turn their attention to him, and his group of powerful friends."

They all liked the idea.

***

"Death is not good. Oh, death!

Truly, death is bad. Oh, death!

I wrote a letter, the letter never got there. Oh, death!

I sent a wire, the wire never got there. Oh, death!

Death is truly bad."

-Oku Animmo {Martha's heart}.

"I curse the pain in my heart for you.

I curse the longing for your touch, which will never be filled.

I curse your sweet words, which I will never hear again.

But is the pain in my heart not proof that I loved you?

Is the longing for your touch not sweet?

Were your sweet words not testament of that love?

Should I then curse your memory or celebrate our love?

Why do you bring a smile to my face and tears to my eyes?

Alas! My pain is proof of my love.

Should I let go of your memory to let go of the pain?

No! For I shall endure the pain to keep the memory."

-Oku Animmo {Martha's heart, a perspective on death}.

"As above, so beneath.

The great eternal moment, presented to you, you who have received the gift of the fourth dimension.

Should the living not envy you, oh, death, and the dead, for the great eternal moment?"

How then, shall the living access the fourth?

Let him that is wise, understand.

For death is the natural path to the fourth, but in the quantum realm, a path is laid out before the living.

Let them that seek, find.

For the answers above are also beneath."

-Oku Animmo.

***

At Reginald's mansion near Aztec, about half a dozen luxurious cars lined the parking spaces, far from the entrance gate, away from prying eyes.

In the living room, Wardens D'Agostin and Jackson stood guard in suits. Also present were Victor and the four servers standing still on each wall, their minds deliberately ignoring activities around them, only paying attention to calls for service. Victor freely observed the proceedings.

In the centre of the room, hanging from harnesses fastened to iron hooks on the high ceiling, were six young men and ladies ranging in age from sixteen to twenty-five. Each of them had needles with thick syringes inserted into their veins, each in both arms; all of them sobbing quietly through their gagged mouths.

Under them stood Reginald, Maha Pinto, Derrick Obiojor, Dibia, and His Majesty and his consort. They were all dressed in formal wear, the men in suits and ties, but there was nothing dignified about them. They looked like a board of directors that had been trapped on an island without food or water. Their eyes looked crazy with some sinister craving that nothing wholesome could quench.

"Does scripture not say," Reginald began, "it is the glory of God to conceal a matter and that of kings to search it out? Are we not gods ourselves? The future belongs to only those that have the audacity to take it."

The crazy sinister smiles on all their faces broadened. They all looked high, their wide grins dripping with lust and greed.

"Those among the living that tap into the great eternal moment shall have life everlasting. Let us fellowship and drink of this gift, for the future shall be ours and all men shall bow to us."

While Reginald spoke, Jackson clicked a button on a remote in his hand and the gray light liquids were injected into the 6 youngsters hanging from the high ceiling.

As they started to react, Victor went underneath the captives with a knife and cut them deep all over their bodies, as high as his hands could reach.

When the blood began to drip down, Reginald concluded his speech.

"Let us engage in this fellowship of life and death, because, guys, we will play both sides and we will win. Let the shift begin!"

"Let the shift begin," they responded.

They all held hands in a circle and properly positioned themselves under their captives, with their mouths open as each drank in their fill of the skooches gorged blood of their victims. As they drank, they all began to growl and howl like animals and started screaming at each other, licking the blood off each other and tearing off their own clothes. Each tore off all their clothes, down to the underwear, including his majesty, as they continued to howl and scream. Then they got on their knees, twisting weirdly, some continuing to howl while others licked the blood off the floor.

***

Maleek woke up in the bathtub, wincing with pain and his head ached. He rubbed his forehead.

While he pondered what he was doing lying in the bath, he quickly remembered how he got there and immediately prepared his mind again.

"Look straight, expect to see something at every turn. Look straight, look through," he thought.

As he stood up slowly, he assumed there'd be the most hideous entity outside standing there when he opened the curtain. He held his breath and opened. Nothing was there.

He walked into the room, trying hard to make his body language seem like he wasn't expecting to see anything unusual. From the corner of his eyes, he generally observed a pair of shoes in the corner, worn by an invisible body, tapping impatiently. He turned on his music app and started dressing. The tapping feet walked toward his phone and then the music stopped. He maintained his composure to observe the phone, staying in character and remembering to register enough inquiry on his face to seem as natural as possible. "Merryl Streep the fuck outta this bitch!" he thought.

"What the hell is up with you?" he said loudly to the phone, started the music again and returned to his dressing, keeping his eyes generally casual and keeping his mind prepared for the worst.

It turned off again. He looked back and sighed.

As he turned to pick it up again, all the walls around him and the floor disappeared, briefly. It happened so suddenly he experienced vertigo, which made him brace for a fall.

"Fuck!" he muttered. Before he could catch himself, his eyes darted toward the direction of the tapping feet. In that very instant, the pair of legs flew at him, Bruce Lee style.

He was out cold.

When he woke up, he found his way to the bed and decided to stay there till the effects wore out. He wouldn't even get up to pee. Fortunately, his mattress had an absorbent waterproof protector. When finally, his bladder couldn't handle it anymore, he relieved himself on the bed, and then heard a couple of voices laughing.

"Damn, this fucker determined to sleep through this shit," he heard a voice say.

Another voice chuckled lightly. "Maybe, we should cuddle up with him and see how good an actor he is, eh?"

Immediately, his body became cold, and he stiffened. It was one thing to pretend not to see, but how was he supposed to control his body's reaction? He started to panic and his heart beat faster, loudly. He knew he was made and prepared for the worst but was still too scared to raise his head and look. For the first time, he wondered how this would end for him, battered and hospitalized like Burke, or dead like Delroy. Burke did survive, but he wasn't prepared and certainly didn't want that kind of beating.

"I'm just gonna have to wait this out," he thought.

After a short while, he heard yet another voice.

"Hey."

He ignored it.

"Hey, Maleek," he continued, with a more soothing voice, "I know you're scared but not all higher dimensionals are bad. The others are gone, it's just you and me."

Maleek desperately hoped that was true.

"I'm going to touch you, okay? Don't be afraid."

Maleek still ignored it, his eyes now open and darting but not looking back. He felt a poke on his shoulder that made his skin run even colder. He remained frozen and refused to believe he was hearing entities talk. He ignored him, still.

"Okay, we'll do this my way then," the entity said.

Maleek did not remember getting up, he simply saw himself seated and facing this entity.

He looked and dressed exactly like a Kenyan Maasai, shiny dark skin, lean, 6'4", bare-chested and only wearing his red, beaded shuka, with a fimbo in hand.

Initially, Maleek was scared to make eye contact, but he reassured him. "I won't hurt you. Like I said, we're not all bad."

Maleek finally dared.

"See?" he heard. As the entity spoke, Maleek noticed that the full image of the being stood in front of him, motionless, like a virtual image, but also scattered around the room were copies of different sections of the man's body, like cropped motion images only showing different parts of him, the pair of eyes, ears, two legs, two hands, etc. When he spoke, the full image before him remained still while his mouth copy on the ceiling moved.

"Who are you?" Maleek asked.

"You can call me Fardeena."

Maleek looked him over and looked around his room for the various body sections floating around.

"Are you Maasai? Why are you dressed like that?"

The eyes on the wall looked Maleek over too, understanding his simplicity.

"Maleek, what would you say is the two-dimensional version of a sphere?"

"A circle," Maleek responded.

"Yes. And if you turn that circle on its side, what do you see?"

Maleek thought for a bit before answering, "A straight line?"

"Yes. And what do you think is the width of that straight line?"

Maleek thought for over ten seconds before responding, "I'm not, I can't say. If it has any width at all, doesn't it then become 2D?"

"Exactly. Now imagine explaining your 3D world to a bi or mono-dimensional being."

It made sense to Maleek.

"What kind of beings would exist in the bi or mono dimensions?" Maleek asked.

He didn't answer. Instead, the mouth on the ceiling smiled.

"Okay, so what do you want with me?" Maleek changed the subject.

"Nothing," Fardeena answered.

Puzzled, he asked, "You're in my room, how could that be nothing?"

"Whatever it is you call a room, I'm not there. Sometimes waves mix with each other causing an interference, that's what's happening here. You could say we caught on to your vibration and saw you needed a bit of help. Pure coincidence, in a manner of speaking."

"What's happening to me?" Maleek asked.

"What you did gave you a brief ability to see the outer spaces or higher dimensions. None of it will make sense to you because your primary vibrational frequency is limited. How ever you see me now is just the best way your mind can comprehend it."

Maleek took a bit to take it in.

"What do you see from the higher dimension?" Maleek asked.

"Looking into your plane? Everything. In all possible permutations and combinations and further permutations and combinations of each outcome; everything that could ever be and that could ever happen, all trillions and trillions of them, all at once. As I see it, all roads are taken, all outcomes occur, all possible timelines and their resulting outcomes are seen at once. I know the end from the beginning because I can simply pick up one particular single strand of your timeline and see its start to finish. While you see your life as a timeline passing, I see the entire bulk of it, in all its quadrillion possible outcomes, all at once."

"Doesn't that make you a god of sorts?" Maleek asked.

"To you, I would be a god but, as above, so beneath."

Long moments of silence followed.

"Can you make this stop? Please? I'm tired of getting knocked out."

"Yes, I'll cut the effect short for you."

"Thanks," Maleek said and immediately, the man disappeared.

***

His young mind had noticed. His mom and dad only gave him that serious look when he was being naughty. Now, his mom's once loving face seemed unwelcoming. Sometimes, she just stared at him, as if searching for the true face of the evil spirit that posed as a little boy. When they got too distracted with their sorrows, and the boy's tantrum began to flare due to neglect, they both had to force themselves to walk the finer line.

"It's not the boy's fault," Luca reminded Chiara, and himself.

"But isn't it though?" She countered. "We both heard him, 'I'm Nina and I'm Adank and when I die, I shall return again.' Isn't he in control? 'Cause that sounds like control to me. Who's to say he isn't a full-grown creepy entity masquerading as a child?"

Luca knew she was right. "He's our son. He came out of your womb. I know it's difficult, but we can't lose this fight."

Chiara was about to continue when Elias walked in, sulking, clearly seeking some attention. Chiara exited the room, after giving Elias a gentle touch on the head before walking out.

Luca picked him up and sat him on his lap, rocking him gently as he continued his research.

In the search bar, "Abeekoo" didn't return anything sensible. After various combinations, he finally tried "Abeekoo children that die and return" and got the Wikipedia page, "Abiku."

Abiku meant "born to die." It referred to the spirits of children who die before reaching puberty, repeatedly. It was also believed that the spirit returned to the same seed bearer to be re-born, again and again.

He paused to look down at Elias, who had been looking at the screen before looking up at his father, with such an aggressively sweet innocence that immediately melted Luca's heart. His eyes became wet with tears.

"Papa, why you crying?" Elias asked.

Luca raised the boy and stood him on his thighs and looked him straight in the eyes.

"Elias, Adank, Nina, I love you. Your mom and I love you so much, with all our hearts. You mean everything to me, and I can't, we can't go on with this pain anymore. Please tell me what to do to stop this. I don't want you to die again."

Elias himself then started crying.

He wasn't sure to what extent the child understood him or if he was just crying because he saw his dad cry. Elias reached in and wiped his tears with his small hands and leaned in to kiss him.

"Papa, don't cry."

***

As Elias cried with his father, Adank and Nina felt his pain in that eternal moment.

In the Wasteland. Adank, Tana, Kester and AJ dragged their feet through as they searched, all wishing they could still cry, if only to find an outlet for the heavy pain and despondency they felt. But they were on a mission and of course they knew it was already over in the same eternal moment.

They found them, the cold ahus of the six men and women.

The routine was different. There was no swallowing. They dragged the six cold ahus, split between themselves, and matched straight to the first enforcer they found.

***

When Brazile checked the doorbell app on his phone, he saw Maleek's face from an angle but didn't immediately recognize him.

"What you want?" he asked through the ringer speaker.

"Uhm, hi, I'm looking for Brazile," Maleek answered.

"What you want?"

Maleek thought for a bit on the right answer and then raised the ezi into view.

He held it there a few seconds before the door unlocked and opened slightly. Brazile observed him with some curiosity through the slightly open door, then shut it again to undo the chain and let him in.

After he entered, Brazile observed him more closely.

"Don't I know you?" Then it hit him, "Ah, Officer Pelvic Bone."

Maleek's countenance fell while Brazile got immediately worried, as he made the Reginald investigation connection.

"What you want, Officer?" Brazile demanded.

"For what it's worth, I'm not here on official business, sort of."

Brazile observed him without responding, his impatience getting more visible.

Then Maleek reached into his phone and got out an inbox message from his social media account and showed him.

"The fuck is that?"

"It's for you. I don't understand it myself, but a lot of shit's been going on and I don't know what else to do," Maleek answered and extended the phone to him.

Brazile looked at the message, the account name showed "Luca," but the message read "Brazile can be trusted. - Kester, aka, Iceman."

"You know Kester? Where he at? You lock him up?"

Maleek first looked back at him with some surprise. "Uhm, Kester, uhm, you mean, the Iceman, right?"

"Yea?!" Brazile was getting very irritated.

"He's dead. He's been dead almost two months."

Brazile wasn't sure how to process what he heard. "What do you mean 'dead'?"

"He's dead. I saw his autopsy report. He overdosed on skooches."

Brazile was dazed and honestly saddened. "Wait, so how the fuck you got a message from Kester if he dead? The fuck you want, officer?"

Maleek observed the ezi on him too, then held up his own and walked closer to him. "I think we both know you know what's going on."

After Brazile took a breather and calmed himself down, Maleek told him everything.

Brazile sat in silence for a bit.

"Reginald killed Seventh?" Brazile was upset, scared, and angry.

"And Kester too. Although that's just a suspicion for now."

"Damn." Brazile shook his head.

"And I'm suspended indefinitely, not sure if my department or even the FBI has the mind to pursue this to completion, and who would blame them? I even feel crazy hearing myself talk about it."

While Brazile's mind raced, Maleek continued, "and I know you still work for him. I'm not sure what's your deal with the governor but I know you supply him skooches."

"Been keeping a tab on me too, huh?" Brazile asked.

"Not long. Had a short stakeout outside, once. Before all this shit went south"

Brazile shook his head and they both continued to ponder in silence.

"I can't stop working for Reginald. If I don't wanna be unalived, I gotta keep doing my shit for him. But why did they ask you to trust me? What's going on?"

"How's this even possible?" Maleek was truly incredulous. "You really don't think it's Kester actually writing you from, where, the great beyond?" Maleek added with visible sarcasm.

"Animmo," Brazile whispered.

"Huh?"

Brazile ignored him and continued, "despite all you just gone through, you still skepting. Well, if Kester sent you, I guess we should confirm."

Suddenly, Maleek tensed up. Recalling his experience back at home, he wondered if he was literally about to meet the dead. He thought of the images he saw that night with Ebuka. Ebuka. He made a mental note to reach out to him.

Brazile double checked the door to make sure it was locked and noticed the tension on Maleek's face.

"Don't worry, the dog's eye goo let you see and interact with other spaces," pointing his fingers around horizontally, "but this skooches trip will only take us to the nether lands," pointing his fingers to the ground. "That's all we need it for."

"So, you're about to call who, Kester?" Maleek asked.

"Yes."

"From the dead?"

"You did say he died, right?"

Maleek nodded.

"So?"

"Okay," Maleek said and shrugged.

Brazile sensed his spook and laughed at him, lightly. He understood though, anyone would be scared in the situation.

"Don't worry, it's not like the movies."

He got a mug from the kitchen and filled it with water, put it in the microwave and ran it till it boiled. He got a second cup and poured out a little into it. He then took a tablespoon of skooches and stirred it into the hot water till it mixed completely before topping it up with a little cold water from the fridge.

"Whose blood is that?" Maleek asked when he got out the little red tube from a drawer.

"Does it matter?" Brazile replied.

"Is it safe?"

Brazile sighed and shook his head and went ahead to mix it in.

"It's the blood of twins. It's the best mix for this specific kind of trip for the powerful connection it can create."

He poured out a little into a shots glass, then poured out the water in the other mug and poured half the cup of mixed skooches into it, each could make a full gulp.

"And yes, it's safe. We might be underground, but all customers still want good shit, no?" Brazile reassured.

He handed Maleek one cup and took his and the shots glass back into the sitting area.

He then took out two new pins from a chest, sprayed some disinfecting alcohol on them, and handed Maleek one.

"Now, we gotta create an atmosphere and then be in the mind space to make the connection, cool?" Brazile asked.

"Cool."

"So, that pin is to prick your finger and give a couple of drops into this small cup. We both gotta do it since it's we both need to make the connection."

Maleek understood. They both pricked their right index fingers with the needles and let two or three drops into the cup. Brazile added more water to it, mixed well and then carefully poured it on the ground, making a full circle around them both.

Inside the circle, they both sat down, Burmese style, facing each other, Brazile taking the lead. They both then stirred their cups gently by swirling before downing in one gulp and dropped the cups outside of the circle. They held hands and closed their eyes.

As usual, the take-off was quick and smooth.

At first, it was an ease, a care-free removal from self. Maleek inhaled deeply and smiled, with the freedom of a playful, innocent child, like when he ran around his dad's freshly mowed lawn in the springtime. Then he felt further removed from self, with his eyes still closed, his sight began to be filled with vision of interesting things, as if they were open.

Suddenly, he felt a rush of love, like a hurricane, pouring through him, as all the elements of his persona crumbled and were blown away, his pride and fears, successes and failures, achieve-ments, identity, opinions; everything got blown away. Nothing remained but him, a force of life, in its true and simplest form, buzzing around like an electron wave. Simplicity.

He was locked in observation of his simple self, without the added weight of life's experiences, DNA, or physiology, but bare, a form that fundamentally remained true regardless of prevailing circumstances or even evolutionary stage. In that moment, he too understood it, nothing matters, nothing matters above all; and in that same moment, he also realized, both he and Brazile were one and the same. Two different instances of the same program.

He wanted to stay there, in that place with that singular understanding, where life was life and nothing else, life in its elemental form, unclogged, not yet collided with living, or thrown at an instance of conception. He could stay there forever. They both continued to hold hands as they basked in that fellowship, in the eternal oneness, evidenced by their state of divine simplicity.

After a while, he felt Brazile's essence tug at him and then pull him out of that space, deeper into another experience.

In Maleek's closed-eye vision, it became pitch black again before gradually, images began to appear, men and women of various ethnicities and time periods.

Suddenly, that background changed, like everyone was transported to a different scene, but same faces he'd originally seen. This time around, they were somewhere that looked like a medieval marketplace. He and Brazile seemed to be standing at the entrance, also the exit of the market, shaped like a cul-de-sac. Right there at the neck of the market was a small medieval looking canteen. Brazile first saw it and walked in, beckoning on Maleek to follow him. He did.

As they headed to sit, they saw the people seated with plates of food and drinks in front of them, but no one was eating or drinking. Brazile walked to a table and sat, Maleek followed his cue and sat too.

Maleek couldn't believe his eyes, that body he had seen in a body bag, back in Jisike, where the entire thing started, there, seated in front of him was a different version of him. It was Andrew Jackson, with a shadow mark on his forehead. To his left, opposite Brazile, was Kester, looking the very same way he did in his autopsy report, still frozen.

There was a subtle hum in the air, like a blend of everyone talking in hush tones but he couldn't make out a single specific thing being said and also, he noticed no mouths moving. Same thing on their own table, everyone's mouth looked closed but, they seemed to communicate perfectly, smiling politely and pleasantly at one another, Maleek and Brazile to AJ and Kester, all mouths still shut, but communication achieved and understood.

Maleek knew what he would do. Wait, and observe for opportunities to deal the governor a blow.

When both he and Brazile opened their eyes, they both had been asleep and woke up to find themselves laying on the floor. It was 2 am.

He first doubted if it was really a trip or just a dream based on expectations drummed into his sub-conscious. However, Brazile had recounted same story to him before he left for home.

He really owed Ebuka an apology. Kester had told him they watched them have sex that night and that it was him that told Reginald.

10

Stanley missed the simpler times, when life was easier and his problems, in hindsight, were really not problems, after all. He remembered the day he ran a red light and almost got himself killed, riding furiously to beat the weekly pizza delivery record. He didn't die and he also beat the record, which came with a cash prize of $100, in addition to his weekly pay of about $200, then. After tax, he spent the rest on pairs of Air Prestos and Phat Farms. He was trying to impress the gals and look cool for the guys. On his way home on the bus, carrying the shopping bags with pride, a group of boys had literally almost slapped him unconscious and took both pairs from him, including the ones he had on his feet, just for added insult. He walked back home bare feet. By the next week, he was so dejected, all fire had left him. He also gave up on the weekly record prize.

He chuckled and shook his head. Sitting in the diner that evening, he wished all the governor wanted was his shoes and nothing more.

As he finished his breakfast, he dialed Mindy Woo's number. Again, it went to voice mail.

He went back to social media and scrolled away as he continued to eat. He stopped on one of those split screens with the commentator on one side and a video on the other. The caption read, "Ghost caught on camera."

"Oh, my God, guys, this shit is craaaazy. Many ya'll been sending me this and asking me to comment on it. I don't really believe in ghosts and all, but my hommie swears it's legit."

As the video on the other half started to play, it showed two men, from some distance, at the back of a store having what seemed to be a heated argument. As they talked, one of them got lifted in the air and thrown at the other man. The video paused again and as the guy started commenting again, Stanley scoffed and scrolled to the next one, then scrolled away, absent mindedly. He scrolled through a few more videos that didn't get his attention. Then he came upon another video, promo of a Collegiate Governor's Ball, hosted by Pinto Inc., and featured some celebs, private sector players, and especially the governor.

He paused to take stock of his situation. He knew the current plan was not well thought through and certainly not sustainable, not even for another week. He'd started skipping meals just to ensure he was able to cover his motel bills. He decided to try Maleek's number again.

***

"Hello?" Maleek answered, his voice groggy.

"Hi, Detective? Did I wake you?"

"Who's this?"

"It's Stanley Weppler. From Arizona State Prison Annex."

"Yeah, hi. What's up?"

"Yeah. Uhm, I heard you got suspended from the case. I saw the stuff on TV."

Maleek remained quiet, wondering where it was going.

"I guess that came out wrong. Look, what I'm trying to say is, you know, I hadn't stuck out my neck or anything before you and the FBI lady asked me to do so. Now I've done it, and the governor and Angela know I was involved. As a matter of fact, my colleague, Mindy, has vanished. Like gone missing. I'm not even sure if she's alive or dead."

Silence.

"Hello?"

"I'm here," Maleek answered.

"See, Detective. I did what you asked and now I'm in trouble. Can you please, please help me? I know you're suspended and all, but can I still get that protection or some assistance? As you know, the people I'm running from are also my employers, so I can't go home cos I'm freaking out and I can't go to work either, which means I have no money coming in. I really need help."

Silence, Maleek continued to think.

"Hello, Detective, you there?"

"Where are you?" Maleek asked.

"Agua Caliente."

"Are you mobile?"

"Yes, I am."

"I'll send you my address. Come on over."

"Thanks," Stanley replied, relieved and sighed as he hung up.

***

They made love while Elias took a nap. It was usually his go to when Chiara was sad, and the daily stress was eating away at their connection. He would take time out to get them to talk and try to end it with love making, even if they were not exactly in the mood.

Later, while Chiara lay on her side of the bed, Luca was going through his social media account when he noticed, in his in-box, a message from a user he didn't know. It read "Who this," preceded by "Huh?" and then by a message from him that read "Brazile can be trusted. - Kester, aka, Iceman."

"Was zum Teufel!" he muttered and sat up.

"Was ist los?" Chiara turned back to him to inquire.

He showed her the message. "I didn't send this. I don't even know who this is."

He clicked to Maleek's profile and looked around.

"This guy is American. I think he's a cop too. But he didn't even message me first, I did."

"Could Elias have been playing around?" Chiara asked.

"Even so, it shouldn't be this specific. What four-year-old talks like this?"

Then it hit them. The message was indeed too direct and specific to be fun and games. Something was up. Just then, Elias found his way to their room, rubbing his eyes, full of sweetness and innocence. He smiled at both of them and climbed into their bed. Chiara reached out and kissed him.

"Hey, buddy," Luca rubbed his hand lovingly through his hair. "Did you send this?"

Elias looked at it for a bit and nodded.

They both exchanged glances, confused.

"Why did you send it?" Chiara asked.

"Adan and Nina told me to. They said I'll be good if I send it."

Adank and Nina, again.

For a minute, they both remained silent as Luca continued to peruse Maleek's profile.

"Hey, buddy, why not go watch cartoons in the living room? Mommy and I need to talk."

He obeyed.

Chiara shut the door behind him.

Luca went back into the inbox and did a voice dial.

"Hello," Maleek answered.

They were both quiet, not sure how to continue.

"Hello," Maleek answered again. "Is this Luca?"

"Yes, this is Luca," he finally answered.

"Okay, cool, cool. Hi, Luca, how are you?"

"I'm fine, thanks. Who are you please?"

"Huh?"

"Who are you?" Luca asked again.

"Uhm, you messaged me, bro and if you remember, I asked you the same question."

"Yeah, you did." He let out some frustrated sigh as he remembered again. "Yeah, my son….", he paused again, not sure how he'd sound to the stranger.

"Yeah, Kester did say he had Adank send the message. Come to think of it, I didn't ask how he did it."

Luca and Chiara's eyes lit up and burned with teary confusion.

"What the fuck is going on?!" Luca screamed into the phone.

"Yo, chill!" Maleek spoke up but reassuringly. "What do you mean?"

"What kind of a sick game are you playing? And all the way from America? What is wrong with you? You want money? Is this a game?"

Silence.

"Hey, look, your account initiated the message okay. Have I said something to upset you?" Maleek asked.

"Adank was my son, and he's dead. So again, I ask you, what the hell do you want?"

Maleek was silent, then sighed.

"Jeez. Look, I'm real sorry, but my life has been every bit as confusing and frustrating. I guess I thought you'd have been aware, since the message came from your account. Again, I'm sorry. I should've been more delicate."

Luca tried to calm his spinning mind.

"Aware of what? And you said Adank sent the message and I'm saying Adank was my son and passed away over four years ago. So how could Adank have sent the message?"

After a few seconds silence, Maleek finally spoke. "Hey, look, bro, I don't know where to start. Strange things have been happening and as crazy as everything sounds, that message from your account fit into the puzzle, even though we still have no idea what the whole picture is."

"So, what you are saying, Adank, my dead son told you he personally had this message sent to you, from my account?"

"Kester, I mean, someone else but yes, for all intents and purposes." Maleek answered.

Luca remembered once more. "Me. I am Nina and I am Adank and when I die, I'll be back."

"I see," Luca said.

"Look, my name is Maleek Shapiro. I'll text you my number. If you ever need to talk. I know what you're hearing sounds bonkers, but I feel you're aware the world ain't as black and white as we thought. There's got to be at least something you know."

"Yes. Thanks" Luca responded and hung up.

Luca and Chiara just stared at each other, both desperate for answers but neither with words to express their bewilderment.

Just then, Pastor Oseyi called.

"Hello, Pastor Oseyi."

"Hey, Luca. How you doing?"

"I'm good." Chiara also voiced her presence as they quickly went through the pleasantries.

"So, I have an update. Abikus usually carry a soul gift."

"A soul gift?" Luca sought to clarify.

"Yes. A soul gift. I honestly don't know what it is, but from what I heard, it literally could be anything, as precious as diamond and as commonplace as a stone or plastic spoon."

"Pastor, can you please be a bit more specific?" Chiara asked.

"Okay. So, it's like this. The first one to arrive, in this case, Nina, would've formed an attachment to something, anything, but it's usually very brief. What they do is that they mark it as a soul gift and leave it as a present for their next iteration or version. It represents their bond to one another and to the afterlife. When they come back, they instinctively know where it is and usually, they will find it and contact it, at least a few times."

"Okay," Luca answered. It was starting to make sense.

"You have to find that soul gift and destroy it, burning should be fine. It's the only way to break the bond and keep your child from dying, at least by that path."

"So how do we identify this soul gift?"

"I have no idea. Like I said, it could be anything. You'd just have to let your mind or memory get to work. Yeah, it could be anything but it's definitely in that house, especially since you've not moved since you got it."

"Can't we just ask him?" Chiara asked Luca.

"That's another thing," Pastor Oseyi continued, "he'll most likely not tell you. I mean, you could try, but they hardly tell. Although I've heard that sometimes, after many returns, they might start getting weary of the pain they cause their parents and disclose it but like I said, that's rare."

Long pause.

"Pastor, something else just happened."

They told him about the interaction with Maleek Shapiro and what he said Adank told him.

"So, meaning he has a way to reach Adank?" Pastor Oseyi asked.

"Huh?"

"Think about it." Pastor Oseyi continued, "We know Adank and Nina are able to communicate with Elias. And now, an adult has said the same thing. Meaning, he has a repeatable way of reaching Adank."

The light went on for Luca. He decided then he would book the earliest possible flight and head to America. If anyone would talk to Adank, it was gonna be him.

After Pastor Oseyi got off the call, he messaged Maleek for his address and told him he was coming to visit.

***

"The universe has already existed.

The lightening has already passed.

Your story has already been told.

You have already lived, and you have already died.

Today, this moment, is merely your linear point of observation.

In Animmo, you will observe it, not as linear, but from the fourth dimension.

However, let him that is wise take heed, for in the quantum realm, a path is laid before you.

As above, so beneath."

-Oku Animmo.

"Are atoms, even though whole and independent, not still part of a cell?

Are cells, even though whole and independent, not still part of an organ?

Are organs, even though whole and independent, not still part of an organism?

Are organisms not part of larger communities?

Are communities still not part of larger entities?

Oh, man and his simple ways!

For why should it be different for him?

Does he not know that just as he exists in the third dimension, wholly and independent, he also exists in the second and first dimensions?

Is he not aware of his higher self, the "him" in the higher realms?

The same him. The one and the same, traceable through his higher dimensions all the way to the one singular source.

The one and the same. The eternal source.

To the living, you must seek out your chi.

For your chi is your personal copy of the eternal source."

-Oku Animmo.

***

In Animmo, they called it different names. "The well," "the river," some even called it "there."

The moment you stepped in, it became like an infinity pool that seemed to stretch far beyond the horizon, like a vast ocean, the end vanishing out of sight in every direction you looked. It was Animmo's playground, a place where the soul came to make merry and bask in the eternal simplicity of life and rejoice in the oneness with the eternal source, that singular source of all photons.

Together with the others, Tana, AJ, Kester, Adank and Nina all played in it, like children, bursting with innocence and eternal life. Then they all froze, in that eternal moment, in rejoicing, for the beauty of their oneness and understanding of their source, in that eternal moment that also lasted for all eternity. The living called that part, "heaven."

***

At home, Elias sat on his mother's laps, her arms around him, holding him with a gentle but subtle desperation. Elias' head rested on her chest, staring in his father's general direction, with a peaceful and beautiful smile on his face. He too, in that moment, was in connection with Adank and Nina as they played. The happy feeling was nowhere as intense as for those in Animmo, as it would have been if he was united with them. Instead, it was a dulled down version, like that whiff or scent that you perceive out of the blues that brings back good memories and makes you smile, only stronger, so its unmistakable and still powerful enough to give the child a deep longing to unite with his other selves, his previous iterations.

Luca observed him, happy for the perceived tranquility he saw on the boy's face. For the first time, he wondered if it was the fear-laced urgency with which they had approached the matter that it needed, or more understanding. Was the universe not typically full of so-called aberrations, outlier events and manifestations? Who was to say the spiritual realm couldn't exhibit same?

Chiara pressed him a little closer to herself. Elias leaned in also, lovingly, and raised his little finger and twirled her necklace around it playfully. She inhaled the scent of his hair and kissed him again. They were already packed. Their flight to Arizona was in less than five hours and Elias would be going with Luca.

***

"Best to die with a smile on your face.
   Best to die with understanding.
   -Oku Animmo.

***

That same medieval canteen was where they met. Neither Reginald nor Kester or AJ had smiles on their faces. Instead, their expressions were an unfriendly kind of plain. The type you gave to your least favorite co-worker.

Sitting opposite him, they both just stared at him while he looked from one to the other, locking eyes, like an unfriendly but polite stare down, while everyone else mostly smiled with their companions. In their stare down, they did communicate.

The plan was almost complete. AJ and Kester needed to drive up deliveries and ensure they had enough supply for the ceremony. In no earth time, it would all be over and the hammer over Kester's girl and two kids would be lifted, and he'd leave Sarah and Jessica alone too.

***

Back from the skooches trip, Reginald stood in the bathroom, nude and bent over in front of the mirror, holding on to the sink. As he came to, he staggered a little, looked around and smiled at himself. He focused on his reflection in the mirror, looking himself over.

He smiled again, closed his eyes, and deliberately transported himself back to the canteen. AJ and Kester were no longer there. He stood up from the seat and walked outside of the canteen. At the neck of the cul-de-sac, he took a turn and kept walking, with a wicked smile on his face.

When he approached a part of the path that dipped and on it was a puddle of water, he hit an invisible wall when he tried to jump over. He surely would have loved to go further but that was already tremendous progress.

When he opened his eyes, he was still in front of the mirror. No fresh skooches drink, no circle, no contact on the other side needed. He was starting to come and go as he pleased. Soon, it would all come to fruition.

"Let the shift begin," he muttered and then chuckled before walking into the shower.

***

Sarah lay on the couch, eyes open and staring into nothing. The TV was muted with images she paid no mind.

The door bust open, and Jessica entered quickly and locked the door behind her, looking very worried.

"What is it?" Sarah asked, alarmed.

Jessica turned off the light, leaving the TV as the only source of light.

"What the hell, Jessica? What's going on?"

"Shhhhh," Jessica shushed her gently. "Mom?"

"Yes."

"Listen, one of those guys with the governor from that other day?"

"Yes?"

"Well, he's in the car parked outside and I think he's been out there, watching us."

"What?! Where?"

"Out the window, you can see him in his car," Jessica responded.

They both went to the window and parted the curtains. In the black SUV downstairs, Victor sat there, window down. He noticed the slight illumination from there and looked up to see them too.

Then he raised his hand and motioned a gunshot with his fingers, at them.

They quickly closed the curtains.

"My God, what have we gotten into?" Sarah lamented in a low voice.

"Should we call Officer Maleek?" Sarah asked.

"But, Mom, he ain't a cop right now. What's he gonna do? Please, let's not do anything to piss them off. I'm sure it's just a warning, to remind us they're watching. Maybe he'll go away.

***

Linda opened the door. Her face was disapproving instantly.

"Hey," Maleek said, supplicating.

"Well, well, well, if it isn't Officer Pelvic Bone," Linda responded, mocking gently.

Maleek smiled and made a face.

"How are you, Linda?"

"Come on in." She stepped aside and let him in. "I wondered when we'd see you again."

"I'm sorry, Linda. Things have been sorta side-ways." He leaned in and kissed her on the cheek. She reached in and hugged him.

Just then, Ebuka came out from the inner room.

They looked at each other for a bit, Ebuka still visibly angry.

"Hey, Ebuka."

"Sup."

"Look, I'm really, really sorry. I acted like a complete asshole. I'm sorry my head went there and I'm sorry for hitting you."

"What? You hit him?" Linda asked out loud before turning to Ebuka, angrily, "He hit you? Why didn't you tell me?"

"Oh, shit, he didn't tell you?"

"Why didn't you tell me?" Linda demanded.

"I didn't wanna talk about that part. But don't worry, he tried it, and he found out."

She turned to Maleek who quickly added, "Yup, he did put my lights out."

He turned back to Ebuka.

"Really, I'm sorry. Just that a lot of shit's been going on and got too much for me. I got confused and snapped. Let me make it up to you?"

"We'll see," Ebuka responded.

The rest of the day, they had a quiet evening, drinking and catching up.

"Babe, we need to do skooches with Maleek. I swear, it'll change your perspective."

"Oh, yeah? Well, count me in then," Linda answered.

***

An enforcer had earlier informed him, on the Ofuuku's orders, to do his transports in his own domain, and without cold ahus.

In the eternal moment that he walked from Oluku back to his domain, he imagined several scenarios of how it might all play out.

He wondered if he'd still go into Oluku if he wasn't compelled to. He admitted he enjoyed the place. He wondered what Reginald was up there, planning, but ultimately, he hoped he'd be there to welcome him to Animmo.

AJ sighed and recited, "I plead the everlasting doors, may death be permanent, and this death be mine." On the other side, Zino lapped it up quickly out of the mist.

The mist was supposed to disappear, but it lingered. Suddenly, the ground and building shook like something heavy fell from the sky.

Both Brazile and AJ felt it at once, as both their domains shook. In that eternal moment of their connection, they both felt it's presence, that same familiar evil presence. AJ knew enforcers wouldn't lie, but he had not expected to still receive a visit from the Ofuuku.

Another thud and then followed by that sharp, nerve grating shrieky claw mark scratching around his domain, like a hungry predator teasing its victim with a lick before tearing into its flesh. Its presence first filled the whole place and shortly after, consumed it entirely in an aggressively tangible way. The atmosphere became choking, Brazile started struggling to breathe, like there possibly couldn't be room for another entity in that space; like having your throat and lungs on fire while running for your life; but all this you felt in your soul. The soul torment made the living think of suicide. Even AJ, in that moment, wished he could die again just to be rid of it. Brazile threw up and begged it to stop.

As the presence lingered and its claws continued to scratch around AJ's domain, AJ finally let out a scream as he couldn't bear it any longer, and then his domain door blew open.

Everyone within a four-block radius of Brazile felt it, most intensely for the people closest to him who started screaming as well. In the neighborhood, fights broke out and pets went crazy. Some people sat on their own and just screamed out loud. They all felt the oblivion, the void, tangible and aggressively tearing at the very core of their beings.

The scratching finally stopped. Silence. AJ didn't know what to expect so he prepared, once again for the second death, just in case. He opened his eyes and looked out his domain door and there was the Ofuuku, on its one leg, the ugly thing, an embodiment of everything one should not have words to describe. The fucker was hideous; and it had his own face. Kester had not mentioned that part but then again, how many have faced an Ofuuku and remained dead to tell the tale?

Its glare was hypnotizing, like you couldn't look away unless it allowed you to, and neither could AJ. In that moment, it was Brazile who had the mortality to shed tears and throw up again, still pleading for it to stop.

"Why do you look like me"? AJ asked, supposedly in his thoughts, but the communication was received, however, ignored. It continued to stare deep into his soul, as if scanning, searching for something so intensely that AJ felt perused, like his soul had literally just been audited, like a book flipped through, page by page.

It finally let the gaze go. Its business would not be with them two. It had simply come to establish contact. It hopped away and its presence left. Both Brazile and AJ fell on the floor, catching their breath and soul, and grateful for life and death, respectively.

As Brazile stabilized, he started to notice the commotion in his building. When he went outside, people were outside of their apartments, standing in the hallways, some crying and hugging, some were on the phone with emergency responders, everyone looked alarmed.

Outside, there had been car crashes of various kinds, and some cars had crashed into and burst the fire hydrants.

"What's going on?" Brazile muttered.

"You didn't feel or hear any of that shit?" another neighbor retorted, incredulously.

"But seriously, what the fuck was that?" another asked.

"That was clearly some paranormal, some kind of alien shit," another responded.

"Jesus, it felt like a part of my soul got harvested," another replied.

Brazile went back indoors.

***

Sarah clutched her phone to her chest, peeping through their curtain slit, as she and Jessica watched the officer talking to Victor downstairs. She had called 911 against Jessica's advice.

Not long after they started talking, the officer and Victor both looked upstairs to their direction, exchanged a few more words, and did a fist bump. Jessica's heart sank. The officer looked up at them again, shook his head and walked back to his car and drove off.

"What the hell? Where's he going?" Sarah asked, frustrated.

"Mom, I told you Reginald owns them all. You shouldn't have."

"Why? Why shouldn't I? Should he own the entire department? That's not normal, Jessica. Can he just sit there and scare me in my own home? That ain't right!" Sarah's eyes teared up.

Jessica understood her mom was just expressing her helplessness. It was one thing to lose a son, but another to witness his murder, yet again, another to know who killed him and even worse still, to see that person walking around, a free man, without any consequences. Then, the unchastised offender returned to offend some more. Who wouldn't be frustrated?

By the time Jessica peeped downstairs again, Victor had just stepped out of his car, angrily slammed the door and was storming upstairs. She ran to the room.

Victor didn't knock. He simply kicked the door open. Sarah screamed in horror and started trembling when she saw Victor come in, already holding his gun. She clung onto the curtains like some kind of sanctuary. As if for effect, Victor cocked his gun.

"You called the cops?"

"Hey, mister, please, I don't want any trouble."

"Well, it's too late for that now, ain't it?"

"Look, mister, leave...." She started but couldn't finish as Victor closed in and backhanded her. As she was falling, she held onto the curtain for support, but Victor grabbed her and pushed her forcefully on the floor. The curtains snapped off from their rods and she hit the ground, screaming as she fell over and started sobbing.

Victor holstered his gun once more and knelt beside her and started choking her out. "He's the governor, you stupid bitch! What did you think will happen?"

Victor then dragged her up by the neck and pinned her to the wall, still choking her. Suddenly, she struck him and started struggling, kicking and screaming. He then punched her hard, in the stomach and then released her neck. She fell to the ground, landing on her knees and crying out in pain, clutching her stomach. He gave her another dirty slap.

She fell to the side, crying, but keeping her head raised in anticipation of his next move, maybe so she could try blocking some of it.

"You stupid fucking cockroach! If we choose to watch your house, shut the fuck up and say thank you. You wanna call 911 again?"

He brought out his phone and dangled it around on her face?

"Go on, take the phone, call 911."

Sarah's eyes had almost betrayed the situation, but Victor didn't notice her eye movement on time. Just as he turned, following her gaze, Jessica came into view, swinging a baseball bat at his head. He was out cold.

She quickly checked in on Sarah before she picked up Victor's gun and put it on top their shelf. She then got a silk scarf to tie his legs and cuffed his hands with the handcuffs they found on him.

"Mom, are you alright? I'm sorry I went to find the bat in AJ's room."

Sarah continued sobbing helplessly, trying, weakly, to push her away. Jessica pushed her hands off and forced her into an embrace, and just let her sob, then started sobbing herself.

"I'm sorry, Mom. I'm so sorry."

They took a couple of minutes to calm themselves then, Jessica called Maleek.

***

Luca prayed fervently on their drive from Tucson International to Jisike. If he found no solution on this trip, he wasn't sure what next to do. For the first time, he allowed himself to acknowledge something he'd been avoiding. If Elias died, he would never try again. Either Chiara tied her tubes, or he'd have a vasectomy. He wasn't sure he'd have any strength to go on or even any more love to give.

On the radio, songs played with commercials, one of which was of the governor's ball.

***

Maleek arrived with Brazile. Victor was still tied up but awake. Jessica had searched every inch of him for everything on him and had removed them to a safe place. She'd also gagged him with a sock and small scarf.

After the men moved Victor to the chair and firmly secured him to it, Maleek ungagged him and tried asking some questions.

"What's your name?"

Victor simply looked back at him and then at all of them, one after the other, shaking his head, as if truly feeling sorry for them, for their impending damnation.

He smirked, "I pity you. I pity all 'ya. The gov's gonna fuck ya'll, hard."

"Hey, focus!" Maleek snapped at him and spanked him on the head. "What's your name, or do we just call you governor's boy?"

Victor spat on him, hitting him directly in the eye.

Maleek blinked as much out and wiped the outer corner with his shirt.

"Don't bother with him." Brazile said. "Not sure what the governor's got on them or did to them, or whatever. I dunno. But this guy, Maurice and a few others, they're like his zombie bulldogs that go anywhere and chase anything and seem to fear nothing along the way."

Maleek gagged him back up. He then went to whisper to Jessica.

"Please take a few things you can gather quickly. I know a place you two'll be safe."

They both did, Sarah moving as quickly as her bodily injuries would let her.

While they packed, Victor stared daggers at Brazile.

Looking back at him, Brazile knew his future with the governor was over.

They left victor tied to the chair.

"Where are we going?" Jessica asked as they all settled into the car.

"A safe house that's off grid, even for my department. Your mom will also have a nurse to tend her wounds." Maleek replied as he rubbed his eyes once more. Victor's spit had hit him right in it.

"This guy's gonna blow me to the governor, and he's gonna send guys after me." Brazile lamented.

"So, what you wanna do?"

"I dunno. They're gonna come find him and once he talks, it's over for me."

While rubbing his eyes again, Maleek had an idea.

"Jessica, say, do any of your neighbors have a nice friendly dog?"

"Yeah, Kate has an old bulldog. But she can't do nothing. It's old as shit and just lays around."

"That'll be perfect." Maleek said.

"What you thinking?" Brazile asked. "Yo! What you thinking?" he asked again as it hit him, what Maleek might be thinking. "How's that gonna help?"

"We might as well leave him a present." Maleek answered. "Jessica, can you please show me to Kate's place?"

***

Kate's place was the building behind them, on the second floor. The dog was outside on the porch, just outside their door. As Maleek pet the dog, Jessica engaged Kate when she came outside, keeping her distracted after telling her he owned a bulldog just like hers and was thinking of getting another. Maleek diligently rubbed all five of his fingertips on the dog's eyes, in the corner, right on the caruncle.

***

Back in their apartment, Victor was still seated and bound where they left him, although the chair had moved a little. Maleek walked in, with Jessica behind him.

"You guys just go about taking whatever and walking all over whoever, right? Well, I hope this truly opens your eyes." Maleek said as he held Victor's chin in place and rubbed all five fingertips in his caruncles, in both eyes.

Maleek then went into the kitchen and washed his hands from start to finish, twice, with soap and very hot water.

He drove Sarah and Jessica to the safe house.

***

Jessica had hit him very hard on the head. He made a mental note to get to the doctor once he got himself free. After shaking his head hard a few times, trying to clear the dizziness he felt, he decided to try let his head rest so he would have more clarity to plan his getting out.

He slept off.

Victor was hearing his neighbor's chant. The same neighbor from his childhood. It was a chant the old woman did every night. It was supposed to be religious, not sure what her religion was, or what god she worshipped, but it terrified him. Every night when he heard her pray, right next to his room, across the fence both families shared, he sometimes got so scared he swore he could feel Aoyin, a boogeyman from his childhood, was in the room and had come to eat his brain. He endured that ordeal every day until the day the old woman passed away.

At first, when he heard the old lady died, he was happy but at night when it came time to sleep, he was relaxing in the room with his cousin when he thought he heard that same chant.

"Did you hear that?" His cousin asked first.

"What? You heard that too?" Victor asked, terrified.

"Wasn't that same chant the old woman used to chant? Ah, I'm leaving." His cousin left the room quickly.

He begged his parents to let him sleep in the living room or join his sister in her room.

"You're ten. Grow up!" his mom would bark at him.

At a certain time every evening, he made sure he stopped drinking water early so he wouldn't need to pee at night, so he wouldn't even have to crawl out from under the sheets, how much more leave the bed.

Every night, he heard her chants, in low tone, but had become modulated, which made it sound more ghostly. The chants would go on from about 9:30 pm, his bedtime to about 11. He wouldn't be able to sleep until it finished.

This went on every day, for almost two months until one day, it accidentally started blaring, which scared the shit out of him and alarmed the entire house, so much that his mom came running into his room.

Turned out it was his older sister all along. She had hidden three tiny Bluetooth speakers around different hidden places in his room, with the volume set so low it couldn't be heard outside the room. Every night, she would play the record of the old lady's chant from her phone. On the fateful day, she accidentally turned up the volume, blowing the whole thing.

The punishment his sister received was story for another day, but he heard that same chant. It took him a bit to realize he wasn't dreaming but seemed he was really hearing it, for real. The sound was present.

He opened his eyes.

He was clearly still tied up, in the same apartment, but he wasn't alone. There were people around and there were also things, or people, blocking his view but the people or things in his view looked like sketches of people, like those Disney cartoons from the 1930s. Then he realized he was somehow inside of those moving sketches-like people, like he was in them and them in him. Then the sketch people moved, and he saw a bit more clearly. Looking around, he still couldn't identify where the chant was coming from.

The living room was crowded, with Sarah and Jessica and AJ, with second, third, fourth and fifth versions of all three of them, all about different activities, all of slightly different heights and body weights, all moving about freely, clearly oblivious to their many other versions in the same room. At the same time, those different versions of the trio he saw seemed to be in a different space from another set of creatures in the room.

He saw an animated man, currently being knitted into existence. The knit man was just about over half-way fully knitted, with the knitting needles and yarn extending out of the current knitting point. Knit man whose bottom half was fully done, was seated with other weird things, around a table, over a game of spades. Around the table also were a one arm, permanently raised in the Nazi salute fashion; a giant so big, only his thighs were inside the apartment. His knees and below would be in the apartment beneath them and the rest of his body above was upstairs and beyond. When it was his turn, he would bend all the way to drop its card. There were also two others that looked just like Sarah and Jessica but much bigger and stronger versions of them.

"Da fuck?" Victor said under his breath at first but was still audible enough to be heard.

None of the entities paid him attention. None of them had ever experienced being seen by third dimensionals. To them, the 3D world was like background noise or fixtures.

The card players continued their game, making sounds that didn't flow like any normal language he'd heard. The closest he could bring to it was probably a much faster version of those African click languages, only much, much faster.

The knit man's knitting had finished but started again as soon as it finished. Even when it was but a few strands of yarn, its presence was still clearly there, and the game continued as if nothing out of place was going on with it. The knitting started and finished, repeating again and again.

"What the fuck kinda sick shit is this?"

The raised arm dropped. Then the "not" Jessica and Sarah paused and looked at each other as if asking, "Did you hear something?" The knit man turned in its chair to observe Victor. They all just stared back at him, curious, like how a group of humans would stare at a talking chair or a dog flying an aeroplane.

"Those fuckers drugged me," Victor thought. He might have been seeing things, but he still recognized Sarah and Jessica, no matter how different they looked or felt.

"Hey, you. Yeah, I'm talking to you, cunt. You better untie me or I'm gonna cut your mother in pieces while you watch. Or maybe I'll have my way with you first, while she watches. How bout that?" He finished with a wicked smile.

The giant bent so low to observe the person threatening them that Victor looked up and noticed its large face had passed through the ceiling, covering it almost entirely. The giant's face was rather hairy and rough, like from the stone age.

When he looked down again, the Sarah look alike was standing right in front of him, curiosity had become mixed with anger. They had understood what he said. She raised her finger and made to poke him in the eyes. He blinked.

Those with visible mouths dropped their jaws. The knit man lunged at him, choking him in the neck, however, the pressure he felt on the neck didn't feel like yarn, it was strong, like being choked out by a giant fighter, and so strongly he feared his neck might snap.

On the other side of the building, a neighbor's eyes had caught Victor through the open curtainless window, tied up at first and then as the drama started, but seeing only Victor.

In the apartment, the rest of the entities had surrounded Victor.

"He can see us," said Jessica look-alike.

"Please let me go," Victor muttered through with the hand still choking him.

"Please?" the Jessica look-alike asked. She looked at him intently and waved her hand over his face and in a second watched his entire timeline. She then called the others' attention to it, and they watched too.

Suddenly, all their images, as he saw them, changed to hideous monsters with fangs and claws. One after the other, they each sank their claws into him and cut him deep, from his head to his toe, again and again.

One of them cut him loose and the handcuffs also dropped. Then Victor stood up and staggered hurriedly out the door and down the stairs, his blood dripping after him. He knew he was running but maybe he wasn't sure, because the entire mob never seemed to leave his side. From how he saw them, he was running but like he was running in one spot. It was as if they were all still standing in place, clawing at him one by one. However, he could still see clearly, he was on the move. He ran past his SUV and didn't even contemplate trying to get in. He kept running and ran into the road.

The bright flashlight that came at him was still no match for the horrors he was running from.

The observer from the other apartment had watched him run downstairs, into the road but, quickly turned his face away when he too noticed him run in front of the heavy truck.

By the time the truck came to a halt, Victor's mangled and partly shredded body parts was all over the road, with a trail of red following the tires. The observing neighbor ran to the bathroom and threw up.

11

They were all seated at the dining table, Luca and Stanley with Maleek seated next to Brazile, who looked lost in thought.

"You good, bro?" Maleek asked.

"Turns out AJ's been doing transports," Brazile said.

"Huh?" Maleek asked, disbelieving.

"Skooches. They come from the other side."

Maleek was first shocked but considering all he'd experienced; it made some sense.

"All this while, I was wondering what happened to Kester and AJ, I didn't even know I'd been doing transports with them." His eyes filled with tears.

Maleek felt sorry for him. "How did you find out?"

"The other day while I was collecting, we met the Ofuuku."

"The what?"

"Look, the governor is involved in shit you cannot understand. This goes beyond money."

"What about the prisoner swapping and forced prostitution?" Stanley asked.

"I'm not deep with him in everything, bro. I just collect skooches and deliver to where he instructs," Brazile said. "But what I'm telling you is shit is about to go down. Too many people been dying of skooches and now the Ofuukus have become involved. So, either the governor is about to do something he cannot come back from or well, I dunno."

They sat in silence for a bit. Maleek proceeded, after noticing the haste in Luca.

"Hey, Brazile, you remember I had spoken to you about Luca and that message I showed you?"

"Yeah. So, what's up bro? I didn't quite make sense of what Maleek was saying. Can you run it by me again?" Brazile asked Luca.

"Of course." He told them everything.

Brazile seemed like he'd be more familiar with such a concept while Stanley wondered for a bit if he'd not cast his lot with a bunch of wackos. But who would lie about the death of their own child?

Brazile pondered on this new dimension to Animmo he'd not experienced before.

"Ah, so somehow Kester and AJ met Adank, your son, who just also happens to be an abiku, and he used his own connection to his living, uhm, self to then contact you to reach me? Wow." He chuckled lightly and shook his head in disbelief.

"Yes," Luca continued. "And we figured that since, clearly you guys have a way to reach him, if you could help me get to him. So, we can break this tie." Luca answered.

"You sure it can be broken?" Maleek asked.

"I don't know, but I hope. I have no other choice." Luca sounded desperate.

Brazile agreed.

He first went back to his place to get some more supplies.

Back, after he'd done all the preparations needed, Maleek and Stanley remained in the living room while Brazile and Luca went into Maleek's bedroom, where Elias was sleeping on Maleek's bed.

On the bathroom floor, Brazile made a wide enough circle with one of the mixes and he and Luca sat in it, Burmese style, holding hands, after they each drank their portions of prepared skooches.

They took off quickly.

Luca saw himself standing beside his wife in their backyard one cool spring evening in Lauterbrunnen. It was the first week of their marriage, their honeymoon was in full swing and in fact, they'd just had another round of very intense and passionate sex that made him feel like a bad boy, in a good way. He stood beside her, him in his boxer's shorts, while she wore her undies and a big shirt on top. His hand was on her waist as they looked out to the lush greeneries clinging onto the mountains.

Then he felt a rush of wind from behind him that pushed him and also somehow became a part of him too, like he moved with the wind. He turned back and saw himself, as if out of body, still holding his wife and smiling.

Swooosh! The wind blew on, as if carrying his entire consciousness with it, down and speedily along the Alpine valley. He even felt the wetness from the waterfall as he travelled up to the snowy mountain tops. He travelled not of his own accord but instead a mere part of the rushing wind. In that moment, he realized he had no ability to resist, nor did he even have the ability to want to.

The wind then blew into an opening in the rock that formed a sizeable pocket full of trees. In that forest, as they blew past the trees, he felt his speed slow and his parting the trees to pass through, like a man walking in a thick bush and using his hands to part the branches. Suddenly, the wind all rushed out of the enclosed forest and up into the sky where it calmed and became still. The stillness became alive, aware, sentient, understanding its nature of stillness and therefore celebrated it by remaining still, just being.

In becoming one with the stillness, his own self-awareness evaporated into the still air around him. There, he exploded in joy that could only be described as pure ecstasy. He stayed in that ecstasy for what seemed like an eternity.

Brazile took him by the hand and pulled him on.

He closed his eyes and opened them again. As he did, he saw himself walking along a medieval marketplace. As he and Brazile walked down the bustling market, he saw a clock merchant ahead. He led the way and walked in. In there, they saw clocks of various sizes and from various times, from centuries past and future.

Brazile nudged him and pointed toward the attendant stand, where, standing side by side were Adank and Nina. In that moment, he was filled with a measured kind of joy. It wasn't overflowing, yet the sorrow he also felt for having lost them was just as measured. Neither of them shed tears, nor did anyone run into the other's embrace. Instead, they just walked slowly toward each other, maintained some space between them and just smiled from one to the other, no lips moving.

In their silent communication, Luca understood. The abnormality of his plight was not discussed, neither was the fairness of the situation nor sufferings endured. It was simply what it was. Luca desperately wanted to ask but for some reason, he couldn't. The will to express it didn't even exist.

Nina and Adank were as clear as adults, like communicating with his own peers. He silently pleaded once more for Elias to be spared. If he wasn't allowed an explanation, what about reconsideration? There was no response communicated back from them on that either. Instead, they re-assured him of their love and their gratitude to have known him and Chiara. They made him understand his love for them was a good love. They expressed gratitude in meeting him in that realm and then politely showed him the door.

As he departed, he didn't feel awkward or disrespected by their reception. He understood. The dead were simple and had no need for the quirks of the living and their emotions.

As he came to, he was happy to have seen them but no, he'd achieved nothing on Elias. Would it even make sense repeating the trip? And to then do what, beg them again? Their response was clear, and he knew it was final. As he staggered back to the living room, he quickly grew frustrated again knowing he'd made no headway for Elias.

Elias.

He was no longer asleep on the bed. Maybe he was playing with the dog again.

In the living room, Luca got startled as his gaze first fell on a rather emaciated and eerily menacing figure standing in his way.

"Jesus!"

"What?" Brazile asked. "Oh, shit!"

Dibia looked ready to play a vampire or some undead creature in a movie, no makeup needed. Behind him was Maurice holding a handgun with a silencer, and four others, wearing tactical gears, with some intimidating assault rifles.

"What's going on?" Luca asked in his heavy Swiss-German accent, scared and disbelieving.

"Ah, you must be the boy's father," Dibia said with a wide grin that had nothing to do with pleasantries, like a real live version of Mr. Burns, if *The Simpsons* was created by M. Night Shyamalan.

"Excuse me? Who are you?" Luca asked bravely.

"Just do as he says." Brazile nudged him and gave him the warning eyes.

Stanley was on his knees with hands raised, sweating bullets, while Maleek lay face down, with his hands tied behind him and his face badly bruised. He'd clearly been hit repeatedly.

Luca looked around worried, "Elias!"

"Oh, not to worry," Dibia said and reached behind him to reveal Elias, crying.

Luca made to head for the boy but was stopped as the guns turned to him.

"Yo, easy. Dibia, what you doing, man? What you want?" Brazile spoke up bravely, hands still raised.

"Care to say what you're doing, cavorting with the governor's enemies?" Dibia asked in his usual calm but menacing manner.

"Cavorting? Governor's enemies? Dibia, what are you talking about?"

Dibia looked insulted and was not about to be taken for a fool.

He turned to Maurice, "Would you be so kind?"

Without hesitation, Maurice shot Brazile in his right knee cap. He bawled over in pain, letting out a scream and grabbing onto his knee.

Luca's face dried up with fear as he turned to Dibia who returned a casual but stern look as if to say, "I hope you realize I'm not here to fuck around."

"I asked you a question."

"Huh? I mean, what question?" Luca stole a quick glance at Maurice to be sure that wasn't a cue to shoot.

"Are you the boy's father?" Dibia repeated.

"Yes, I am."

Dibia seemed to smile at him with some admiration. "You are most lucky."

"I'm sorry?"

"To have had such wonder of a soul proceed from your loins, multiple times. You are truly blessed."

"Aha. I am blessed. Thanks. So, uhm, can I have my son now back, please?"

"Actually, he will be coming with us," Dibia responded.

"Over my dead body!" Maleek said in a grunt.

Dibia turned to Maleek and observed him for a bit then decided, "Maurice, I believe our friend here would like us to do him a favor."

Maurice walked closer to Maleek and shot him point blank in the back of the head, execution style.

They were all stunned. Stanley's life flashed before his eyes. He'd never seen anyone get killed, especially someone he knew. Brazile himself, for a bit, forgot about his own injury. All three of them were stunned, all just stared at dead Maleek, disbelieving. Maleek was the reason they were gathered. He couldn't possibly be dead.

As Maleek's body lay there, hands still tied behind his back, his eyes remained open, and blood oozed all over his expensive rug. Stanley, still on his knees, threw up all over himself.

Luca went on his knees, begging. "Look, mister, please let me and my son go. Whatever this stuff going on with your governor is, I'm not involved. I don't even know the governor. I'm not even from here. I'm from Switzerland, I just came to see him for a problem about my son."

Dibia spoke calmly, "You're more involved than you realize, my good man. But don't worry, I intend to spare you. We may have need for you, yet."

Maurice walked to him and shoved a needle in his neck and injected him with something. He passed out immediately.

One of the four others picked up Luca and slung him over his shoulder. Dibia held sobbing Elias, heading toward the door then stopped and turned to Stanley, as if an afterthought.

"What do I do with you now?"

Stanley glanced up at him and turned his face away, as if trying to will himself invisible, or maybe be forgotten.

Dibia turned to Maurice, "Any suggestions?"

Maurice walked over to Stanley and slammed the butt of his gun on his head, knocking him out.

***

"The souls of all the dead gather in Animmo.

What is the soul but a slate of personality, filled with experiences?

Each path walked, each decision taken, each experience lived, is merely a thread in the eternal bunch, all branching out from the same one eternal source.

In Animmo, all shall return to the same, and truly be one again; all a compilation of various experiences of the same one life.

In Animmo, all is one! In the singular eternal moment, all the dead shall therefore meet all the dead."

-Oku Animmo

***

The united soul, the combination of all experiences lived on earth, the complete picture per eternal moment, the collective cosmic consciousness; fellowships with itself in Animmo. The fellowship is filled with the souls of all that have ever lived and died, a true fellowship of oneness. In that fellowship, there is no judgement.

For when all paths are walked, and all roads are taken and all lives are lived, the full picture is received without prejudice and is celebrated. In the higher realms, this full picture is the record of the universe experiencing itself. It is the record of being.

There, Tana fellowshipped with AJ, Kester, and everyone else. There, Tana also met Victor, an indiscernible pile of human flesh. They recognized each other, however, that moment was only a reflection of the simple facts of their individual and collective lives, no malice or quarrel. None of it mattered.

***

Reginald looked through the different labels on various blood vials. He picked one labelled "Triplet #T016" and turned it into the prepared skooches. Among the collection was all manner of labels describing different blood donors and mixes: foetus, new-born, late-stage hospice, revived near-death, virgin, firstborn, last-born, one, two and three generation in-breeding, etc. He took one labelled "#G3M-026," a three-generation vial of son, father, and grandfather and turned that in as well. He mixed the potion and downed it in one gulp.

He braced himself against the bathroom sink and held fast, gripping it tightly as he first started to drop toward the ground to doze off, but he withstood it and raised himself up again. His heart beat rapidly and his vision was first blurry when he opened his eyes. He also felt sick in his stomach and had to forcefully will himself back to normalcy. After he stabilized, he looked up at himself in the mirror. His pupils glowed bright gray. He observed himself for a bit before going to switch off the light. In the darkness, he saw only the burning gray colored flames in his eyes in the mirror and smiled.

In that darkness, he closed his eyes and performed yet another at-will awake travel.

***

"Oh, the foolishness of man, for he thinks he is in control.

Does he not know that it's all one story?

All who have lived and died have merely played parts in that singular story.

Like notes in a musical composition, each contributes to the one rendition.

If you have your eyes open, close them. If they are closed, open them.

For you see and understand nothing.

Do stories really end or do characters merely enter and exit?

For no story ever ends until the one story has ended.

Oh, the foolishness of man, for he thinks he's in control."

-Oku Animmo.

"Oh, the foolishness of man, for he thinks he is in control.

Has he not heard that all roads must be taken?

He's not aware all paths must be followed.

All that could be, must be.

All that could be said, must be said.

All that could be done, must be done.

It is the law of the higher realms.

Oh, the ignorance of man!

All paths must be followed.

That is how the maker knows the end from the beginning."

-Oku Animmo.

***

Inside of Reginald's subconscious, it was pitch black.

Suddenly, a very bright and piercing flicker of light flashed across in an instant, in the distance, and in that moment, illuminated the entire area and revealed an uncountable number of transparent glass balls, stacked on top one another. The balls were of different opacities and ranged from completely transparent to very dense and dark.

The light flicker was bright and strong enough to register in every single glass ball.

Reginald's mind's eyes observed the balls with patience, in that eternal moment in which the light flashed.

As Reginald looked from one ball to the other, he noticed their opacity, shade, brightness, and color of the light that emanated from each ball. He observed the light source again and noted how it differed from the light produced by the different balls. He heard a sound, like that of a metal bolt being undone. Then the glass balls all started rolling out, toward and away from him. He raised his leg and stepped on one, it was quite dense and produced a faint but present oxblood colored light.

He bent and picked it up.

Pitch black again.

As it brightened, he saw himself standing at the neck of the same cul-de-sac, the canteen just a stone throws away. He turned to his left and walked toward that same bush path he had attempted before. When he came to the point where the small pool of water gathered, he reached out and felt around. That invisible wall was no longer there.

As he crossed that point, he felt a dizziness rush through him. He felt sick in his stomach and paused to try throwing up but was unable to. He tried to stabilize his breathing and walked on.

He then came to a path that across from it, in the distance, was what looked like paddle boats being rowed by hand, carrying people on a small body of water.

Suddenly, he saw himself on the other side, and in the midst of the multitude, from where he could also see himself, still watching from near the bush path. On the side with the multitude, he walked shoulder to shoulder with them, each one shuffling as fast as the crowd moved.

He turned casually to see the person to his right and froze when he realized it was him. Everyone around him was him, in different clothes and body sizes and even from slight to noticeable differences in face, height, and body weight. Then also noticed himself, as a woman, also of varying features, temperaments and personalities.

He stepped back and started running. Suddenly, it was as if his consciousness transferred from the running one to another of himself, who watched the running him run.

The perspective of his mind's eye changed again, and he saw himself standing on one side of a line while a fast slide show of all his various selves rolled by like a huge carousel. He saw himself from his present age, he scrolled past rapidly and he saw himself get progressively younger, past his teenage and infant years, past his birth and down to his conception. He briefly scrolled past his conception point, but it became empty. He sensed there was content there, but he just couldn't see them. In the points between conception and birth, the versions of himself he saw looked like adult sized humanlike androids or humanoids. From birth, then he looked like a normal baby.

As he kept watching the multiple versions of himself at the different ages, he suddenly realized he was in an infinitely large chamber, filled with the innumerable variations of himself, in their varying degrees of differences in height, weight, skin tone, ethnicity, gender, and so on, and each variant, with its own innumerable sub-variants of ages, temperaments, moods and dispositions and so on.

All of them were him, all of them were being rowed across the small body of water to the other side. All of them, him, were dead by different means.

At the point with the officer, by whose order the line forked, his consciousness observed from the point of view of him that was next in line. He stared at the officer and pondered its highly sophisticated human-like features. Also, the humanoid officer was him.

Suddenly, his consciousness transferred to the officer who in turn abruptly turned around and looked straight at him from across the pond to the bush path where he stood.

"Get out of here," the humanoid barked at him. His voice sounded like loud thunder, which startled him and jolted him awake.

When he came to, he was still standing on his feet. Feeling sick, he hurried to the toilet and threw up.

Before turning on the shower, he paused and deliberately travelled again. He still easily got to the neck of the cul-de-sac. He returned quickly and smiled.

"Let the shift begin," he muttered and turned on the shower.

***

Brazile's eyes were hot with tears when Dibia and his team left. For the first time, he had dared take a stand against Reginald and he knew he would regret it. He also knew that if Reginald's plan for Elias came through and he was able to ingest the boy's blood, there'd probably be no stopping him and his goons. With Maleek dead, the others captured, what were the chances of stopping the governor? Was there any use in trying?

He quickly prepared a skooches mix, untied Maleek's body, and laid it facing up. He let a few drops into his mouth, unsure if that would achieve anything, he was already dead after all. He then drank the rest and quickly assumed the Burmese styled seating position, making sure his fingers were touching Maleek's body. He took off immediately.

***

Brazile saw himself in a valley. It was arid and narrow, with rock elevations on either side. It was shadowy too, very shadowy, and not from cloud covers, there were no clouds, but from the rock elevations themselves, it seemed, or maybe the sun was far in the horizon, just about to set.

He'd not walked that path before, but he knew where he was headed.

***

Maleek suddenly found himself there. In his physical appearance, he seemed to walk on his two legs like everyone else but deep in his present consciousness, he still felt the rope that bound his hands and legs together behind his back. It was a shock to him. He knew there were dangers to being a cop, but he'd always considered himself lucky enough to be one of the ones who'd retire. In that eternal moment when he appeared at the crossing, his entire life played out before him.

"How could I be dead?" he whispered to himself. He thought of Luca, Elias, Stanley, Brazile, people who'd all gathered because he'd asked them to. When he sensed the unlabored acceptance of the situation coming, he screamed out in desperation.

"Fardeena!"

"Fardeeeeeeeeeeennnnaaaaaaaaa!" He let out again, loudly and in deep anguish.

His scream did get fleeting notices from the passing dead, as a few of them glanced casually at him but they all continued trekking, unbothered and diligently toward their destination, the forked line ahead.

Suddenly, from behind him, a path cleared, and he felt a force pull him back to and into a different space, an enclosure covered in what looked like translucent wall papers made with images of his final memories. The enclosure felt like his own personal chamber out of which he may have emerged into the crossing. From there he was pulled further back, down a corridor and suddenly burst out into an open space with blinding light. When his sight normalized to the light, he found himself in what looked like a giant court-room, shaped like a soccer stadium and filled with countless mul-titudes of the Maasai he had experienced earlier. They numbered as far as the eyes could see in every direction he looked. They all spoke almost in complete unison, like with the sound of a united multitude.

"Please help me, I was shot," Maleek pleaded.

"I know you were shot," Fardeena replied in that same united crowd voice.

Maleek paused for a bit to acknowledge his disappointment in Fardeena's reaction. He did say he wasn't malevolent but maybe he also didn't care at all.

"Help me, I need to go back. Can you help me?"

"And just how do you think that will work?" Fardeena asked.

"You're a higher dimensional, right? Doesn't that give you access to manipulate time and space?"

"Yes, it does," Fardeena acknowledged.

"So, help me. Send me back."

"It's not that simple," he quickly continued as he noted Maleek's frustration. "The living think they have free will, but the truth is, and as it's written, all roads must be taken and all paths must be followed. All that could be, must be; all that could be said, must be said; and all that could be done, must be done. It's the law of the higher realms and it cannot be changed."

"Gee. Talk about Medes and Persia," Maleek whispered to himself as he understood with clarity, but he refused to accept it.

"Are you telling me that I must remain dead?"

"The most I can do is swap your timeline with one where you didn't die but that'll simply be a swap and would still amount to the same thing. And I can only swap with a timeline from the same branch, so you still must die at the point where you died."

"Can't you just raise me from the dead?" Maleek insisted.

"Yes, I could but there would still remain countless timelines where I don't raise you from the dead and you remain dead. All paths must be followed."

Maleek had no other angles to approach. He gave up.

A Fardeena, one notably different from the others by the design of his shuka, spoke up, gently but loudly enough to be heard by the infinite multitude.

"While our guest has no more questions, shall we bid him farewell on his crossing?"

The silence was clearly awaiting his answer but instead, Maleek had nothing else he could think of.

"I have one." Brazile startled Maleek, as the infinite Fardeena turned to observe him.

"Brazile. What is your submission?" Fardeena asked.

"What are you doing here?" Maleek asked. Brazile ignored him and turned to the infinite Fardeena.

"There is still a way. He can return by inter-dimensional transfers."

While Maleek wondered what it could be, Fardeena showed no facial inquiry.

"And what do you understand that to be?" he asked.

"You can swap his life here with one from a timeline where he didn't die, but the prayer or request to bring him back wouldn't also exist, even if he had died." Brazile stated boldly.

"Yes, that is true. However, you must understand that it still fundamentally changes nothing. Because all paths must be followed, he will still die in an infinite number of timelines where that prayer is not made. It will only seem different in your third-dimensional world."

"That works for me, I accept," Maleek said. "If it's from a line where a prayer to come back doesn't exist, that works for me."

"So be it," said the infinite Fardeena.

***

Brazile came to slowly. Not having slept well the past couple of days plus his gunshot wound, the fatigue had hit him. He had initially made to continue sleeping but woke up finally after a nudge. As he opened his eyes, the memory of Maleek dead and with a bullet wound in his head had just freshly returned in that very instant. Opening his eyes to see Maleek lying on his side and with eyes open, looking straight into his eyes startled him.

"Jesus!" He screamed and jolted as he scrambled to get up, hitting Maleek in the groin by accident.

Maleek screamed and grabbed his crotch, in pain.

"Jeez!! You trying to kill me again? What the fuck?!"

"Holy shit, it worked?"

"Apparently, it did," Maleek said as the pain eased and he was able to stand slowly.

Brazile observed him for a bit and went in to hug him. They locked eyes, silently expressing their own versions of gratitude.

"Thanks, man. Thanks for coming after me. It's like you basically raised me from the dead."

"Hey, we gotta do what we gotta do, eh? Too much at stake here," Brazile replied.

"Thanks all the same."

They both nodded at each other as their eyes expressed and received the unspoken gratitude once more.

"But if the timelines swapped, why do we still remember?" Maleek asked.

"I dunno, man? Maybe to let us know we experienced a miracle?"

That response was good enough for Maleek.

"What are we gonna do now?" Brazile asked.

"Nothing else, bro, I've got to get after those guys. They're not dying on my watch. Meanwhile, you've got to get to the hospital, ASAP! I'll drive you."

As they headed out, Maleek called Destiny and asked to meet.

12

It was red carpets, lights and cameras of various news and entertainment reporting crews at the civic centre, downtown Phoenix. Various celebrities, politicians, business leaders and so-called influencers stood before various camera crews as they gave interviews.

Inside the venue, the drinks flowed heavily, and people mingled happily, all compliant with the black-tie dress code. The large screen TVs in the corners showed events happening outside. On one of them, Maha Pinto, appeared with a wild look in his eyes that should have caused any rational person some concern, but everyone was having fun and being polite.

The MC made a few announcements before welcoming a boy-band from the early 2000s on stage.

***

Several floors below, Stanley and Luca were tied to the chairs they were seated on and gagged. In another office in the corner with a glass door, Elias sat on the bed, watching cartoons and had his back turned to the door. In front of Stanley and Luca were a couple of TVs also showing events from inside the auditorium and outside the center.

Stanley's head couldn't stop racing. He thought of the other possible choices he could have made, like not reaching out to Maleek or going over to his place, maybe even not sticking his head out in the first place for Tana and the girls, telling Maleek and the FBI lady to fuck off, but he still ended up tracing it back to if he just hadn't met Michelle, he'd have left Jisike a long time ago. He saw Maleek get his head blown off so there was a good chance same would happen to him. He'd also seen and heard too much, so why would they leave him alive, especially with a governor that doesn't like loose ends? Tears dropped from his eyes.

With his eyes still wet and vision blurry, he looked up at the TV and for a moment, wondered if it was Angela Blaine he saw walk by in the background. He squeezed his eyelids together to press out the tears to see better, but it had passed.

Just then, the door opened and in came Angela and Wardens Jackson and D'Agostin.

They only briefly observed Luca. The trio showered Stanley with all their scowling and disgust and their shaking of heads.

"My God, Weppler, you are even more pathetic than you present to be," Angela mocked him, running her eyes over him and settling on the vomit stain he still had.

"Fuck you, you stupid cunt!" Stanley said, feeling brave.

Angela first looked shocked, and then burst out laughing, frankly amused. "There you are. I knew it was in there, somewhere.

Was that the best you could do?" She reached in to cuddle his face in a rather condescending manner and held tightly while he tried to pull away.

"Hmm? You stupid little boy," she added.

She looked down at the vomit stain again, shook her head, and walked out, laughing, leaving Jake and Linda behind with them.

Jake stood closer to him and leaned down to his eye level, resting his hands on his knees.

"By the way, Michelle? I mean your wife. She says hi. I have been keeping her company. You know, showing her how real men do it."

Jake watched him closely, slight confusion registering on his own face as he noted no reaction from Stanley.

"I see you found your dream woman. Enjoy!" Stanley responded, with mockery.

Jake shook his head at him. "You're gonna die today, Weppler, and by God, I hope I get to off your sorry ass."

That threw Stanley off. He simply looked away and once again, weighed his choices.

***

Maleek and Destiny arrived at the Civic Centre in one of the many city police patrol cars around, fully dressed in PPD uniforms. They then proceeded to walk through a back entrance to the venue with ease and casual familiarity, drawing no attention to themselves.

***

Inside, the buzz was exciting, and everyone seemed to be in a great social mood. As they ate and drank, Reginald sat on the stage with a female host in an interview styled setting.

"For every year we've done this, at least during my administration, we've continued to try harder to reach the youths and upcoming leaders of tomorrow. You know how it goes, it's easy to get carried away with the movers and shakers and heavy weights, like my friend Maha Pinto. But when a government takes deliberate actions and puts infrastructure in place to actively reach out to the upcoming and younger businessmen and women, we will all be better for it. Its best to catch them, young. Wouldn't you say?" Reginald asked as he licked his lips.

"Certainly, Governor," responded the anchor before turning to the guests. "Now, as a final part of this segment, I've been informed that a special, separate meet and greet session will be going on and will actually happen while the merriments here continue. Thirty lucky people, all selected at random, will have a chance to move to another section where they'll be able to converse one on one with the top sponsors of today's event, including the governor himself and of course, his majesty."

The crowd applauded cheerfully.

She continued, "Right? A chance to mingle and speak with the great minds here today and table some things before them, yes?" She asked, giving the audience a happy challenge.

"Yes!" they responded.

The anchor continued, "Also, if you're one of the lucky thirty, you also get to walk away with a check of fifteen thousand dollars seed money toward your business, courtesy of our group of sponsors."

The crowd cheered even louder.

"So, if your seat number is displayed on the board, well, congratulations!"

Then, a set of thirty numbers, between 1 and 450, appeared on the large screens, arranged in incrementing order. Various cheers erupted from the different corners and then, the whole audience erupted in cheers and applause too for the winners.

The anchor continued, "For the lucky winners, and I really do envy you, please turn around and walk toward the gold statue by the east entrance. Some ushers will meet you there. Remember to take all your belongings with you as you will certainly not be coming back here."

The crowd cheered some more as the thirty lucky men and women, ranging between twenty-one and thirty, all made their ways to the muster point.

As they all walked into a make-shift space, they stood around in excitement as they waited for the last of them to enter the room.

"We'll be right with you. Let me just make sure the conference room is ready," one of the ushers said. He then stepped out, shut the door and locked it.

"Did he just lock us in?" one of the closest to the door asked. He walked up to open it and confirmed. "It's locked!"

When he turned around to the rest, he saw a lot of them suddenly looked sick and drowsy. Then they started slumping to the ground, one by one. He worried but didn't have time to remember to scream. He too inhaled it and slumped shortly after.

After the vent's air flow reversed and cleared out, the attendants opened the door to let in about five heavyset men who lifted the unconscious victims one by one to another room. In there, they were all laid on emergency hospital beds and quickly strapped up with needles to bags of thick liquid skooches hanging from the drip hangers.

Later, in a separate room with an adjoining door, Maha Pinto, Derrick Obiojor, Dibia, and His Majesty, with his consort had been joined by Reginald, as the boy band was back on stage, performing.

Two of the attendants wheeled in two of the victims, still strapped to their hospital beds and the tubes still in their arms. They had both become conscious enough to know they were in danger. The attendants then removed the clips from the bags hanging onto the drip stands and the skooches flowed into them, as they both sobbed.

"My brothers, how far we have come," Reginald started while they all smiled at him, still with the ravenous hungry looks in their eyes. Today, we'll surely reach the required threshold for our journey into the next realm. Call it eternal life, call it cheating death, all I know is that soon, we will be able to look death in the face and simply walk by."

The rest smiled even more broadly, getting giddy with impatience.

"Yes. Soon, we will rule the rest of them all. Let the shift begin," Reginald finished.

"Let the shift begin," they responded.

The bags had emptied into the victims, and they were each in their trance experiences. The attendants then pulled out pocketknives and cut them both all over and quickly walked out the door.

All six of them went to town, three on each victim, aggressively sucking the blood from their bodies while their majesties lay on the ground, facing up and simply opened their mouths while the skooched up blood dripped in. They both moved their feet around back and forth, playfully like children, as they drank.

As usual, they knew to stop before their victims began to freeze over.

They repeated it four more times.

After having drugged and drank up the blood of ten victims, they were all completely drenched in blood, could hardly stand from the exhaustion of too much consumption, and were delirious. They all smiled crookedly at one another and staggered like a bunch of overfed vampires. Then they began to giggle uncontrollably and howl like dogs once again.

Suddenly, Dibia saw himself inside the body, or maybe in the mind of a wild dog, running with its pack. He then realized the other pack members were Reginald, Derrick and the royals. They had been chasing a mid-sized tiger. Then they cornered it and tore it to pieces. As they devoured the last pieces of the tiger's flesh, they then suddenly saw themselves in front of the medieval canteen.

They quickly snapped back into their human consciousness and then realized they had all made a collective travel. They howled some more.

"Let the shift begin!"

"Let the shift begin!"

***

Maleek and Destiny were inside the auditorium. People went back for seconds and thirds and the drinks flowed endlessly. People were starting to stagger about and some even had drunk enough to start getting improper.

The host announced the official merriment had ended and it was time for the unofficial one. The DJ returned to his set and the black-tie event became as a night club. Heavy drinking and dancing commenced.

Where they stood, both Maleek and Destiny knew something was amiss. The guests acted like mindless enjoyment zombies. They both easily walked through the crowd, looking for another entrance to the back area.

***

AJ and Kester were in the wasteland. After they picked up the tenth cold ahu, they dragged themselves, weighed down by the feeling of desolation in the wasteland, to go deliver the cold ahus to enforcers. A couple met them on their way.

"Surrender them and go back to your domains. The Ofuuku is present."

They both understood.

"See you now," Kester said.

"See you now," AJ responded, and they both walked back to their domains.

***

When the door opened, Linda and Jake walked in with Dibia, who was still all soaked in blood. From how Luca remembered him, the creepy deathly aura about him had become layered upon by a deranged giddy look. Dibia looked like a happy and fulfilled demon.

Linda went into the other room and brought Elias out, forcefully, and handed him over to Dibia. He started crying uncontrollably and made to rush for his father, while Dibia held him back.

Luca started protesting by violently shaking his chair back and forth, with tears in his eyes.

Dibia observed him briefly before walking back to ungag him. Stanley remained gagged, watching them.

"Mister. Please. What do you want with my son? Why can't you let us go? Look, I swear, I won't say anything. I don't even know anything. I'll just go back to the airport and head on home. Please give me back my son."

"Mister?" Dibia started.

"Sutter," Luca answered.

"Sutter. Of course. Are you familiar with Oku Animmo?"

Luca's face said no.

"Of course not. You see, all roads must be walked. All paths must be followed. All lives must therefore be lived."

"Okay, and what's that got to do with my son?" Luca challenged.

Dibia educated him. "You see, just as life is lived by billions of people, all happening at once, the same way, some believe that individuals re-incarnate and live different lives. But your son here, you see, possesses a unique ability. He can be several people at the same time, all by himself. It's like his own way of following all paths and living all lives. Such, my dear ignorant father, is the beauty of the abiku."

"Well, you're wrong, he doesn't live all the lives, he still lives them one by one," Luca countered.

"Oh, no, my unlearned young man." Dibia retorted. "You see, in the higher realms, he does. I mean, live all the lives at once. You, we, all of us, merely experience him one after the other because of the third dimensional limitations." He knew Luca had no idea what he was talking about. He signaled to Linda who gagged Luca up once more.

They exited with Elias.

"Wait. Come back. Come back here!" Luca shouted his muffled screams after them. After they left, he started crying, completely letting it all go.

"Ah, my son."

He shoved himself back and forth violently, hoping to break the chords he was bound with. Nothing.

In his frustration, his struggle knocked him off his chair and he fell on the ground, the chair collapsing with him. He struggled some more to force himself free, still nothing.

"God, please help me. Don't let them kill my son," he let out in a prayerful groan.

Stanley just looked on at him, himself helpless to do anything through his own bind and gag.

About five minutes after that, the door opened again, but cautiously. Destiny's head popped in first. Initially, they weren't sure how to react to seeing her. Then Maleek followed in.

Both Stanley and Luca were stunned. It was like they both experienced a real-life dolly zoom effect. Stanley wondered if he had drunk or consumed something that would've made him hallucinate. He looked back at Luca and saw he too was equally dazed.

Maleek ungagged them while Destiny pulled a pocketknife and cut their bonds.

Maleek had actually briefly forgotten he had basically died and come back to life. While he was excited to see them, they both simply stared back, dazed.

"You guys alright?" he asked.

"Why are they staring at you like that?" Destiny asked.

"You died. He shot you. I saw it!" Luca stated.

"Yeah, bro. How are you alive?" Stanley added.

"What the hell they talking about, Maleek?" Destiny asked.

"It's a long story. I'll tell you but now ain't the time."

Both Stanley and Luca both tried to focus on the events at Maleek's place to be sure they did remember correctly.

"For now, we need to move fast. Where's your son?"

Luca's shock at Maleek quickly switched to fear for Elias.

"Elias!" Luca screamed and rushed for the door. Stanley still continued to stare at Maleek curiously.

"Woooow, where you going, buddy?" Maleek asked Luca, trying to stand in his way. "That's what we're here for. Just point us in the right direction and we'll take it from there."

" That's fine. He's my son. I'll go too."

As they talked, the door opened again, and Jake and Linda walked in.

"Who the fuck are you?" Jake demanded.

Suddenly, Linda jumped on Destiny who was reaching in to draw her weapon. She flew in with a kick and knocked it off her hand and quickly delivered another blow before Destiny could recover.

Shortly after Linda jumped Destiny, Jake and Maleek both drew their guns and shot at each other, while also ducking to avoid each other's bullets, Stanley and Luca also doing the same.

While Maleek missed Jake, a shot from Jake's gun knocked Maleek's gun out of his hand. While just in time, Jake's bullet finished as he tried to fire the next shot. As Maleek made to dive for his gun, Jake threw his at him and jumped at him. They kicked and hit each other as they both struggled to be the first to reach the gun.

While Maleek and Jake engaged each other, Stanley jumped into the fight with Destiny, rushing Linda with a very angry punch that knocked her sideways. Linda set once more, trying to try her best in taking on both Stanley and Destiny.

Bang!

In all that commotion, Luca had simply picked up Maleek's gun and shot Linda in the head.

Everyone was startled silent. Destiny, Maleek, and Stanley all stared at Luca and then each other. Taking the opportunity of their distraction, Jake dashed for the door and quickly got away but not before another bullet from Luca struck his left arm. The rest ducked, fearing Luca's bullets.

"We have to go find my son, please, before it's too late," Luca demanded.

Maleek reached closer, gently and took back the gun from him. Destiny picked hers up while Stanley took Linda's.

They headed out the door, cautiously.

The entire path was clear. The music and dance from the hall were still going on. On the ground were blood drops that led them on Jake's path. They followed it. Maleek wasn't sure what to expect, as they didn't know what kind of fire power the governor had on his side, considering the assault rifles that were brought to his place, and not to even mention the tons of police men around. There was no going back, regardless.

Jake's blood led them to a closed door. They all paused for a bit to contemplate what they might find on the other side, and yet again their choices. Luca opened it, the only one without much hesitation.

The general image from inside the room settled on them gradually. There were at least seven men armed with assault rifles, including Maurice with his handgun, all pointed at them. Standing around Elias, in a semi-circle were Dibia, Derrick, Maha, his majesty and consort and Reginald, standing in their middle.

Warden Jake Jackson also stood there, still holding his arm tightly while his blood still dripped, scowling at them. Angela Blaine stood beside him.

Dibia and the others who'd been at Maleek's house couldn't help but stare at him. Maurice also remembered the very moment he shot him in the head. They all saw him bleed out.

"I see our friends have arrived," Dibia said. "And I also see cockroaches have become more immune to their bug spray," he said, giving Maleek a rather confusion laced condescending glare.

The four also had their guns pointed at them, in return.

"Why don't you drop those things and end this futility. You are desperately outgunned, if you haven't already noticed," Dibia chided.

The four guns remained pointed.

Dibia smiled and turned to Maurice, who in turn pointed his gun straight at Elias' head.

Elias closed his eyes and prayed silently, "Adank, Nina, help me."

All their guns lowered.

Dibia waved them in. They walked in slowly and the door shut behind them.

"You must be Mr. Sutter," Reginald added. "We all, must thank you for your sacrifice."

"I reject your thanks; I have made no sacrifices. I want my son back! You don't even know anything about him."

"Oh, but we do. You see, you spoke to one of my own and let's say we've had him bugged for a long time. We've been listening and we've been waiting for your boy."

"You can't kill my son over your silly superstitions," Luca said.

"Really? Superstitions?" Reginald countered. "Same superstitions that got you on a plane to come see people you've never met? Is he not Adank? Is he not Nina? You should rejoice, for when we kill him now, he'll be back." Reginald finished with a wicked smile and winked at him.

Luca was overcome with rage and made to lunge at Reginald, but Maurice quickly shot him in the thigh, dropping him to the ground. The rest turned their guns to Destiny, Maleek and Stanley, who all lowered their guns to the ground, carefully.

Reginald continued. "Let me explain it to you. There are powers and doors and realities beyond your wildest mundane and fucking meaningless imaginations, and your son here, is a primary key that unlocks the door to higher realms and yes, eternal life." He walked closer to Luca and continued. "Your son, being an abiku, is a mere third dimensional representation of what a higher realm would look like, and his blood, for me, for us, is the gateway."

"Please don't kill my son," Luca said, sobbing. Reginald merely shook his head at him. He then turned to Maleek. "Detective pelvic bone." He laughed. "Perhaps its good you're all here. Witness the power of true human transformation. He then turned to Maurice to loosen the drip grip on Elias.

As Maurice reached in, suddenly the whole building shook. They all braced. It seemed like a heavy object had fallen from the sky.

***

In the immediate neighborhood around the Civic Center, it was as if a forcefield of sadness and desperation went through. All the dogs in the neighborhood began letting out a deep groan cry. They almost sounded like humans, humans mourning for their dead. Cats began scratching everything, jumping around and going crazy and the people around were filled with an intense sense of anxiety, and as if deep wells of sorrow had just been opened in every one of them. Many people started crying for reasons they couldn't understand. Many not crying were filled with dread, which was worsened by reactions of people around and the cries of the dogs.

Thud! Everyone in and around the center heard and felt it.

Suddenly, the temperature got hotter and multiple times more humid. The air was still too, as if a mighty glass dome had been placed on that part of the city.

People continued sobbing, screaming. Others begged it to stop.

A few put knives to their throats while yet, a few others jumped off their buildings.

"What was that?" His majesty asked.

Thud! It got much closer.

In the party hall, the music was still blaring loudly while people squirmed around on the floor, filled with all manner intense negative emotions. The DJ went crazy and started chewing off the mixer keys. He pulled so hard his teeth fell off. He continued chewing on the keys, hard, with just his bleeding gums.

Back in the room, Reginald noticed the drip had not been turned on and wanted to rush for it.

Thud! The final one. It had arrived.

From outside the civic center, it looked like a massive boulder had swung at the building from an angle and destroyed a large part of it, across several floors.

From inside the room, they saw as a chunk of the wall ripped off. By then, everyone was toppled in despair.

As they all looked out, each one even though in severe pain couldn't still take their eyes off the entity, a dark, gray sinewy, giant on one leg, tattered and wretched looking. The malevolence it carried with it was palpable. Also, each one that gazed upon it saw his or her own face, a most vile and depraved version of themselves.

"Why do you look like me?" they all wondered in unison, as with everyone that ever gazed upon it.

The Ofuuku seemed to know who to target.

***

"For to take away death is to be formless.

So shall be the fate of those who would seek to manipulate death and the dead.

For their path shall be with death for death to keep its form.

Be warned, for death is for the living but the dead do die, still.

It is wise for the dead to bury the dead.

What is the second death?

In what ways do you kill they that have already passed?

As all paths must be taken and all roads walked, and all lives lived, so shall the sorrows of they that experience the second death be multiplied.

The sorrows and desolation of the wasteland, combined from all the infinite possible paths shall all be centered into that one singular eternal moment.

In that singular eternal moment shall they dwell.

This is the second death."

Oku Animmo.

***

Reginald witnessed, as his consciousness was multiplied into an infinity of the possible variations of himself, and for each variation, it was also multiplied by the infinite number of possible timelines.

For each of the infinite instances of himself, from conception to birth, each of the various ways he could have been aborted, to all the possible ways he could have died, from infancy to old age, he experienced the emotional, psychological and physical pain of their deaths, whether sudden or impending.

The infinite death experiences were all combined into one concurrent time block, yet still experienced one after the other, second by second, according to the nature of the physical world. Heavy fever, bodily pains and severe malfunctions of every possible body organ, from the top of his head to the soles of his feet, combinations of various types and cases of mental anguish, all the road and domestic accidents, plane crashes, natural disasters, suicides, etc., that he died of in his infinite possible timelines, he experienced all of them in that singular block of time in which the Ofuuku swiped its claws; all together, yet, one-by-one.

However, as the others observed it, blood spattered all over.

For all that witnessed, it was as if they watched innumerable lifetimes end in death. For each of Reginald, his majesty and consort, Maha Pinto, Dibia, Derrick and all their armed men, in the moment the Ofuuku swiped its claws, it was as if the infinite number of ways in which each person could die, all happened to each of them, all at once, yet separate from each other.

When the tension ceased and Maleek, Luca, Stanley, Destiny and Elias had all sprung back to easy consciousness, the water sprinkler was on and the alarm was blaring.

The bodies of the entire crew, including the governor, scattered around in pieces. On all their faces were looks of intense terror. Stanley noticed both Angela and Jake Jackson's heads were severed and lay on the ground, facing each other, both clearly in that look of eternal pain.

Luca went to the bed and gently pulled the drip out of Elias' arms and hugged him tightly.

***

In the days that followed, Maleek took time to rest and went to check on Brazile in the hospital.

***

"I want a divorce." Stanley finally broke the silent treatment pact with Michelle.

She also cried when she heard her Jake was dead but got more furious when she heard he only came at her just to punish him.

***

When Stanley made it back to work at ASCHA, Mindy was there too. A new management was also in place.

"So, where you been hiding, girl?"

"Houston, bro. My aunt lives there. Had to disappear."

"I feel you. I wish I had disappeared too."

"But you're still here, you survived, right? Nothing lost." She offered.

"True that."

He asked her on a date shortly after.

***

In the wasteland, the dead feel the anguish and pain of all the living. For those that die the second death, as it is written, their anguish is multiplied by the infinitely possible timelines of their existence.

Reginald was assigned his domain, with these terms, in the wasteland.

AJ, with Kester and Tana already knew this. In that eternal moment, AJ went back to his domain and rested his soul.

***

They'd already been back in Lauterbrunnen over a week. Luca's emotion was a perfect mix of gratitude for his son's life, and confusion for not knowing when next they'd lose their child yet again.

Chiara had heard the whole story. She too was relieved and grateful for Elias's survival, but she too couldn't help but wonder how long they had.

They were in the living room, Luca sitting by himself, his bullet wound treated and still healing, while Chiara rocked Elias on her lap. She held him close to herself, tightly. She finally admitted to herself that she had lost all hope as the tears from her eyes fell down her cheeks and landed on Elias' forehead.

Elias' toddler eyes seemed to light up with determination. Then he raised his head to observe his mom for a bit. They locked eyes, in love, then he smiled at her, kissed her on the cheek with a resounding smack and then rested his small fingers on her necklace.

She leaned in to kiss his face again. As she raised her head up, his hand grabbed a firm hold on her necklace, weighing down on her neck. She tried to take his hand off, but he wouldn't let go.

"Elias, let go, you're hurting me." She tried again, but he wouldn't budge.

"Elias! Let go, you're hurting me."

"Elias, let go!" Luca added and came closer to remove his hand, but Elias remained stubborn. As they tried harder to force his hand away, he screamed suddenly at them. When they got startled, he reached in with his other hand as support and yanked off the gold chain.

"Ouch! Elias! What is wrong with you? That really hurt," Chiara said, her feelings hurt also.

Luca joined in, demanding, "Elias why did you do that?"

Elias, still holding the chain in his hand turned to them both and replied, "soul gift."

"Excuse me?" Chiara said.

"Elias, what did you say?" Luca asked, disbelieving, tears in his eyes.

"Soul gift." Elias repeated. "I want to stay. I don't want to die anymore."

Both Luca and Chiara were initially stunned silent, then both burst into tears, hugging and kissing him.

A while later, Pastor Oseyi and Christof already around, Luca prepared a small fireplace in their backyard.

"It doesn't need to melt. It just needs to burn," Pastor Oseyi said.

Chiara led Elias to the fireplace and asked him to drop it in.

Elias hesitated at first, they all saw the separation pain on his face. He finally let go and as the necklace hit the fire, Elias slowly crumbled to the ground, crying, as if with the understanding of an adult. Chiara wanted to rush in to comfort him, but pastor Oseyi stopped her.

"Don't. Please leave him alone. He must walk this path by himself."

They watched him sob with deep groans for over an hour. All four of them inevitably joined him on that journey, even though it was just emotionally. They all cried with him.

***

In Animmo, Nina and Adank were together in an embrace, also in much pain because of the separation from Elias.

Suddenly, their pain ceased.

As they disengaged, they both noted the translucent hue on Adank was gone. They were pained by the separation but glad to understand what the new realities would bring Luca and Chiara.

***

Elias finally stopped crying, wiped his tears and ran into his mom's arms, Luca joined them. All of them hugging and kissing as both Christof and Pastor Oseyi joined them in a joyful embrace.

EPILOGUE

E buka thought about him sometimes. He'd heard the story in the press about Maleek's death. He still missed him, his company and some days, he longed for the night they had with the skooches. Those thoughts made him smile, even the memory of their fight. The only true sad memory was the day he'd opened a link in Linda's message. It had simply read, "Disgraced former JPD officer, Maleek Shapiro, murdered!"

On a warm Saturday evening, in one of those timelines in which a prayer for Maleek's return was not made, Ebuka focused his thoughts on him again and smiled.

***

"We thank the maker for life.

We thank the maker for death.

For as the egg goes to larva, to pupa, to butterfly, so shall life go into the next phase.

The next phase cannot begin if the current does not end.

You must exit the third to enter the fourth!

As above, so beneath.

-Oku Animmo."

The end.